Get hooked on the Loon Lake mysteries
from Victoria Houston . . .

Dead Water

"[Victoria Houston] puts me right there in the Wisconsin heat and cold, lets me know what the fish are biting on, lets me spy on the interesting characters of Loon Lake, and most of all, spins an intelligent and captivating tale. I look forward to more and more."   —T. Jefferson Parker, author of *Silent Joe*

"Victoria Houston's love for her Wisconsin setting—and her wonderful characters—is evident on every page of her fine series. Loon Lake is a great get-away, even if it does keep me up at nights."   —Laura Lippman

Dead Creek

"Fans of a well-drawn regional police procedural will want to read this novel. All the subplots smoothly return to the main theme and there are plenty of suspects to keep the audience guessing about what is going on and who is the mastermind behind the mysterious events. With this fine novel, Victoria Houston will hook readers and make them seek her previous stories."   —*Painted Rock Reviews*

"What a great story! A book that fishermen of all ages (and species) are sure to enjoy."
    —Tony Rizzo, legendary Northwoods fishing guide and author of *Secrets of a Muskie Guide*

"Murder mystery muskies! The *X-Files* comes to Packer Land."   —John Krga, dedicated Northwoods "catch-and-release" muskie fisherman

Dead Angler

"Who would have thought that fly-fishing could be such fun? Victoria Houston makes you want to dash for rod and reel. [She] cleverly blends the love of the outdoors with the thrill of catching a serial killer."

—*The Orlando Sentinel*

"As exciting as fishing a tournament—and you don't know the result until the end." —Norb Wallock, North American Walleye Anglers' 1997 Angler of the Year

"Houston introduces us to a cast of characters with whom we quickly bond—as fly-fishers and as good citizens—in the first of what I hope will be a long series."

—Joan Wulff, world-class fly caster, and cofounder of the Wulff School of Fly-Fishing

"A compelling thriller . . . populated with three-dimensional characters who reveal some of their secrets of trout fishing the dark waters of the northern forests."

—Tom Wiench, dedicated fly-fisherman and member of Trout Unlimited

"Should net lots of fans . . . a good catch."

—*The Star Press*

Dead Water

VICTORIA HOUSTON

Victoria Houston

BERKLEY PRIME CRIME, NEW YORK

This is a work of fiction. Names, characters, places, and incidents either are the product of the author's imagination or are used fictitiously, and any resemblance to actual persons, living or dead, business establishments, events, or locales is entirely coincidental.

DEAD WATER

A Berkley Prime Crime Book / published by arrangement with the author

PRINTING HISTORY
Berkley Prime Crime edition / June 2001

The Penguin Putnam Inc. World Wide Web site address is
www.penguinputnam.com

ISBN: 0-425-18003-4

Berkley Prime Crime Books are published
by The Berkley Publishing Group,
a division of Penguin Putnam Inc.,
375 Hudson Street, New York, New York 10014.
The name BERKLEY PRIME CRIME and the
BERKLEY PRIME CRIME design
are trademarks belonging to Penguin Putnam Inc.

PRINTED IN THE UNITED STATES OF AMERICA

10 9 8 7 6 5 4 3 2 1

*For Judith Cooke,
the kindest and dearest of friends*

one

"The true trout fisherman is like a drug addict; he dwells in a tight little dream world all his own. . . ."

Robert Traver

Lost Lake. June 15, a Tuesday. Eight-twenty A.M.

The sky was peach that day. Peach scudded with wisps of periwinkle blue. An innocent sky. A sky that assured Paul Osborne nothing was wrong in the world. *You dummkopf,* he would find himself saying before eleven that morning, *never trust a sky.*

The sea kayak was taking some getting used to, and he wasn't sure yet that he liked it. Of course he could never tell his daughters that. They must have shelled out a thousand bucks or more for the boat, a Father's Day gift handmade of red cedar and trucked to the backwoods of northern Wisconsin from Swan Lake, Montana. Osborne knew he was lucky: No one in Loon Lake had ever seen such an elegant two-cockpit seventeen-footer.

Still, he felt awkward: waist-deep in water but wearing a skirt, not waders, legs immobilized with only his upper body free to move, hands occupied but no fishing rod, not even his five-weight fly rod. Nothing about the damn thing felt natural.

Maybe it was being imprisoned below water level that bothered him. Maybe it was knowing the kayak was allowing him to cruise into wilderness where even canoes couldn't go that made him feel he was violating nature. Or maybe it was instinct. Whatever it was, he felt uneasy. Uneasy yet compelled to keep pushing deeper and deeper into the swamp guarding the lakeshore.

"Ease up, bud, this is what a kayak is meant to do," Osborne told himself, thrusting aside the sense that he was disturbing something he shouldn't.

Dipping one end of his paddle and ignoring the rustled warnings of the weed bed underneath the calm surface, he slid the kayak over menacing shadows of submerged boulders. His eyes scanned the dense underbrush. What made the bog impervious to any other boat also made it a safe haven for nesting loons and the blue heron. A sighting of either would make his morning.

Osborne inhaled deeply. The air, fragrant with pine and spring grass, made him feel alive, alert, and exquisitely tuned to the signs and murmurs around him. He spotted a break in the wall of brush off to his right and let the kayak drift toward it. The water deepened as protective branches of tamarack fell away to expose a creek of good width. Something familiar in the pattern of trees and rocks tugged at the back of his mind. When had he fished here?

Suddenly he swung back on his paddle, pulling the kayak hard to the right, nose pointing north. Seeing the shore from that angle jarred loose the memory. That massive boulder to the east of the opening—he knew that rock, even though it had to be over twenty years since he had accidentally drifted into this watery trail. Suddenly, as if it were just yesterday, he remembered boosting his two young daughters out of the old wooden canoe so the three of them could sit on the big rock and eat bologna sandwiches, the sun easy on their cheeks and foreheads.

Maneuvering the kayak so he could see upstream, he studied the opening. The cedar and spruce hiding the entrance had grown and changed, but the same gap in the marshy border exposed the same creek, the same heart-breaking beauty of a path that shimmered as it twined north between spires of tamarack and skeletal fingers of dead pine. That year, he and the girls had canoed north to where the stream ended in a spring-fed pool tucked so deep into the tamarack forest that Erin, his youngest, had named it Lost

Lake. Hard to believe she was over thirty now with children of her own.

Only an exceptionally high water level from the spring runoff of a heavy snow that year had made it possible for the three of them to reach the tiny circle of perfect water. Osborne edged the kayak upstream. Was Lost Lake still there? Or had beavers reworked nature? Erin would be tickled to death if he could bring her and the kids back in here. Osborne felt a grin spread across his face.

A flash over his left shoulder caught his eye and he ducked, rocking the kayak. But it was only a great blue heron not expecting visitors. As he watched, the gaunt, gangling bird unfolded like a giant origami sculpture coming undone. Then, tucking in its loopy neck, the great blue circled up and over to disappear behind the tamarack tips just as Osborne realized he was holding his breath. He exhaled. Fifty years of fishing the Northwoods, and that was as close as he had ever gotten to one of the prehistoric-looking birds. Jeez, he thought, maybe this kayak wasn't such a bad idea.

He glided forward, feeling at one with the boat for the first time that morning. The solitude was bordered with a soft trill of birdcalls and a burbling of water. Fishing had addicted him to this kind of peace, a peace he was learning to substitute for the seduction of single-malt scotch, a peace he could find only near water. It restored his spirit when he felt the clutch of loneliness.

Sunlight and shadows drew him deeper, and the kayak slid through the rusted arch of an old culvert. Osborne ducked to avoid wolf spiders nesting in the dark recesses overhead. Nearing the end of the tunnel, he could see, less than a hundred yards upstream, the rusting girders of an abandoned railroad trestle that marked the entrance to Lost Lake.

As the kayak emerged into a patch of sun, dragonfly wings caught the light bouncing off the water. Hold on there. Was that a green stone fly hatch? Tiny helicopters with double sets of wings whirred overhead. No . . . maybe little yellow sallies? Osborne peered up intently, regretting again the lack of a fly rod, not to mention his polarized sunglasses. He looked down but all he could see were a few dead mayflies drifting on the surface. If the bug life was tantalizing any trout, the water, dark from the tannin of pine needles, was hiding its treasures. He'd have to come back with his waders to be sure.

What a shame, he thought, but he grinned, marveling for the umpteenth time at how his belated return to fly-fishing was changing his life.

Raising his paddle to let the kayak drift, he studied the insects. He was determined to learn the Latin names of the damn things. First, of course, he had to learn to recognize them in plain English. One, then another fish slurped. One splashed behind him. He spun around. A trout? A brown? Or a brookie? He sat rock still, not even breathing, hoping it would jump again. His eyes raked the surface for a betraying dimple. The water ranged from one to three feet deep here. That splash was loud. Could a young muskie be feeding in such cold water?

Letting his breath out slowly, he lifted the paddle from the water. Tamarack crowded his peripheral vision, spilling their spring needles in frothy strands studded with cones. What a juicy moment: He could feel the dark water alive beneath him, charged with larva hatching and fish feasting. Overhead, the peach sky had morphed into a crisp new blue. White clouds scudded. Utter quiet prevailed.

"Peace and solitude, bud, life don't get no better than this," whispered Osborne, relishing the bad grammar of his fisherman's mantra as he let the kayak drift.

A scream split the silence wide open. A full-throttle human scream.

two

"Only dead fish swim with the stream."

Anonymous

Osborne froze, blood drumming in his ears.

"Hel-l-o-o," he hollered, once he recovered from the shock of the scream. Had someone fallen out of their boat? Who could possibly be back in here?

No answer.

"Hel-l-o-o-o," he tried again, his voice booming into the silence of the woods around him. The scream still reverberated in his head. Whoever it was sounded terrified. But no one answered his calls.

Just as Osborne thrust the kayak forward, a slash of orange rounded a curve beyond the trestle. Another instant and the slash became a kayak moving swiftly toward him. Above the cockpit, a woman's face twisted with fear and exertion as she pushed over the still water. Mouth gaping, shoulders heaving, she looked like she was strangling on her own breath. Behind her sat a small child in a bright blue life jacket.

As the kayak neared and slowed, Osborne recognized the strong-boned Swedish face under the short frizzy hair.

"Marlene! What on earth—?" He pulled his kayak toward her.

"Oh, Doctor . . . Dr. Osborne." She slowed to a stop, heaving as she spoke. Tears were streaming down her cheeks.

"What is it, kiddo? Is someone hurt? How can I help?" Even as he offered assistance, Osborne felt inadequate, his legs locked in place in the damn kayak. He couldn't jump out to help if he had to.

Marlene Johnson was the same age as his oldest daughter, Mallory. She and her parents had been patients of his years ago, but the elder Johnsons were now dead a good ten years or more. Marlene had not lived in Loon Lake since her marriage to a man from Stevens Point. Osborne vaguely remembered Mallory saying she had seen Marlene, now divorced, at a recent high school reunion.

"Oh my God, oh thank God," Marlene gasped, looking back as if she were being chased. "Someone's dead. Back there." She pointed toward the trestle with her paddle. "We've got to get out of here. The face . . . it's too awful . . . it's . . ."

"Marlene," Osborne spoke sternly. The woman was on the verge of hysteria. "Settle down. Now take a deep breath." At the look on her face, he repeated himself louder. "I mean it," he said, "take . . . a deep . . . breath."

Osborne may have retired from his practice, but he hadn't lost his skills. Years of dentistry had vested him with a tone of authority designed to stun frightened patients into stillness. Early on he had learned that adults calmed quickly when treated like a child.

Marlene was no exception. She relaxed ever so slightly.

"Okay," said Osborne, as if rewarding her, "I will go back and see what the story is, but first I want you and your youngster here to take it easy. Can you do that?" His eyes fixed on hers for an answer. She nodded.

"You're safe, Marlene, nothing is going to happen. If you found a dead person, they're dead. That means they're not moving." His tone softened.

"You're absolutely right, Dr. Osborne," she said, smiling at his little joke and breathing easier as she wiped the wetness from her face. Then her eyes widened again. "But what if the killer saw me?"

Osborne studied her, deciding not to express the opinion that someone had been watching too much TV. "Listen, kiddo." The sternness crept back into his voice, "If you found a body back there, chances are it's a hunting accident. You're in Loon Lake, Marlene, not Milwaukee. Besides, you didn't see anyone, did you?"

"No . . . but that's no hunting accident."

A little face leaned out from behind Marlene. He couldn't have been more than five years old. "That dead lady lost her pants."

"I did *not* intend for my son to see what he saw," said Marlene, switching from fear to anger. Her tone implied it might be Osborne's fault that she had stumbled onto something ugly.

The sudden change in Marlene's attitude triggered an equally sudden and unpleasant memory of his late wife, who had a talent for placing blame elsewhere, elsewhere being him. Some folks learn to drive defensively; Osborne had spent thirty-odd years *living* on the defense.

Enough of this, was his immediate thought. "I wouldn't worry, Marlene." He worked at keeping an edge out of his voice and resisted the urge to tell her the kid was in much better shape than she was.

"Why don't you and your son head for my place and call the police. The house is open. My dog is loose in the yard, but he's friendly. The phone is in the kitchen, and I want you to see if you can reach Chief Ferris, okay? She knows exactly where I live. If you can't reach her direct, let the switchboard know where you are and what's going on. Then help yourselves to anything in the fridge—a pop or some iced tea. There's hot coffee on the counter, too. I'm going upstream and take a quick look. Okay? Can you manage that, Marlene?"

"I . . . how do I get out of here, Doctor? We came in from Shepard Lake, but I don't know my way out this direction. Once I got past that body, I couldn't bear to go back. And be very careful. Someone may be back there, y'know."

"Don't worry about me. I've done this before," Osborne assured her. "The way back is easy. Just head straight downstream, bear right as you enter the bog, and that'll take you to the channel between First and Second Lake. Take a right through the channel markers into Loon Lake, then a left down the west shoreline. My dock is the sixth one down, the one with two rocking chairs."

"Got it." Marlene raised her paddle. Sitting up straight, the fear out of her eyes and the redness in her cheeks subsiding, Marlene took on an air of competency. Her son's eyes were sparkling. Osborne could see this was all great fun for him, blood and guts included.

Osborne pulled his kayak tight to the bank so she could glide past. Then he thrust his paddle deep into the water. He had forgotten to ask where the body was, but it wasn't necessary.

No sooner had he emerged from under the trestle than he heard, even before he saw, the cloud of flies to his immediate right—a distinctive sound he remembered well from his tour of duty as a forensic dentist during the Korean War. Twenty feet beyond the cloud, the stream widened to become Lost Lake, but he was no longer interested in the lake.

Osborne pulled up to halt the kayak. He let it drift toward the bank. The air was pungent with death. But it was the sight rather than the smell that pulled at his gut: Loon Lake was so small, the odds were great he was about to encounter someone he knew, someone who hadn't expected to die and whose death would cause grief to others he knew. He just hoped he didn't know them well.

At first glance, the corpse appeared to be standing on its head, the face turned away from him toward Lost Lake. The lower torso, buttocks, and legs were naked and hung up on a tag alder bush. The upper back and shoulders still wore a woman's halter top, and the head was tipped down onto the bank, almost but not quite touching the water. She couldn't have been dead too long as the color was not bad. Certainly not black, thank goodness. The last two nights' temperatures had dipped into the low forties, and the days had been cool. That would help, too.

The limbs were splayed as if someone might have tossed the body through the air. He looked up. They had. She either fell or was dropped from the trestle. Could this be someone who was taking a walk along the old bridge only to be hit by a stray bullet from a hunter? Not with hunting season five months away. Osborne's stomach tightened. Marlene's theory was looking good.

With a quick thrust, he drove the kayak onto the grassy bank, unsnapped the skirt from around his waist, and boosted himself up, out, and into the water. He decided to walk in the shallows as much as possible so as not to disturb any footprints or other sign that might be left near the body.

Osborne crouched to study the corpse from the back. He thought he could detect an entry wound at the back of the head: a blackish red bubble of dried tissue that stood out against the light-colored short hair. He'd know for sure in a minute. That could rule out suicide. Tough to shoot yourself in the back of the head.

He stood up, chagrined he did not have his tackle box. Too many years of people mistaking the *Dr.* in front of his name to mean *doctor,* not *dentist,* along with too many years of being asked to remove fishhooks from noses, ears, and eyes, had taught him to always approach water with a pair of latex surgical gloves in his tackle box. He sure could use those now. Osborne patted the back pocket of his fishing khakis, hoping against hope he had a pair tucked away. Nope.

Spotting a dead tree limb on the opposite bank, he opted to use that instead. Extending the branch, he prodded the left arm. Limp. Rigor mortis had come and gone. That would put time of death at or over twenty-four hours ago, but— given the amount of maggot activity he could see plus the color of the corpse—still within the last forty-eight hours. That would make sense. He could not imagine anyone in Loon Lake missing more than two days without everyone in town knowing.

Taking as few steps as he could, Osborne hiked up to the

back of the tag alder for a better view of the lower body. The lab in Wausau, sixty miles away, was much better prepared than he to assess many details including time of death, the nature of the assault, and the exact weapons used, but his training in dental forensics might help speed up the identification, maybe even point out a few more mitigating factors, something always appreciated by Loon Lake Police Chief Lewellyn Ferris.

And she needed every advantage she could get over the goombahs in Wausau, who had a habit of trying to weasel in on interesting cases, either for publicity's sake or to pad the bill for their services. In Osborne's opinion, the Wausau boys relished giving Lew a hard time simply because she had nailed a job two of them had applied for. He knew that in their feeble minds, a dutiful Northwoods female, mindful of the alpha male culture of the region, should have declined the position when it was offered. Not Lew.

She embraced it with enthusiasm, gender politics and all. And the politics were an ongoing issue as Loon Lake, population 3,197, was too small to have its own crime lab, though it held its own when it came to crime. Or so Osborne had learned since helping Lew out on two earlier occasions. Those two occasions had also shown him an easy route to Lew's affections: She loved whatever he could do to save her time, paperwork, and money by limiting the involvement of the Wausau boys.

From where he stood now, Osborne got a good view of the chest below the halter top. Blood had pooled along the left rib cage, indicating the victim was deceased before she flew off that trestle.

He stepped around the buzzing flies to view the right side of the body. That's when he saw what had terrified Marlene: the blown-out face. Not a great sight for a five-year-old. Not a great sight for a sixty-three-year-old retired dentist either, forensic experience or not. He looked away fast, then looked back. Had to be a high-powered rifle to do that kind of damage. Made him think .30/06, but he'd let Wausau answer that question.

Even though most of the upper face was missing, the mouth and portions of the lower jaw were intact. The mouth gaped, making the teeth easily visible. Osborne knelt again. The canines and the lateral incisors looked vaguely familiar. The lower front teeth were crowded, a pretty distinctive pattern there. With several fillings visible, the mouth appeared cared for. He had a strong hunch he had seen this mouth before. If so, he would have a record in his files. Thank God he had hidden those when Mary Lee tried to force him to throw them away.

Osborne leaned back on his knees. So . . . a woman from Loon Lake with a nice smile. A sick sadness flooded his chest as he stood up. Thrusting his hands deep into his pockets, he stood staring at the still, pale form, committing the details of its position and location to memory.

Osborne turned to wade quickly through the stream and pull the kayak into the water. He had to get Lew out here right away. With that thought, the sadness gave way to a sheepish eagerness: The murder would generate just the opportunity for which he had been hoping.

To be honest, more than one opportunity. Given that Lew felt she did her best strategic thinking in the trout stream, and given that she did not like to fish alone, chances were excellent that if she deputized him to work on this case, she would have to include him in her fly-fishing. That could be every night. She had done so in the past, which had improved his fly-fishing immeasurably, not to mention increased the number of trout flies (tied by Lew) added to his box. Her ability to forecast a hatch—*and have the right trout fly along*—impressed the hell out of Osborne.

But his urge to help the Loon Lake chief of police went well beyond improving his backcast or learning the hatch. The simple fact was that assisting Lewellyn Ferris bought him time to be around a woman who had no idea he adored her.

As Osborne leaned to lower himself into the kayak, he scanned the landscape one last time. Marlene had seemed so sure someone might be back here. He heard nothing except the flies buzzing and a few random birdcalls. Not a branch, not a blade of grass moved in the still sunshine. A few yards away, Lost Lake looked as peaceful as heaven.

He gave the body a once-over. From this angle, he could see the eagles and turkey buzzards had already begun their work: myriad puncture wounds stood out in sharp relief along the curve of the bare shoulders, so close to the ground that he had almost missed them. His eyes lingered. Something was too familiar in those patterns. Much too familiar.

Shoving the kayak aground and slogging back to the corpse, Osborne dropped to his knees for a closer look. This was not the work of vultures or eagles. No sirree. The Northwoods held many surprises, but that did not include birds with canines, molars, and incisors. Yet he was looking down at four bites, almost symmetrical, two on each shoulder.

Four bites from four *different* sets of teeth. Human teeth.

three

"An expert is a person with whom you go fishing, and if nobody catches anything, knows all the reasons why."

Anonymous

Marlene ran onto the dock just as Osborne pulled up in the kayak. Osborne had forgotten the woman was six feet tall. She was strong, too, reaching without hesitation to give him a hand up, then help him hoist the kayak from the water. Behind her, Mike, his black Lab, was bouncing happily.

"I take it you reached Chief Ferris?" said Osborne as they boosted the wooden craft onto their shoulders and started up the river rock stairs toward his house. She nodded. Mike took off ahead and disappeared.

"She's on her way," said Marlene. She turned to look at him, her eyes dark with concern. "Wasn't I right? That was no natural death, do you think?"

"I agree with you . . . but it's Chief Ferris who makes the call," said Osborne, reluctant to say more until Lew could check it out. Word spreads fast in a small town, and he knew Lew would want to control just how many details were out there. "She may ask you to keep this quiet for a while, Marlene."

Marlene trudged in silence for a minute. "Do you think she was raped?"

"I have no idea. The Wausau lab will test for that. One thing I do know, which ought to make you feel better, is this: That individual has been deceased at *least* twenty-four hours. I saw absolutely no sign of anyone lurking, not even a crushed blade of grass. That body came off the trestle sometime yesterday at the earliest. So don't you worry that you and your son saw something you shouldn't have or that you were observed by anyone."

Marlene's shoulders relaxed under the weight of the kayak. Even her stride up the rock stairway was suddenly firmer, lighter. Osborne smiled gently at the sight of her relief. He felt like a good father. "Turn right at the gate, head toward the garage, and watch for Mike mines."

"Mike mines?"

"Dog poop."

"Ah." They walked forward in silence. At the gate, Marlene paused to adjust the kayak. "My son is in your kitchen with a strange man," she said, her voice cheery. "He seems to know you. He walked right in without knocking."

"Oh yeah? Tall guy?"

"Very tall—with a stuffed fish on his head. Robby is fascinated."

"My neighbor, Ray Pradt," said Osborne. "Did you see that trailer home as you paddled toward my dock? That's his place. You remember Ray, Marlene. He's just a couple years younger than you and Mallory."

"*That's* little Raysie?" said Marlene. "Last time I saw him, he was four feet tall. My God, he's grown!"

Osborne chortled. "Yes, he has." At six feet five and in his early thirties, Ray would be mortified to learn that an attractive single woman remembered him as little Raysie. Whoa, Osborne couldn't wait to lay this one on his pal. Little Raysie. Wait till the guys at McDonald's heard about it; the seven A.M. coffee klatch would have fuel for weeks.

"So what does Ray do these days, Dr. Osborne?" She tried to sound nonchalant.

"You mean, why does he wear a fish on his head?"

Marlene laughed.

"Well . . ." said Osborne, hesitating only because he always got a kick out of describing Ray to adults who spent their lives making sensible decisions. "Ray Pradt is considered one of the finest fishing and hunting guides in the

Northwoods. He guides for muskie and walleye in the summertime, ruffed grouse, duck, and deer over the winter. He has clients from Chicago, Milwaukee, even Saint Louis and Kansas City. People who won't fish if they can't fish with Ray."

"You sound like you're bragging about a son," said Marlene, a soft smile on her face.

"I do?" Now it was Osborne's turn to be surprised. "Then I didn't mention the grave digging. God knows why he does that."

"The *what?*"

"Oh, it's the goofiest thing," said Osborne, easing the kayak onto the ground beside the sawhorses and pausing while Marlene did the same. The boat was deceptively heavy. "Yep, Ray's got the franchise on dead Catholics in Loon Lake. He insists he loves it." Osborne mimicked his friend's spiel: " 'A grave a week on average, double that over the holidays, and triple 'tween Christmas and New Year's. Mackerel snappers love to check out before tax time, doncha know.' "

At the look on Marlene's face, Osborne eased up. "Well, it is steady work, and it does augment his income between seasons."

"Jeez," said Marlene, "and his father was a surgeon." Her tone implied that being a doctor's son should somehow insulate you from career choices such as grave digging. Osborne shrugged. That was just one of Ray's many contradictions. If anything, his friend and neighbor was living proof you can never predict the future.

"But he's a hell of a fisherman, Marlene." And with that, Osborne made clear the bottom line on Ray Pradt. He knew she knew that in the Northwoods, praise doesn't come much higher.

He chose not to say more: Not to tell her that Ray, his junior by a good thirty years, had taught him more about life than any of his peers, that the two of them drove in Ray's battered blue pickup twice a week to those heartbreaking meetings behind the door with the coffeepot on the front, and that Ray had saved his life on at least three occasions, not counting the drive through the blizzard the night Mary Lee died.

"Who did you say he's married to?" Again the forced nonchalance as she followed Osborne's lead to lift and turn the kayak over onto the sawhorses.

"Ray?" Osborne repressed a big grin. He had been asked this question in so many ways and on so many different occasions it was ridiculous. Why don't women just flat out ask if a man's available or not? Even his daughters stepped around such matters, though they were hardly oblique when it came to their interest in *his* love life. Mindful of Marlene's childhood friendship with Mallory, Osborne decided to take it easy on her. That plus the fact that her day had not started out so well.

"Confirmed bachelor," he said. "Too bad, too. The man is an exceptional cook." Osborne stopped there. She would have to discover the rest on her own. He reached for a large blue tarp that lay nearby and threw one end of it at Marlene.

"That's so funny," said Marlene. "I would never have guessed Ray Pradt would turn out this way. He was such a serious kid when we were growing up. I would have thought he'd turn into someone quite different—"

"Oh yeah?" Osborne interrupted, intrigued to hear speculation on Ray from someone who had known him as a child and hadn't seen him in years. A bad judge of people too often himself, he loved to hear others make the same mistake.

"Oh . . . college professor, history or philosophy . . . something like that. You know, responsible father of four."

"Well, he may be all of those in a certain sense," said Osborne. "You should get to know him again, Marlene." She gave him an odd look, her mouth opening then closing as if she had decided not to ask a certain question. Instead, she finished tying down the tarp on her end.

Calm now and over her fear, Marlene was not a bad-looking woman. Tall as she was, everything was firm, muscled even. That was something Osborne liked about his daughters' generation: These women looked healthy, quite the opposite of Mary Lee and her crowd. What was with the women in his age group, anyway? They were either overweight or bird-boned. Out of shape, weak, and hardly a one could hold in her stomach. Excluding Lew Ferris, of course. But then he figured Lew to be a good ten years younger. Too young for him, unfortunately.

"Marlene," said Osborne, directing her back around the garage with a wave of his hand, "what the heck were you doing in that swamp? That's a darned remote area, y'know. Not many folks find their way back in there."

"Are you kidding? Lots of people know Secret Lake. That's what we kids called it. There's a path from my cabin on Shepard Lake—I own my parents' old place—that takes you back in there. You have to portage a little ways over a patch of Consolidated Paper land, but that's not hard to do. Dad rigged up kind of a wheelbarrow contraption for our boat, and the two of us would fish almost every day when I was a kid. Great crappie hole—summer and winter.

"So, anyway, that's what I was planning to do with Robby this morning. Beach the kayak, fish off an old log that was my favorite spot when I was a kid, and . . . gosh, that body . . . I didn't see it until I was on top of it, and it just scared the living daylights out of me. Thank God you came along."

"Halt! Who goes there?" boomed a man's voice suddenly from the screened-in porch that fronted Osborne's home.

Ignoring the intruder, Osborne put a hand on Marlene's shoulder. "You're sure you're okay? And Robby?"

The latter half of his question was answered by Robby himself. Dashing out the front porch door of Osborne's house, he rushed up to his mother, bouncing on the balls of his feet. "Mom, can I go fishing with Ray? He knows where I can catch a five-pound walleye. Can I please, huh? Please?"

"Robby," said Osborne, "want a pop?"

"Sure. Whaddaya say, Mom?"

"I want to hear you thank Dr. Osborne for the soda pop first; then I'd like to hear you say '*May* I please'; and, Robby, you know we don't call grown-ups by their first names; it's *Mr. Pradt*," said Marlene, looking over her son's head at Osborne with a question in her eyes. "As far as fishing, let me think about it." Osborne could see she wasn't entirely sure it was wise to trust the well-being of her only child to a man wearing a stuffed trout between his ears— even if she had known him when he was short.

Just then, Ray stepped out from the porch. He was looking exceptionally well put together in a pair of creased hunting pants, the rust-colored cotton duck contrasting nicely with an olive-green fishing shirt, sleeves rolled up and an embroidered walleye glistening on the left pocket. He may have even trimmed his beard, thought Osborne, as the auburn curls flecked with gray looked more tailored than usual. The prized hat must have been left indoors as Ray's head was bare, the rich bounty of auburn curls that matched his beard gleaming in the sun as if freshly shampooed.

An easy grin highlighted the humor in his dark-brown eyes as Ray loped toward them. Whether it was the care he had taken that morning in the shower or simply the sunny loveliness of the day, Osborne could see from the sparkle in Marlene's eyes that Ray was looking particularly handsome.

Or maybe it was Marlene. That was it. Osborne watched Ray straighten all six feet five inches of his lanky frame and suck in his gut as he thrust a large hand toward the woman. "What the heck are you doing looking so doggone beautiful, Robby's mother?" he said, running his words together while pumping Marlene's hand with enthusiasm. "Doc, she ran out before I could ask her her name."

Marlene, simultaneously charmed and alarmed, backed up, stepping on Osborne's foot.

"You're Ray Pradt," she said, her voice less certain than

when she was talking to Osborne. "Don't you remember me?"

Ray's eyes looked her up and down, amused, interested. "Give me minute," he said, staring at her.

"This is Marlene Johnson," said Osborne when it was clear Ray didn't recognize her.

"I *am* a few years older than you—"

"No, don't tell me," interrupted Ray, raising his hands as if to stop her, "you look at least five years *younger*."

Marlene blushed a deep red. Osborne shook his head; there was something about Ray that ladies liked right off the bat. On the other hand, Ray never played his hand quite right once he had his foot in the door. In the two years they had been fishing and kibitzing together, Osborne had learned more about women just from watching Ray's mistakes. Another lesson appeared to be on its way.

four

"The last point of all the inward gifts that doth belong to an angler is memory. . . ."

The Art of Angling, 1577

"Hey, you." Ray leveled a stern look at Robby over his mug of hot coffee. "Knock, knock."

The youngster, delighted to find a grown-up capable of communicating on his five-year-old wavelength, swung his legs so hard he could barely stay in his chair.

"Who's there?" said Robby with a grin so wide it framed three missing teeth.

Osborne looked away from the kitchen window where he was watching Lew's cruiser pull into his driveway just in time to see a smile break on Marlene's face. Robby's pride in letting Ray know he knew this game was so infectious, Osborne followed her lead with an understanding grin of his own.

Ray, meanwhile, having positioned himself across from Robby at the round kitchen table, sat with his legs crossed, arms folded, and fish hat resting in front of him, while his face did its darnedest to look serious.

"Canoe," said Ray.

"Canoe who?" The short legs kicked faster.

"Canoe come out and play?"

"Oh, you!" Robby slammed one fist on the table and hit his forehead with the other. If there was ever a question of Robby's fishing with Ray, the look on Marlene's face sealed the deal.

She's a Northwoods woman all right, thought Osborne. Probably married and divorced a city boy and relieved to finally find a man who could do for Robby what her father had done for her. Yep, chances were good the little guy would see a cane pole, a bobber, and one of Ray's famous egg salad sandwiches before the week was out—not to mention a stringer of big, fat walleyes. Ray might have to poach to make Robby's dream come true, but poaching was just one of the illegal acts that Ray could indulge in when absolutely necessary.

"Doc." Ray looked over at Osborne with a sideways glance. "Any problem my hearing what you have to say to Lew, or do you need me to leave?"

"Stay right where you are," said Osborne.

As he spoke, the back door opened.

"Turns out I *do* have a missing person," said Lew in her clipped way after Osborne had finished describing the scene at Lost Lake. She had taken the chair next to Ray at the kitchen table and gratefully accepted a microwave-warmed mug of black coffee. She was hardly relaxed, however, positioning herself on the edge of the chair and swallowing the coffee in gulps.

Osborne couldn't take his eyes off her. The police department's summer uniform of khaki pants and a matching shirt, buttoned to the neck and anchored with a forest-green tie, set off the warm brown of her skin, lightly toasted by a late-spring sun. Her mouth was generous, smiling easily, exposing the even whiteness of her teeth. Osborne could never get over the fact she had the blackest eyes, the liveliest eyes of any woman he'd ever known. Right now, those eyes were focused on him.

It had crossed his mind in recent weeks that Lew had a way of filling a room. At least, *he* was acutely aware when she was nearby. Not a small woman, Lew Ferris stood about five feet eight inches tall, with a figure Osborne described to his oldest daughter, Mallory, as "trim, extremely fit, and with enough upper-body strength to slam a two-hundred-pound drunk to the deck so fast he'd never know what hit him." This morning her khaki shirt was tucked neatly into the belted waistband of her smooth, narrow-legged trousers, but not so loosely that Osborne wasn't aware of her breasts pushing against the crisp cotton.

Even though Lew had a tough edge to her—she had been brusque in her introduction to Marlene—she exuded confidence, a subtle warmth, and something more. Erin had nailed it. As a Loon Lake wife, mother of three, part-time lawyer, and chairman of the Loon Lake school board, she knew people. Better than that, she knew women. It was Erin who had commented to Osborne after watching Lew during a county commission meeting when she was being grilled on her annual budget that she considered Chief Ferris one of the few women she knew to be "happy in her skin."

Osborne was not sure exactly what that meant, but he knew he was happy when she waved to him if their vehicles happened to pass going in opposite directions, when she invited him to share a trout stream on a calm summer night and, at the moment, he was doubly happy that she was inhaling coffee in his kitchen. At the same time, he was refusing to think how deeply pleased he would be if she drafted him to be a deputy on this case.

"Just as I was leaving the office after Marlene's call," Lew was saying, "Phil Herre stopped in to tell me he and Georgia haven't been able to reach their daughter, Sandy, for a couple days now. She's got her own place, so they didn't worry too much at first, but when she didn't show up for a nephew's baptism yesterday, they got concerned. And she hasn't been answering any phone calls. He asked me to go with him to her town house on my way out here, which I was happy to do. . . ."

The kitchen was quiet as Lew took a long sip of her coffee. "No sign of the woman. She's got a bassett hound, and the poor dog was left in the house the entire weekend. Phil said it was not like Sandy to leave him with no food or water, having accidents all over the place—"

"Sandy Herre?" Osborne interrupted. Bracing both hands on the kitchen counter where he stood, he dropped his head, thinking hard. That mouth, the crowded teeth on the lower jaw . . . it had looked so familiar. "Sandy Herre," he repeated himself. "Excuse me a minute."

Osborne hurried around the garage to the little room off the back where he cleaned fish. Using his shoulder, he shoved at an inside door that opened reluctantly to a narrow storage area running across the rear of the garage. Here he had hidden the old oak files that held all the dental records from his practice. Mary Lee had insisted that he throw them out. Instead, when she was out playing bridge one night, he had enlisted Ray to help him hide them back in here. Fortunately, she had never thought to look in this musty, cobwebbed room.

The files were meticulously organized. He had separated his thirty-five years of dentistry into decades, then alphabetically within each decade—a system that had evolved from his habit of making up new files for each patient every ten years or so.

He loved these files. They spoke to him of his pride in his work and his affection for almost all the people that had needed him. He and Ray often joked that the dental file was to Osborne what the headstone was to Ray: a point of departure for a good story. And if Ray insisted that the inscription on a headstone was a clue to character, Osborne could argue that what he found in a mouth was a metaphor for a life: sparkling clean or crummy with unnecessary plaque; teeth broken and left unrepaired or strong from healthy habits; every space accounted for or gaping holes where teeth should have been, holes left open for reasons beyond the owner's control.

To find Sandy Herre, he had to go back only seven years. He was lucky she was there. Anything more recent than five had been left with the young dentist who took over his practice.

Osborne pulled the file and opened it to find a set of

full-mouth X rays taken when she was sixteen. Turning toward the light from the doorway, he held up the narrow strip of white cardboard with its small gray black inserts. As he studied the X rays, he could recall Phil Herre's voice as he, a man of modest means, and his daughter had decided she could live with the slightly crooked lower teeth because the bill for orthodontics would have crippled the family's finances.

Lew rose from her chair as Osborne returned to the kitchen, the question in her eyes making them seem even darker. She said nothing as Osborne stopped and looked at her, his right thumb cupping his chin as his index finger pressed against his pursed lips. He cursed his autonomic nervous system as he had so often in his life when emotion reduced him to silence. Feeling his eyes tear up, he cleared his throat, but no sound came out. Where should he start? Sandy was just a kid. Only twenty-three. Younger than his daughters. Phil and Georgia would be devastated. And they were such good people. . . .

Ray spoke first, laying a firm hand on little Robby's shoulder, which caused the child to quiet down instantly. Osborne was always amazed at the intuition of young children: Robby's eyes, watching Osborne, were as worried as his mother's.

"Ah, so it *is* Sandy." Ray's deep tones filled the silence. Osborne nodded.

"Hmm . . ." Ray looked down at the table as he twisted a curl of his beard; then he glanced around at the group, the easy humor gone from his face. "This will be one tough grave to dig." His voice was matter-of-fact yet soft in the quiet room. "She was a good . . . kind . . . woman." Ray had a way of drawing out his words when the situation was serious.

"Good, kind, and dead," said Lew, with not a little anger in her voice. "Son of a bitch." She set her coffee mug down hard as she spoke. "Bring that file along, Doc?"

Osborne nodded.

She walked past him to the door, then gave him a side-long glance. "Got time to work on this?"

He nodded again. Funny how life turns on a dime.

"Ray." Lew stopped and turned, her right hand resting on her nine-millimeter SIG Saur holster. "Nobody knows that damn swamp better'n you. What's the best way to get there from here?"

"The best or the fastest?"

"You know what I mean."

"Let's look at a map. Any chance of suicide?" asked Ray, unfolding his long body from the kitchen chair.

"Nope," said Osborne, "not unless you can shoot yourself in the back of the head. And, Lew, I suggest you call your bug man right away. If you can get him in to set time of death, you can probably shave two to three days off your billing from the Wausau boys."

"Good idea, Doc. Bob Marlett is terrific with maggots, best in the region, and he lives just over in Point. Boy, if I can get him up to the site before we bag the body . . . well, let's just hope he's not on vacation."

Marlene, who had been leaning against the kitchen counter behind her son's chair, suddenly brought both hands to her face and burst into uncontrolled sobbing.

"Oh, golly," said Osborne. He set the file down on the table and walked over to fold his arms around her. "There, there." He patted her heaving shoulders as if she were one of his own daughters. "Marlene . . . kiddo," he murmured into her ear, "take it easy. I'll tell you what. Mallory is driving over from . . . ." He paused, deciding not to tell her where Mallory was coming from. "She'll be here later today. Why don't I have her give you a call? You two can catch up. Take your mind off this. How's that, huh?"

He looked over at Lew, expecting her to follow his attempt to console the young woman with something reassuringly official like a request for a brief statement. Instead, he found her watching him with a peculiar look on her face. A look that made him acutely aware that he had his arms around a young and attractive woman. It was a look he had never expected and one he would mull over again and again in the coming days, secretly pleased each time.

five

"At the outset, the fact should be recognized that the community of fishermen constitute a separate class or subrace among the inhabitants of the earth."

Grover Cleveland

A quick study of the *Wisconsin Gazetteer*, an atlas of back roads that Osborne kept in his car, along with a suggestion from Ray, pointed them in the direction of an old logging lane running parallel to the abandoned North Central Railroad tracks. With luck, they could park close to the body.

Lew waited while Osborne double-checked the contents of his black bag, making sure he had all the dental instruments he would need for an on-site exam. He slipped Sandy's file in, too.

"Call the Herres, Lew?" he asked before they left the kitchen.

"Not until I'm absolutely positive."

"Doc," said Ray, walking them out to Lew's cruiser, "I'll take care of Marlene and Robby . . . put their kayak in my truck and give them a ride over to her cottage. But I stopped by for a reason." Ray thrust his hands into his pockets and looked at Osborne with unsmiling eyes. "I hope you don't mind; I have a favor to ask for one of my clients."

"Sure," said Osborne, opening the door on the passenger side of the police cruiser and wondering why Ray looked so uneasy.

"I would like to borrow your Browning, if I may."

"My twenty-gauge?" Osborne, who had just bent to climb into the car, straightened up to stare at his friend. Ray knew better than that. The Browning was one of his treasures. He

had purchased the Belgian-made side-by-side shotgun with the small inheritance he had received from his father. The Browning was more than a gun; it was a cherished relic. He loaned it to no one, not Erin, not Mallory. Not even the man who had saved his life.

"What are you doing after you drop off Marlene and Robby?" asked Lew, buying Osborne time to consider the request.

Ray checked his watch. "It's ten-thirty now. I have to meet my client at the gun club at one. Doc, it's that Gabrielle from Dallas. Her fiancé is taking her wing shooting in Ireland, and he has some fancy twenty-thousand-dollar shotgun from Holland & Holland. She wants to impress him, and I had mentioned your Browning—"

"Do you have time to meet us at the site in half an hour?" interrupted Lew.

"I can do that." Between his question and her questions, Ray looked a little discombobulated.

"Let me think about the gun," said Osborne, still perplexed by the request. He knew all about the client. Ray had been thrilled to book the flashy Texan who was staying at the exclusive Dairyman's Association in Boulder Junction. She was paying him a thousand bucks a day for crash courses in walleye fishing, skeet, and shooting clays, courses she hoped would coax a wedding ring out of her billionaire boyfriend. Osborne wavered. If the gun was worth another five or ten thousand for Ray, who could really use the cash, and if it would help to land Hubby Number Four, garnering Ray a serious bonus even, should he be selfish? Ray would take good care of the firearm.

"All right, all right," Osborne called out with some reluctance as Ray was opening the door to the back porch, "you can borrow the gun. Take it out of the cabinet while you're in there. You know where I keep the key."

"Thanks, Doc." Ray smiled and stepped into the house.

"You sure you want to do that?" asked Lew as she turned the ignition key. "The look on your face—"

"No," said Osborne, "I'm not. The last thing I want is that gun in the hands of some overaccessorized blond, but the woman is the best piece of business Ray's ever landed. I don't think I told you about her, Lew.

"Gabrielle Westbrook is a well-preserved divorcée, maybe in her forties, and stalking Husband Number Four—maybe it's Number Five—who the hell knows with people like that. She called Ray out of the blue two months ago and told him she wants this big-game goombah to think she's an expert outdoorswoman. Offered to pay him a thousand a day—"

"A thousand bucks *a day?*"

"Yep."

"That's a lot of money for Ray."

"That's a lot of money for anybody, especially up here . . . and I owe him, Lew. He's been there for me when it counted. You know that. So he can have the damn gun."

And Lew knew exactly why he owed the younger man.

Taking cover under an overhang of the Wolf River while trout fishing late one night, they had had to wait nearly an hour for a thunderstorm to pass. An hour during which Osborne had told the story of his wife's death. He wanted her to know the details of that night because it explained his loyalty to Ray Pradt.

Lew tended to come down hard on Ray, needling him for his bad jokes, his ill-timed bird calls, and his record of misdemeanors, a lengthy list that included repeated citations for poaching on private land and, at the same time or on other occasions, smoking a popular controlled substance. It was the latter that caused her to balk at deputizing Ray just when he was most needed.

Lew might deputize Osborne for help in identifying victims and early clues to cause of death, but when she needed a jump on some nogoodnik hunkered down in an abandoned whiskey still somewhere deep in the Northwoods, she would need Ray, arrest record and all. At least Osborne thought so. No one—meaning no one on the police force or in the Loon

Lake telephone directory—could cut through woods and cross water like Ray. It was as if he had been born with the instincts of an eagle. It had crossed Osborne's mind more than once that where Ray's father had been a cutter of the body, Ray could go to the heart of nature. Unerringly and without fear.

And so he had taken advantage of the lightning strikes over the Wolf River to make Lew listen. Methodically, as if detailing a new technique for root canals, he had described Mary Lee's dedicated torture of the young and not-so-innocent fishing guide.

It started when Ray lucked into ownership of the property next door to the Osbornes' newly constructed lakeside home because he happened to be at a grave site, waiting to fill it in, just as the deceased's heirs discussed their plan to put the land up for sale. Loon Lake being one of Wisconsin's top five trophy muskie lakes, Ray, shovel in hand, made an offer over and above the asking price.

Days later, the parking of the "Pradt Mobile," the scruffy trailer Ray called home, in full view of Mary Lee's living room picture window, was the catalyst for full-scale warfare. The president of the Loon Lake Garden Club was not going to have *that trailer trash* ruin "everything I've worked for in my life."

She wasn't exaggerating. Over the thirty-eight years of their marriage, Osborne had come to realize that he'd married a woman who prized her possessions above all else, certainly above him. Nor was she happy unless she was in full control of any life that touched hers. This meant she was seldom happy.

If Osborne had fine-tuned the art of escape through fishing, Mary Lee had turned negativity into her artistic achievement. The most pleasant remark or gesture from her husband—or a friend—was always interpreted as a cover for some hidden, dastardly agenda. Only her daughters were viewed as benign.

And so it was that Ray met one of the few people who ever hated him.

He took it on the chin. Where Osborne had learned to duck and cover, Ray stood his ground, a sheepish, amiable grin flitting across his features as Mary Lee conducted herself like Rumpelstilskin, stomping along the property line, hands hard on her hips or fingers jabbing into the air, and all the while shouting demands.

"I hear you, Mrs. Osborne," was Ray's gentle response. Just those words and nothing more. One morning, pushed to the edge by Ray's refusal to move his trailer and the Oneida County sheriff's determination that the Pradt Mobile was legally sited, she even called Ray's heritage into question. At that point, Osborne suggested she quiet down. He reminded her it was Ray's mother who had proposed Mary Lee for membership in the Rhinelander Garden Club, a group considered more prestigious because it drew from a population ten times the size of Loon Lake.

Meanwhile, unbeknownst to Mary Lee, Osborne decided to befriend Ray, whom he had heard was a wizard when it came to catching trophy fish, whether muskie, walleye, bass, or bluegills. Inviting the younger man to share a couple beers one night when Mary Lee was out playing bridge, the two men reached a détente, based on mutual regard for the trophy fish each had caught over the years. The détente was tested only once, when it was discovered that Ray was piping his sewage illegally, down a gulley that emptied into Mary Lee's rose garden.

The morning Mary Lee realized why her roses were flourishing was one of the few times Osborne got in the way of his wife's ballistic behavior: "You're winning awards for the damn flowers, woman," he had said, "so put a lid on it."

She was so stunned, her jaw dropped. But Osborne wasn't finished: "The last thing we need is inspectors over there who might drop by here. You hassle Ray Pradt on his plumbing, and I can guarantee I'll be tearing down that gazebo you insisted on building ten feet too close to the shoreline." Mary Lee shut up, though she stomped around the house all day.

That afternoon she went golfing with her girlfriends. Osborne, extremely pleased with himself, strolled down to Ray's dock with a six-pack of cold Leinenkugel's and the news that Mary Lee had been told to back off. Early the next morning, he found a mess of fresh-caught bluegills on the back porch, filleted and ready for the frying pan. Prized catch in hand, he stepped into the kitchen only to be confronted with yet another surprise. During the night, Ray had moved the trailer twenty critical feet, twenty feet that restored Mary Lee's vista and made her happy for an entire day. She backed off Ray for a few weeks after that, but soon she found other matters to niggle about. Basically, his very presence aggravated her, and she made no effort to hide it.

That February, a blizzard blew out of the northwest, closing roads and whipping snow so deep into driveways that travel was hopeless. Late on the worst night of the storm, Mary Lee's viral bronchitis turned deadly. It was four in the morning when Osborne knew he had to get her to the hospital. Desperate, he called the only man with a pickup that could plow through their driveway.

Ray hitched the heavy blade on in thirty-below-zero temperatures and three feet of blowing snow, plowed them out, then insisted on driving behind them to the hospital. "If you go in the ditch, Doc, it's all over." And so the two men did everything they could to save the life of a woman who had made them both miserable.

When it was over, Ray was there to drive Osborne to Erin's to deliver the grim news. On the way, Osborne tried to apologize for all the abuse that Mary Lee had heaped on the younger man, but Ray had only shrugged and smiled. "Doesn't matter, Doc. Never did."

That was as much of the story as Osborne chose to share with Lew, though he suspected she knew the rest.

In spite of the fact that Mary Lee had been a hard woman to live with, her death left a hole in Osborne's life, a well of loneliness he tried to fill in all the wrong ways. So wrong that some mornings he awoke on his living room floor, never knowing how he got home. He had, in fact, a vague memory of being helped one night by a police officer who closely resembled Lewellyn Ferris. Why he didn't end up dead, in jail, or without a driver's license, Osborne never quite knew.

It was Erin who intervened, demanding he get help or lose his children and grandchildren, too. She drove him to Hazelden for rehab. Weeks later, back in Loon Lake, he drove himself to AA. The Loon Lake chapter met every Tuesday night. On his first visit, he entered to find an unexpected but familiar face.

"Hey, Doc," said Ray, "take a seat over here if you'd like."

"Thank you, Ray," Osborne had said, walking past other familiar faces. Several were former patients. Two he knew to be drunks, but the others were a real shock. The room was silent as he took his chair. Then Ray curled his right upper lip and let go with a bird trill that brought the other six people in the room to their knees in hysterics. That's when Osborne knew for sure he could change his life. He went home happy for the first time in years.

"Years?" Lew had asked him as he finished his story.

"You betcha." He was happy that night, too, that he was alive to hear the ripples of the river and see the glow of the moonlight in those dark eyes.

Yep, he owed Ray more than the loan of a gun.

Lew's radio hummed suddenly: "Chief Ferris?"

"Lucy." Lew grabbed the handset. "What's up? I've got Doc Osborne in the car, and we're heading over to a logging road that'll put us close to the victim. Looks like it's about a third of a mile past Fire Number Forty thirty-nine. I'll call in after I see exactly what we've got."

"Fine, but a call just came in from some folks over in Pine Lake, Chief. They found a fatality on the road to their house about half an hour ago. Looks like some woman was out jogging and had a heart attack or something. Wait—hold on a minute, the emergency line is ringing. . . ."

As Lew pulled off the county highway and continued down the dirt road, she held the microphone open, waiting for Lucy.

"That was them again," said the switchboard operator. "Not a heart attack. They looked closer and . . . well, they sound pretty upset. Apparently someone out there thinks she was shot."

"Oh for God's sake," said Lew, "will you please tell them not to touch a damn thing."

"I did, Chief," said Lucy. "Do you want me to get Roger out there?"

"Yes, please, and tell *him* not to touch a damn thing."

"Okay," said Lucy.

"Anything else?"

"Hank Kendrickson called. Wants to know if you can go to dinner and fly-fishing with him tonight. Or fly-fishing and dinner, whichever, depending on your schedule."

Osborne froze. Kendrickson was fairly new in Loon Lake, a well-to-do businessman, who appeared to be in his late forties and who Osborne had met only once. Osborne relied on his cronies at McDonald's, with whom he had coffee most mornings at seven, to update him on local gossip. But when it came to Kendrickson, all anyone had gleaned to date was that the man had plenty of money, drove a Range Rover, and had bought the game preserve over in Hazelhurst with money he made in the stock market. Osborne hadn't paid much attention to the gossip. He sure would now.

"What did you tell him?"

"I said you were booked pretty solid with two murders and a bat loose in a house over on Lincoln Street."

Lew snorted.

"I said you'd get back to him," said Lucy. She was an older woman, kind of a blowsy blond with penetrating blue eyes, early wrinkles from smoking too much, and a no-

nonsense attitude she applied to shield her boss from the ridiculous: the missing pets, angry mothers-in-law, and late trash pickups. Right now, she was doing her best to keep the tension level under control, given that she was well aware that two deaths in one morning was a very serious matter for Lew.

"Jeez," said Lew. "Why does everything happen at once? Lucy, would you mind calling Hank back? Tell him we'll do it sometime next week."

A few more back-and-forths with Lucy, and Lew was able to set the handset back on its hook. "That woman's a pro, Doc. Don't know what I'd do without her."

"So, how did you meet Hank Kendrickson?" asked Osborne in what he hoped was a carefree tone of voice.

"Jerry Redfield put us in touch," said Lew, referring to an elderly man considered the guru of fly-fishing. Lew had learned much of what she knew from old Jerry. "He's learning to fly-fish and asked me if I had time to help him out . . . like I do with you."

She looked over at Osborne, and he thought he caught a sly twinkle in her eye. "Of course, I'm not getting a thousand bucks a day. Just a dinner every now and then."

"Oh?" He hoped he sounded a lot more nonchalant than the awful thud in his stomach indicated.

Osborne glanced at the clock on Lew's dashboard. Holy cow, it wasn't even eleven o'clock, and already he was feeling like he'd been taken apart and put back together. What a Tuesday.

six

*"Fishing is a cruel sport . . . how would you like it if
fish and angler were reversed?"*

Robert Hughes

Hot, still air and a dingy cloud hung over the old railroad
tracks. Osborne felt sluggish as he pushed along behind Ray
and Lew. They plodded, too, as if the thick air was holding
them back.

A recently logged forest stretched off ahead and behind
them. The landscape was grim: a stripped slash punctuated
with scraggly, dying spires of trees that hadn't made the cut
and jagged branches of birch and pine thrown about like a
basket of broken pencils upended from a desk. A by-product
of the paper mill economy, slash was exactly what Osborne
always tried to avoid.

Even though he knew that aspen and fern would soon
take over and green it up again, he found the whole scenario
depressing as hell. The mill had done its damage and would
do it again in forty years. But right now, it was a red pine
burial ground. Even wildlife avoided areas like this: No
cover means no safety.

The three of them were about a hundred yards from the
skeleton of the old trestle when Ray waved a halt. Osborne
and Lew paused, eyes fixed on Ray. He was looking up.
Three turkey vultures circled overhead, their blackish wings
raked back to expose ugly red heads.

"Now those fellas," said Ray, looking up at the vultures,
"those fellas . . . hunt . . . with their noses."

"Which means . . ." Osborne tried to hurry him along.

The long pauses combined with the humidity to make him not a little crabby. Ray ignored the question.

"They never show up . . . until their meal . . . is . . . at least," he turned around to Lew and Osborne and pointed up with both index fingers as if to frame his remark, "at *least* twelve hours old."

"Twelve hours," said Lew.

"At least."

Katydids trilled in the stillness. A bead of sweat trickled down Osborne's right cheek. Ray moved forward about ten yards, then stopped to stare down to his left. The bank dropped away from the rail bed. The clear-cut below was identical to what they had passed earlier: stumps, piles of brush, mounds of dirt, and deep ruts in the sandy soil.

"Those goombahs ever hear of selective cutting?" said Osborne to no one in particular. "Jeez, I hate to see this."

"Costs too much. That new wood jockey running the show in Rhinelander wants to save a few bucks," said Ray. "We're back to land rape."

"Eh, you pick your battles. It's private land, no law against it," said Lew, dismissing the issue. Both men nodded. They knew that she knew that paper mill taxes went a long way to cover the costs of Loon Lake's new jail and offices for Lew and her crew.

"See over there?" said Ray, pointing down at an angle. "I think we got something." Sidestepping down the incline, he moved carefully over to where a barely discernible set of ruts had crushed a bed of brush and run up to the bank, where they ended in a patch of sand. Ray crouched over the sand. "I'd have Wausau take a mold of the tire tracks you see here," he said. "Could be loggers, but why would they be driving off-road when the job is done? In fact . . ." He stood up and cocked his head to examine the ruts from the side. "Looks like an SUV to me."

"How so?" said Lew. "The configuration of the tires?"

"That, and they're too new to belong to a logger," said

Ray. "The tread is barely worn. Loggers *work,* doncha know."

Ray backed away from the ruts, his eyes scanning the ground. "Oh, oh . . . get a load of this. You got footprints, too. Funny . . . the soles are completely smooth. No tread, no pattern, but flat, not heeled like a street shoe. What do you make of that, Lew?"

"You got me."

Lew and Osborne sideslipped down from the rail bed, being careful to avoid the area that Ray was examining. As he walked by the ruts, Osborne shook his head. He would have missed them completely.

"Now isn't *this* interesting." Again Ray pointed. Again Osborne could barely make out any pattern whatsoever. "Whoever it was got out of their vehicle here . . . messed around over here . . . and set off thataway." He looked up in the direction of the trestle. Then he looked down again. "Doc, what ya got in that bag? Anything I can use to measure the depth of these footprints?"

"Depth?" said Osborne. "Depth? How the hell can you see depth in these?"

"Like I said, Doc. When the good Lord gave out eyes, I thought he said 'knives' and asked for some sharp ones."

Lew groaned.

"Okay, okay, I'm sure I've got something." Osborne unzipped his black bag and tossed a probe at Ray. "Here, it's marked in three-millimeter increments. Will that work?"

Ray measured one set of footprints, then another, hidden behind a clump of brush and leading up to the rail bed. At that point, even Osborne could see where the tracks led up, forcing the sandy soil into clumps. Or did they lead down? Osborne couldn't be sure.

As Ray worked, moving slowly and methodically, the haze from the sun and dull buzz of the katydids lulled Osborne into a heavy-lidded sense of sleepiness. Blinking, he tried to stay alert while Ray hovered over another set of footprints. A sudden poke in the ribs startled him.

"Doc!" The smile in Lew's eyes woke him right up.

"Yessiree." Ray straightened up and stretched his back. "Looks to me like the same in . . . di . . . vid . . . ual emerged from their vehicle here." He pointed. "Then took up a burden through the tailgate there." He turned. "And scooted up thataway. Then . . ." He stepped sideways. "Over here . . . we have the return trip. Lighter."

"Can you tell how much of a weight difference between the two?" asked Lew.

"Nope, but it was more than taking a leak."

"Any chance you can state that in a way that I can put it in my report?" asked Lew.

Ray winked. "Sure. Got your notebook?"

Lew reached into her back pocket. Face serious, Ray remeasured, then jotted down each calibration. "If Wausau can't figure it out, talk to a structural engineer. One of those guys can tell ya the weight difference. In fact, talk to Pete Phelan. He helped me file for the patent on my walleye jig. He can figure that out."

"I'll put through something for your time," said Lew when he had finished. "I'll have Roger photograph these, and I'll make sure Wausau takes molds."

"Better make sure old Roger gets out here before it rains," said Ray.

Lew looked up at the heavy sky. The crisp blue of the morning had disappeared in a weather change typical of the Northwoods. "Damn, I'll bet I can't get him out here in time. Ray, you have your camera in the truck?"

"You betcha." In addition to guiding, harvesting leeches for walleye guys, digging graves, and shoveling snow, Ray also picked up a few bucks selling wildlife photos to local printers for their cheap calendars. He always kept a camera jammed under the driver's seat, and while he often hit Osborne up for a tube of toothpaste or some dental floss, he never seemed to be out of film.

• • •

Ten minutes later, they were looking down at the body from the trestle.

"Oh yeah," said Ray quietly. "Doesn't take a goombah to tell you what happened here."

seven

"Fish die belly-up and rise to the surface, it is their way of falling."

André Gide

A small crowd had gathered around the second victim. An ambulance was parked in the grass nearby, but the EMTs were leaning against their vehicle.

"Good," said Lew, "Lucy got to 'em. Looks like they haven't touched a thing."

As Lew and Osborne got out of the cruiser, a man in his late forties, lanky in dusty denim jeans and a well-worn Levi's shirt, walked toward them with his hands in his pockets. A tall, slender woman in equally dusty jeans, a washed-out pink polo shirt, cowboy boots, and long, straight honey-blond hair hurried behind him. Neither looked happy.

"Chief Ferris, I'm Bert James, and this is my wife, Helen." The man extended his hand to Lew. "We found the body. These people"—Bert waved at the others standing in the road—"are guests of ours at Timber Lake Lodge. We run a bed-and-breakfast over there." He jerked a thumb behind him. "So is she." He nodded toward the body that lay on its side, slightly curled, about twenty feet away. His eyes shifted to look behind Lew.

"Dr. *Osborne?*" Bert raised his eyebrows as if to question why his former dentist had arrived on the scene.

"Doc's a deputy," said Lew. "He'll do a forensic ID. I got the coroner out working up another case. Step over here a minute, you two. I don't need all of Loon Lake to hear us."

Lew pulled the husband and wife off to the side of the

grassy lane that ran along a perimeter of meadow edged with forest. "Tell me exactly what happened."

"Let me," said Helen, stepping out from behind her husband. "I found her. I was out looking for blueberries—"

"When was this?" Lew had her notebook open.

"About ninety minutes ago. We've been waiting for you for quite a while."

"Busy morning," said Lew.

Helen continued, "So I had walked over in this direction. We have a trail here that leads to our deer feeder. . . ." She pointed into the forest behind them.

Behind her was a wide meadow. Looking across, Osborne could see the roofline of a log home about a quarter mile away. The trail they were standing on was a grassy lane that snaked west, detouring off the main driveway, which was entered from the highway. He knew the James place by reputation only. The couple had moved to Loon Lake from New York City seven years earlier, built a drop-dead expensive log home, and was now trying to make ends meet by running a B & B. At least that's what the locals said. Murder would not be good for business.

"Ashley went for a run late yesterday afternoon—"

"Ashley?" asked Lew.

"Her name is Ashley Olson. She's from Kansas City," said Helen.

"Good," said Lew. "So we know who this is."

"Yes," said Helen. "I don't know how she heard about us, but when she registered, she did give a name and number in case of an emergency. I've got a call in. It's some woman in Kansas City. I assume that's all right?"

"Fine. I'd like to be the one to talk to her, but right now just tell me exactly what has happened so far."

Helen took a deep breath. "Last night . . . well, see, I *thought* she left the house to go out last night. No one saw her return from her run, but we didn't worry. I just assumed she came back to change while I was in town shopping and then, maybe, went to dinner with friends. I mean, we don't keep track of our guests' activities. . . ."

"Of course not," said Lew. "You're not running a scout camp."

Helen heaved a sigh of relief. It was clear she was feeling very guilty that she had not noticed her guest's absence.

"What friends would she have planned to see?"

"Now, that we don't know," said Bert. "We were talking about that before you got here. When she arrived Sunday, she spent some time looking in the telephone book, and I asked if I could help her find someone, but she said she had what she needed. She was gone for a while yesterday morning, but she didn't say where she went or what she did. She was a very pleasant woman but quite private."

"Right." Helen nodded. "Some of our guests tell you their whole life story, but not this one. It was almost like she had something on her mind."

"So she didn't seem happy."

"I wouldn't go that far," said Helen, "more like she was preoccupied. No questions on where to rent a bike or a kayak, didn't ask about fishing guides, not even restaurants. She just stayed in her room, used the phone in the living room a few times, and then went for that run. Now this!" Helen raised her hands in frustration.

Lew walked over to the body. The other guests still stood in a cluster at a polite distance, watching. The ambulance attendants hadn't moved from where they had propped themselves against their vehicle, arms crossed. Osborne remained standing alongside Bert and Helen. He looked up.

Once again, the birds had gotten there first. A bald eagle circled, the massive head gleaming white in the sun. He thought of Ray's description of the magnificent birds: "Vultures in king's clothing." Not that Ray was down on vultures. He frequently appalled clients by alleging that the birds of prey were proof of the Resurrection: "Hey, they recycle, doncha know . . . turn death into life."

Lew crouched to look at the quiet form, touching the

shoulder with her fingertips to roll the body back slightly. She glanced over at Helen.

"How do you know this is Ashley?"

"That's what she was wearing when she left for the run."

"I see. Doc, come here."

Osborne walked over. The dead woman wore mottled purple and pink running shorts and a pink tank top. The straps of her white sports bra were exposed near the neck. The victim's legs were tanned and rather thick for her small frame. Lew had pulled the body back far enough that he could see there was no need for his black bag: The woman's face had been completely blown out from the side. If there were any teeth, he was more likely to find them in the bushes, in the tree trunks, or on the ground.

Osborne took a quick look at the ground around the body. Teeth, the hardest bones in the body, can survive the most severe physical trauma, including the blast of a bullet. He combed his fingers through the grass near the victim's head. No sign of teeth. Not even much blood. Odd.

"Gunshot wound?" said Lew softly under her breath.

"Yep. High-powered rifle."

"Doc, look at this. . . ." The woman's chest was a bloody mess. "Shotgun?"

"I doubt that," said Osborne. "Looks like knife wounds to me. On the other hand, if the body was out here overnight, could be predators. I don't know, we'll need Wausau for that."

Osborne crouched beside Lew. He spoke in a low, deliberate tone: "I can tell you this: See how the blood has pooled down along her left side? With very little blood and no teeth or tissue in the vicinity of the body, I have to believe this young woman was shot somewhere else, Lew."

"And dumped here."

"Yep."

Osborne watched as Lew let the body fall back in place. As she took her fingers from the bare shoulder, Osborne caught her hand. "Wait . . . look."

"Oh, brother," said Lew.

The two bite marks were unmistakable. Osborne knew without looking that he would find two more on the other shoulder.

eight

"I know several hundred men. I prefer to angle with only four of them."

Frederic F. Van de Water, author

"Here comes another police car," said Bert from behind Osborne. He pointed to the roof of a white sedan bouncing in and out of sight as it crossed the field toward them.

"Oh good, that's Roger," said Lew. "Is this the only access to the area?" she asked Bert.

"No. Our property line ends just the other side of our deer stand, a couple hundred feet past the feeder, due west. The neighbor's road runs in just behind there. In fact, we have quite a problem with hunters trespassing onto our property, if that's a help. We can't see this area from the house—"

"So someone could have driven onto your neighbor's property, walked a few yards this direction to drop the victim, and you would never see anything. Is that correct?" said Lew.

"I'm afraid so." Bert thrust his hands deeper into his pockets. He looked very worried. "But the Bearskin Bike & Running Trail is less than a mile from here, too. I think that's where she went to run. We keep a map of the trail at the front desk."

"Could someone have entered Timber Lake Lodge unobserved and pulled Ashley Olson from her room?" asked Lew.

"That's not impossible, but it's not likely," said Helen. "My desk faces our front door, which opens into the lodge living room. I'm there in the late afternoon and early evening because that's when most of our guests arrive. You have to come and go down the center staircase to reach any of the bedrooms. That's how I saw Ashley leave for her run in the first place."

As Lew stepped away from the body, she studied the lush ferns blanketing the ground beneath the hardwood forest behind them. "Darn! I wish Ray were here to see if there's any sign left in those woods."

"I doubt he could find much the way everyone's been walking around, Lew," said Osborne.

"I'm afraid I tromped around in there myself," said Helen. "I thought maybe someone had been in that deer stand of ours. I didn't think. I'm sorry."

Lew shrugged. "I'll have Roger rope off a half-mile radius around this site. We'll do a foot search through the brush. Doc, would you see if Ray can come out after he's finished with that client of his?" She looked at Bert. "Don't panic if you see a man with a fish on his head poking around out here. He's one of my deputies. Ray Pradt. He's good; he can track a crappie under ice."

"Even if it rains?" Osborne looked up at the sky.

"Yes," said Lew. She lowered her voice so Bert couldn't hear. "I've got a lot more confidence in Ray than some Wausau jabone who wouldn't know a fox from a feral cat."

As she spoke, they watched Roger Adamcyzk climb slowly out of his car. Roger never looked real eager to join the party. Lew had inherited him as her senior deputy, and he was a lifer. Formerly a life insurance salesman, Roger had made a career switch in his late thirties, thinking that being a cop in Loon Lake would ensure a foot on the stool and a light snooze for most of the day. That was twenty years ago. He was right at the time, but Loon Lake changed. The tourist trade took off. Not only was Loon Lake redefined as a "destination location," but the cost of living went up along with an increase in drug traffic, poaching, and domestic violence. Then Lew arrived. Poor guy rarely got a snooze in any longer. Worse yet, he was always assigned the body bagging. Today was no exception.

"Got that other victim on its way to Wausau for you, Chief. Pecore never answered his phone. Jeez Louise." Roger had spotted the woman's legs behind Lew. "Boy, oh boy, guess I shoulda had the van wait, huh?"

"I thought that's what Lucy asked you to do." Lew's voice turned testy.

The look on Roger's face said it all: "Oh, that's what she meant. She told me that one of the techs from Wausau would be here in a couple hours so I just thought—"

"You thought he could use his Jeep?"

Osborne suppressed a smile. He remembered Lew's description of her staffer: "Not the sharpest knife in the drawer." She could say that again.

"Call Lucy, tell her to reach that van somehow. If she has to ask one of the state boys to pull 'em over, that's fine. Just get it back here, Roger."

The older man slouched toward his car.

"And Roger," Lew continued, "no one moves the victim until Wausau gets here. When they're done, be sure the EMTs save every piece of clothing and shoes . . . just like I told you with the other victim. Every item, got that?"

Roger waved.

"Are we waiting for the coroner?" called Bert from where he stood watching, arms folded.

"No. Pecore's at his granddaughter's graduation this morning," said Lew. "Doc here does a preliminary ID and then we send the victims to Wausau for a full workup. A lab tech is on his way from the Wausau Crime Lab to do the preliminary here at the site.

"Thanks, but we won't need you folks." She waved at the ambulance crew. "Crime lab should have a van on the way in about thirty minutes." She turned to the Jameses. "Would you take your guests back to the lodge, please. I'll be down to talk with everyone shortly."

Bert shook his head, and Osborne knew exactly what he was thinking: First, Lew arrives late to the scene, now there's no coroner. What the hell kind of operation is this?

Not being a Loon Lake native, Bert would have no idea that the absence of the coroner was a blessing.

Pecore wasn't well respected in the small town. It wasn't just that people resented the fact that he let his two golden retrievers roam freely through his office and autopsy lab, leading to speculation that one of the pooches might lick a beloved. The man had a darker side to him. In addition to signing off on cause of death, he was also expected to photograph victims of assault and other crimes. Apparently, the confidential nature of his work didn't register. Osborne knew of more than one instance when the guy had shown up at a local bar and proceeded to display official photos of his subjects, particularly if they were young females. It was no surprise to Osborne that when the daughter of one of his closest friends was raped and beaten, the family refused to report the crime rather than risk Pecore's involvement. The problem was that the position was a political appointment; Pecore could not be fired, but he could be avoided.

As if she knew what he was thinking, Lew caught Osborne's eye. "I don't want Pecore in on this. I'll do a point-and-shoot myself and leave the rest to Wausau."

Bert and Helen had just started to trudge down the road, guests in tow, when a black Range Rover came bouncing across the field.

"Who the hell—? He's driving right through my raspberries!" Bert put his hands on his hips, his face reddening with anger. "Is this one of your people, Chief Ferris? Please tell them to stay on the lane."

Lew looked as surprised as anyone. The big, boxy car continued toward them. Finally, Lew could make out the driver. "What on earth is Hank Kendrickson doing out here?" she said. "I hope Lucy didn't tell him—"

"Hey, there." A cheery voice came at them from the car window. Behind the driver, their big heads hanging out the open window, were two yellow Labs. As the big car neared the group, the dogs went crazy, barking and bouncing around in the backseat.

"Keep those dogs in the car!" shouted Lew.

The door opened, and the occupant jumped out. "I spotted Roger in town and followed him this direction. I thought I might find you here, Chief."

Watching Kendrickson advance on Lew, Osborne remembered Ray's take on the jerk: "a Hemingway wannabe." Right on, Ray. Not only did the man sport a squared-off blond gray beard replete with a slightly flattened pink nose, but he was perfectly outfitted in crisp khaki pants, a matching fly-fishing shirt, and a spanking-new fishing hat whose brim sported a cluster of colorful trout flies. Osborne knew without asking that the razzbonya would say he had tied them himself.

Hank continued toward them, his gait an insouciant swagger that Osborne found irritating as hell. He recognized the look on the guy's face, too. It was exactly the type of seductive grin he had alerted his daughters to when they were in their teens, lovely and vulnerable. "Guys like that are dangerous," was all he had been able to say, too embarrassed to let them know exactly what worried him most. But even as he could at least warn his daughters, he didn't dare say a word to Lew. He had to hope she knew.

"Oh my goodness!" Hank came to a skidding halt, smile vanishing at the sight of the curled and bloody human form. He yanked his hat off and clutched it to his chest as if to pay his respects to the deceased.

In spite of his big head, he was modest in height and stocky, with a peculiar posture that made him look like he was perpetually leaning into the wind. The bearded face was topped with a stiff frizz of grayish blond hair. At the moment, hair standing on end and eyebrows arched in shock, he looked like he was plugged into an electric socket. At least, that's what Osborne hoped Lew would think.

Osborne guessed him to be in his late forties. What he didn't have to guess at was the obvious: Hank Kendrickson had the money to look like he had just stepped out of the pages of *Fly Fisherman* magazine, the kind of money that buys a man time to fish Montana, Canada, the Yukon, New Zealand, probably even Russia. Worst of all, Osborne suspected he was infinitely better at fly-fishing than Osborne could ever hope to be. How could Lew not be seduced by a guy like Hank Kendrickson?

"Who is it? What happened?" Hank started to walk forward, but Lew moved quickly to block him.

"Hank." Her voice was crisp, blunt. "What are you doing here? I told Lucy to get back to you—"

"Oh, she did, she did. But as I was leaving your office, I heard her send Roger after you." Hank tried to peer around Lew, but she stepped into his line of vision. "I guess I shouldn't have followed Roger, but I thought maybe it was just routine stuff, y'know."

Osborne wondered just what Hank thought was so routine in law enforcement that Lew encouraged drop-ins.

"I need you to leave, Hank." Lew advanced in such a way that Hank had to back up.

"I-I, well, Lew, I just have to show you something. Hey . . ." He raised his hands at the hostile expression on her face. "C'mon, Lew." He dropped his voice seductively as a charming smile crossed his face. Hank gave a nod toward his car and started to walk to it. "You can take a minute, can't you? I've got it right here in the car." He hurried back to the Range Rover, where the door on the driver's side stood open, reached for something on the seat, grabbed it, and ran back toward them.

"I really do not have time for this, Hank."

Osborne had never heard Lew sound so terse. He moved closer, as if his presence could serve as a buffer.

"Voilà!" Hank waved a piece of paper at her. Osborne looked over Lew's shoulder as she accepted the photo, scanned it, nodded, listened for a polite moment to Hank's excited bragging, and then, her left hand on his shoulder, walked him back to his car and shoveled him into his vehicle. He kept talking and gesturing until she could slam his door shut.

Arms on her hips, Lew blocked the drive as she waited for the Range Rover's engine to purr back into life and for Hank to put it in reverse. Only when the car was moving did she back away.

"What was that all about?" said Roger, emerging from his vehicle as Lew headed back toward the body, a set look on her face.

"Mr. Important caught a trophy trout this morning," said Lew. "A big brown . . . twenty-six inches, seven pounds. He says. He's on his way to the taxidermist with his photo. And it is so special that he had to track me down at a crime scene."

The irritation in her voice made it clear that Big Bucks Hank had just made a big mistake. With luck, it was one from which he might never recover. Osborne relished the moment. Maybe he should feel ashamed at his delight over Hank's faux pas, but he didn't.

"Oh, it gets better," said Lew. "Told me he caught it about ten o'clock last night, fishing the Deerskin . . . south of the dam."

"Really?" said Osborne. "Did he have a witness?"

"Oh yeah, he got some kid who works for him to sign off on the catch. Sign off or lose his job, probably." Lew was quiet for a few seconds as the two of them walked back toward the victim. Then she muttered, "I hate fishermen who lie. Especially fly-fishermen. Comes with the sport, I guess, but I don't like it."

Osborne felt positively gleeful. That should cement her feelings for Hank Kendrickson now and forever. Of course, the guy had caught a hell of a fish, and Osborne could understand why he would want to show it off. Osborne would do the same but within limits. What he wasn't sure about was how Lew knew Hank was lying, but he sure wasn't going to demonstrate his own ignorance and ask.

"Can't agree with you more," he said. "At least he released it." That was the good news about new techniques in taxidermy. A close-up photo made it possible for the taxidermist to replicate a fish using a basic model. The actual fish was not necessary in order to document your trophy catch. In fact, the new process was not only less messy, but it reinforced efforts at conservation. Even so, it was, as a man like Hank would know, a more expensive technique.

"But to push your way in where I'm working, when it's obvious I'm busy?" Lew shook her head. "Men like Kendrickson never take women seriously. No matter what. And that's what I really don't like."

Osborne bit his lip. He took her seriously, way too seriously. A condition from which he was beginning to think he might never recover.

"Lucy reached the van driver just south of Gleason," said Roger. "He's turning back."

nine

"The charm of fishing is that it is the pursuit of what is elusive but obtainable, a perpetual series of occasions for hope."

John Buchan

Down at the house half an hour later, Helen escorted Osborne and Lew to the dead woman's room. She unlocked the door. "I haven't been in here since she left last night."

It was a spacious room with a double bed tucked into the far left corner. A casement window with ruffled white curtains tied back stood open to the immediate right. A white chenille spread on the neatly made bed matched the color of the curtains. Under the window was a small, round oak table covered with a checkered tablecloth and two chairs next to it. A straw purse was sitting on the table. Along the wall beside the bed was an old oak dresser, and to the right of that was a luggage stand holding an open suitcase.

"Here's the bathroom. . . ." Helen opened a door to their left. Small but pristine with white ceramic tile and crisp white towels hanging on the log walls, the bathroom looked unused. Cosmetics and a hair dryer were neatly set out on the counter around the sink. "And the closet." She opened a door next to the bathroom. A black jacket hung in the closet. It looked like silk to Osborne. "Ashley arrived Sunday and was planning to leave tomorrow."

"Do you mind if we take a few minutes to look around?" Lew implied she would like Helen to leave.

"Not at all. When you're ready, I've got the file with the name of a person to contact in case of emergency," said Helen. "Did you want to make that call?"

"Yes," said Lew, looking around. "Is there a phone in here?"

"None of our rooms have phones. You may use my office."

"Thank you. I'll want to see your phone bill for the last few days, too."

Ashley Olson lived in Kansas City and, according to her business card, appeared to own a marketing firm, Olson & Associates. Her driver's license, checkbook, and wallet were in the straw bag on the table. A second check of the bathroom produced a pair of black pants and a sleeveless black blouse hanging behind the door as if the victim had planned for any wrinkles to steam out while she showered after her run.

"Silk. Expensive," said Lew, examining the woman's clothes. "She was planning to look good for someone."

A small bottle of cologne stood among the cosmetics. "That someone likely to be a man?" offered Osborne.

"You never know," said Lew. "If I've learned anything in the last ten years, it's never to presume everyone is heterosexual, Doc."

Osborne noted out loud that the victim had brought along an electric toothbrush, base and all, and she had two packets of floss in her cosmetic kit.

"What does that tell you, Doc?"

"She's health conscious, a woman of habit. Why else would you haul around the base for your electric toothbrush?"

The rest of her luggage included an extra-long T-shirt with matching leggings, a pair of khaki shorts, and two more T-shirts. An interior section of the soft-sided suitcase held three pairs of good-quality cotton panties and a small velvet case. Lew opened the case. In it gleamed a pair of gold earrings, oblong hoops, and a wide gold wedding band.

"Now that's interesting." Lew's dark eyes caught Osborne's. "Why wasn't she wearing her wedding ring? She must have brought it for a reason. She's obviously a woman of some wealth and must own more jewelry. But all she brings is one pair of earrings and this wedding band. . . ." The room was quiet as the two of them pondered the ring.

"Doc, who do you know has a wife living in Kansas City?"

"Or an ex-wife?"

"Or a fiancée?"

"I doubt that," said Osborne, "you don't get married in black. Certainly not in pants."

"Oh yeah? Rick Streater and his wife got married in their turkey camouflage—"

Helen knocked at the door. "I've got a name and number for you when you're ready."

As they walked down the stairs, Lew checked her watch. "Oh, golly, it's after three, and I need to see the Herres. I should have been there an hour ago. This is not good, Doc. That family is in agony."

"Lew." Osborne put his hand on her shoulder. "Why don't I make this call? At the very least, I'll get enough information for you to follow up on later. That way you can get to Sandy's folks right away."

"Thank you." Lew looked relieved. She paused at the front entry to the lodge. "Tell you what, Doc, if you've got the time later, I'll have Bernie's Bakery drop off a bag of sandwiches at my office. We can grab some sodas and compare notes while casting a few over in the Tomorrow River flats. Unless you've got plans?"

"Heck no, that works fine." Osborne was surprised and pleased. The last thing he had expected that morning was to end the day fishing with Lew.

As he sat down to pick up the telephone in Helen's well-organized office, Osborne couldn't help thinking as he did more often these days: Lewellyn Ferris made him feel like a teenager again. Who would ever expect that a man who'd seen sixty could feel sixteen?

But the happy thought was followed by an equally familiar regret: Why did this have to happen so late in life? Why did she have to be so much younger than he? Hank's age, probably. Osborne resolved, as he always did, to keep his secret.

ten

"The fish are either in the shallows, or the deep water, or someplace in between."

Anonymous

"Metro desk, Palmer." The female voice was tight, curt.

"Hello? This is Dr. Paul Osborne from Loon Lake, Wisconsin—"

"Loon *who?* Gimme a break. I'm not in the mood for crank calls." The strident, East Coast accent hit Osborne's ear like a hammer.

A loud click. Osborne held the phone away in amazement. He punched in the number again.

"Yes!" The same voice barked.

"I'm calling to report the death of someone you know." Osborne spoke through clenched teeth, his voice low, measured, and insistent.

This time there was a slight pause. "O-o-kay . . . tell me about it. No, no, wait a minute. Is it someone who lives on this planet?" Her skepticism was a draft of cold air he could feel through the telephone. Did she get calls like this all the time?

"I'm assisting the Loon Lake Chief of Police—"

Again a long pause. The woman on the other end of the line was obviously convinced he was some kind of nut.

"So where the hell is Loon Lake?"

"Northern Wisconsin."

"You've got the wrong newspaper, bud. This is the *Kansas City Star.* Call a Wisconsin newspaper, would ya?"

That was it. Osborne had had enough.

"Listen, young lady, I don't care if you are the star and

the moon and your uncle is the Big Dipper, your name was listed as the emergency contact for a young woman who was shot and killed up here. Now will you *please* shut up and listen?"

Osborne was astounded at the anger that had flooded into his voice. Never in his professional career had he told another adult to shut up. But then never had he been treated so rudely.

"I'm sorry." Her tone changed abruptly. "Wait a minute, let me go into my office. I'm going to put you on hold, Doctor. Please, wait just a minute."

Osborne took a deep breath as he waited. Then he took another one. The blood still pumped in his ears.

"All right." The voice was softer. "Please, who are you trying to call, and what is this all about?"

"A woman by the name of Ashley Olson has been shot and—" said Osborne.

"No!" Gina Palmer shouted into the phone as if refusing to let herself hear him. "No no no no. No-o-o," she keened. "Oh dear God, this can't be."

"I'm afraid it is. She's dead. I'm with the Loon Lake Police and I . . . We are sorry to have to call this way, but we didn't know any other—"

"It's my fault. I knew this could happen. I just, oh God—" she stopped.

Osborne waited a brief moment before asking, "Are you family?"

"Umm. Kind of . . ." The woman's voice trailed off, ending with a peculiar sound. Osborne recognized exactly what was happening.

"Take your time," he said, feeling his own throat tighten. A vivid memory of his calls to his daughters the night of Mary Lee's death flashed suddenly: their silence, the choking, the quiet sorrow.

"Gina . . . may I call you Gina?"

"Of course." The strident tone had disappeared. In its place was the voice of a little girl.

"She gave your name when she registered at the Timber Lake Lodge bed-and-breakfast in Loon Lake, Wisconsin, this past Sunday. . . ." He paused for several beats. "Before I continue . . . for our records, I need to know your exact relationship to Mrs. Olson. Are you next of kin?"

"What makes you think she was married?" The question came at him like a pistol shot. Osborne held the phone away from his ear and looked at it. Just who was asking the questions here? From little girl to velvet hammer in a matter of seconds. Was the woman schizoid?

"I'm sorry, Doc." The voice calmed down. "I'm a reporter. I can't help it. And, um, I've kind of been expecting something like this, so you better realize I feel pretty bad. Like I'm responsible in a way. But I'm upset with myself, not you." She spoke with an easy directness that reminded Osborne of Lew.

"I understand." He didn't, but he'd try.

"You asked about *Mrs.* Olson . . . but it's *Miss* Olson. Ashley wasn't married. I don't know why you thought that. But first, please . . . you must tell me how she died. Was she killed instantly? Did she suffer?" The woman didn't even breathe between questions.

"I-we-we're not sure," Osborne stammered, realizing he had no hope of controlling the conversation.

"You're holding back. Look, Doc, this conversation is off the record. Ashley was one of my closest, dearest friends. I am not going to report anything you tell me, okay? I don't write the obit. But you have to tell me every detail, because I may be able to help you find the killer. See, Ashley has . . . had a penchant for the wrong kind of men. Like I said: I've been *expecting* this. Now, please. Tell me exactly how she died."

If Gina Palmer was good at anything, she was good at making you feel you had to ante up. And for reasons that went against his better judgment, Osborne felt compelled to answer.

"My guess—and I'm a forensic dentist only, and a retired

one at that—is that a high-powered rifle shot to the head may have killed her instantly."

"*May* have?"

"I'm not absolutely sure of cause or time of death."

"Well." The demanding tone rose in her voice again. "When will you know?" Her implication was clear: Not knowing meant someone wasn't doing their job.

"The police chief will get a report from the crime lab shortly. We found Ashley's body just a few hours ago, Gina. This is a very small town up here, and I help out as a deputy when the chief is shorthanded. As I said, I have some forensic experience, but I'm no expert. All I can safely say at this time is we know she was shot and it looked to me—but I could be wrong—it looked like she had multiple stab wounds in her chest . . . and . . ." He stopped before he went too far.

"*And . . . ?*" Too late. She knew he had more to add.

But Osborne balked, remembering that Lew had specifically directed him to keep the bite marks confidential.

"Brutally slashed across the throat and the chest . . . but, again, I may be wrong. There was a lot of blood."

"Revenge," said Gina grimly. "It's a revenge killing. Why stab when you can shoot? I've seen a few murders in my day; I know the signs."

Osborne wasn't sure what to say next. As it turned out, he didn't have to say a thing. Gina had finally decided to answer his first question.

"I've been looking after Ashley's house and her cat, Doc. I'm sorry, do you mind if I call you Doc? I know it's a little familiar but—"

"Certainly not. And her family?"

"She has none. Both parents have been dead for years. She had one sister who was killed in a car accident a year ago and a husband she divorced ten, maybe fifteen years ago. Doc, was she alone when she died?"

"We think so. She appears to have been out for a run."

"That fits. Ashley was a fanatic runner . . . ten miles a

day, sometimes longer. She was in excellent physical shape. She could defend herself, too. She must have been with someone she knew."

"Miss Palmer, is there any chance you might be able to come up here to identify the body and—"

"No problem. I know her lawyer. I'll make some calls regarding arrangements and all that stuff. It's the least I can do. . . . I feel so . . . responsible." Her voice dropped, and Osborne heard heartbreak in her last words. Then a quiet sobbing.

The receiver held tight to his ear, Osborne lowered his head as he waited in the swivel chair at Helen's desk. "Do you have the time for just a few more questions?"

"Look, I'm going to set aside what I'm doing here, take the day off, and get up there as fast as I can. Sure, go ahead, whatever I can do."

"The obvious one: Do you know anyone who would want to kill your friend?"

"I certainly do. Her ex-fiancé."

Ah, thought Osborne, *the wedding ring.*

"And this gentleman is who?"

"Who knows what name he's wearing these days. . . ."

"Michael Winston appeared on the scene four years ago," said Gina. "He rolled into Kansas City flashing a roll of Texas money, made a big hit with the local bankers, and got himself invited to all the right parties. That's where he met Ashley. She liked him immediately, brought him in as a consultant, then they were dating, and before long, he wanted to buy into her company. Every step of the way, she was impressed with the guy.

"Can't blame her; anyone would be. According to his résumé, he had an MBA from Harvard, had been a vice president for several of the big ad agencies on Madison Avenue, his family had made a fortune in real estate down in Houston, yadda, yadda, yadda. She resisted letting him buy in, but she did hire him . . . brought him on board as her right-hand person and CFO. Bottom line? She was in love with the twerp."

"You didn't like him."

"I met him after the fact. I was assigned to write a profile on the guy for our business section. But . . ." Gina underscored her *but* with a long pause. "This was not a random assignment. Her late sister was a copy editor here, and she came to me one day and asked me to do a story on the guy. Chris wanted him investigated. She said she thought he was after Ashley's money."

"She had good reason to think that?"

"Yes. She told me her sister had a weakness for the narcissistic type who would say whatever he had to say to gain her affection . . . and access to her bank account. See, Ashley was a little different. She was moderately attractive, but in her twenties, she had had a type of breast cancer that required the removal of both breasts. Even though she had reconstructive surgery, the scars were deep . . . psychologically very deep. Chris seemed to think she had poor self-esteem when it came to her body. This made her, in her sister's view, an easy target and a very vulnerable woman.

"I thought Chris was overstating the case," said Gina, "but I agreed to look into it. That's how I came to know this about Ashley. I could see right away why Chris was worried. Here was a bright, successful woman who was always attracted to inappropriate men. I mean, we all are to a certain degree. But Ashley seemed doomed to be attracted to flashy, sleazy guys. The list of men she dated before she met Winston was . . . well, one creepola after another. Who knows . . . maybe their father was like that.

"I got the assignment approved, then I called an old friend who's a sportswriter for the *Houston Chronicle* to do some background. He recognized Winston's name and had me talk to their lead investigative reporter. He sent up a batch of court documents, and I had Mike Winston cold: no Harvard MBA, no experience working anywhere close to New York City, the real estate fortune was a complete fabrication. Then I ran a database search on his license plates and discovered he had a felony conviction for penny stock fraud. He got off because his father was a well-connected lawyer, but he was forced to leave town.

"So I made an appointment to interview Ashley about her star performer—supposedly—and I delivered the news. I even had a detective fly up from Houston to document everything. Chris was afraid she wouldn't believe us.

"Ashley was shocked when I told her. Not only had she just made him executive vice president, but she was planning to marry the jerk." Gina's voice took on a darker tone. "And she'd put him in charge of all her financials."

"How big a company is this?"

"*Was*. She sold out six months ago. Good sized, over a hundred employees. She sold it for ten million dollars."

"So she's worth a lot of money?"

"My friend is a woman of substantial means. I would estimate her estate at several million dollars or more, probably a lot more. Her house alone is worth over a million."

"I see." Osborne pondered that information.

"You need to find Michael Winston," said Gina. "My bet is that's why she was up there. He has to be in the area somewhere."

"We've got a pretty big region up here," said Osborne. "He certainly isn't in Loon Lake, because I would know it if he was. But he could easily be in a neighboring town like Presque Isle or Manitowish Waters. I don't understand. What would be her reason for finding him if what you say is true?"

"That I don't know. I'll poke around down here and see what I can find, though. At least I know where to start."

"How did her sister die?"

"Car accident."

"Suspicious circumstances?"

"In my opinion, yes. But no one shares my opinion."

"Can you give me a description of this Winston?"

"He's kind of nondescript really. Not the type to stand out

in a crowd. Medium height, dark hair, very clean-shaven . . . a good Republican face. Nice-looking in a bland, baby-face way. Pleasant smile . . . but plastered on, if you ask me.

"The one distinctive feature I remember about the guy is that when he lies, which he did throughout my interview with him, he has a nervous tic . . . constantly clearing his throat. You know, Doc, I can check the morgue here at the paper for a photo for you folks. We ran a head shot with the story, and I know Michael attended a lot of charity events when he worked for Ashley. I'm sure we'll have some good photos."

"That will be a huge help," said Osborne. "Thank you very much."

There was a sudden silence on the phone and Osborne wondered if they had been cut off. "Hello? Hello?"

A soft mumbling. He could barely hear Gina's voice.

"What? I can't hear you."

She took a deep breath. "I said, I'm sure I'm the reason she's dead, Dr. Osborne."

"Because she fired him? Broke the engagement, I assume?"

"No. She did nothing of the kind. She listened. She refused to confront Michael, but she did take her books to an outside auditor, thank goodness. He was already into her for half a million bucks."

"So he was stealing from her?"

"That's what I called it, but she tried to tell me that they had some misunderstanding, that he thought he already owned half the company and this was money for an acquisition of some kind. Pure baloney. I didn't believe it."

"If she thought that, why did he leave?"

Gina was quiet again. Osborne waited.

"I called him on it. A week after meeting with Ashley, knowing she was in Chicago on business, I confronted him. I told him that if he didn't resign, I would tell Ashley the rest."

"Which was?"

"He had a wife and three children living in Houston, Texas. He heard me all right. He left town the next day. I never told Ashley what I did. She would never have forgiven me."

"Do you think she still wanted to marry him?

"Wouldn't surprise me. She refused to prosecute. She let him run off with all that money."

"Then why on earth would he want to kill her?"

"I'm sure he blames her for all the deals that fell through when he had to leave. After all, if he hadn't tried to scam Ashley, he would never have run into me, and he would have made a fortune here. He had a lot of people conned, Doc, and he could have left when he wanted to, not because he *had* to.

eleven

"As the fish strikes, the line has to be given a little jerk . . . the timing and the pressure have to be perfect—too soon or too late or too little or too much and the fish may have a sore mouth for a few days but will probably live longer for his experience."

Norman Maclean

"Insects always hatch at the nicest time of day," said Lew, inhaling happily as she scanned the view over the rushing water. She had pulled into a clearing beside the Tomorrow River, jimmied open the rear door of her beat-up Mazda fishing truck, and was now standing with her hands on her hips, feet planted wide apart.

"Those flats," she said, pointing to the river burbling fifteen yards off to the right, "are very shallow, very easy to wade. A lot of smooth pebbles and very few boulders—oh golly, look at that." She cupped her right hand over her forehead to shut out the sunlight flooding in from the west. "I don't believe it. We might have a true caddis hatch, Doc." Osborne followed her gaze to the river. The dusky summer sun infused the air with a golden light. Wings shimmered as tiny insects spun across rushing, bubbling, foaming waters.

"I love this time of day," said Lew, "all-hallowed dusk." Her voice had slowed, taking on a husky tone quite unlike her usual clipped curtness. "Whoa! There's a rise!" The woman's enthusiasm made Osborne laugh out loud. "See Doc? Over there!"

Osborne looked hard, trying to see what on earth she was seeing. Years of lake fishing made it no easier to differentiate a rising trout from a riffle. Nor were his eyes familiar with rivers, especially rushing rivers, which are very different from self-contained, predictable lakes.

Rivers are alive, always changing, always moving, pulling you in. Osborne admitted only to himself that he feared rivers, even the shallow ones. The innocent facade of a dry, smooth boulder could easily hide a slippery, dangerous, deep hole. A river was like an angry woman: riveting in her energy, treacherous in her depth.

Lew walked down to the bank of the river, grabbed at the air, tipped her head down to examine the insect in her hand, then lifted her palm to release it. Hands again on her hips, a pleased grin on her face, she watched the tiny flight back over the churning water. Osborne watched her.

The fatigue of the long day, the frustration of the delays by the Wausau boys, the sadness of the meeting with the Herre family, the awfulness of the shattered heads and decaying bodies—all was wiped away. Sheer pleasure shone in her eyes as she charged back up the slight incline to pull off her uniform and pull on her fishing gear, all with the energy of a kid. Too shy to let her see him watching, Osborne looked past her to the river, still searching to see what she saw.

He put on his polarized sunglasses. The surface glare vanished, and the world changed.

"My God, *look* at that!" He couldn't help but echo Lew's excitement. Dozens of trout were rising, catching the emergers, the newborn insects. Everywhere he looked he saw fish jumping. Trout by the score. He never knew there could be so many trout in one stretch of water.

"I gotta tell ya, Doc," said Lew as she untied her boots and threw her waders down on the ground, "this black caddis hatch, you see something like this maybe three times in your life. So hurry up. Let's go play with some fish!"

Reaching behind her, Osborne swept up his waders, boots, fishing vest, and rod case. He turned around to find Lew unbuttoning her blouse. She yanked it off, then pulled on a khaki fishing shirt, sleeves already rolled up. It was only seconds between the blouse and the shirt, but Osborne didn't think he would ever forget those seconds: the swell of her breasts against the cups of her white bra, the creamy skin, the soft shadow of nipple. He ached to touch her with an ache he hadn't felt in years. But even if he never did touch her, it was a thrill to feel so alive again. . . . Still, he would love to touch her. He could always hope.

But he was here to fish not dream. Osborne addressed a more immediate task: He had to tie a new tippet onto his leader. The prospect was daunting and a challenge he preferred to meet in private. He tarried pulling on his waders and boots so he wouldn't feel self-conscious executing sloppy knots in her presence. He knew without asking that Hank Kendrickson could tie on a tippet in five seconds or less. Hank Kendrickson could tie a blood knot one-handed. With help, maybe he could tie one around his neck. The thought was absurd but amusing. Osborne chuckled out loud.

"What are you laughing at?" said Lew walking toward the river, bulky in her waders and vest.

"You," he said, fitting together the sections of his fly rod as she charged into the water, "you're a vision in rubber."

She made a gesture with her right hand that made him laugh harder, then turned her attention to the river. "Oh God, here we go! I'll work that hole up at the first bend, Doc. You take the one straight ahead." She pushed upstream in the knee-deep water. "Remember to stay close to the bank, and don't let your shadow spook 'em, Doc."

He let her forge ahead before he adjusted his polarized sunglasses so he could see through the bifocals. From one of the small left front pockets of his fly-fishing vest, he pulled the two-inch square envelope that held his new tippet. Holding the envelope in his teeth, he threaded the line, clipped off the old, too-short tippet, and set to attaching the new one to his braided leader. Good, done.

He was concentrating so hard, he hadn't even heard Lew

return. Startled, he looked up from where he sat on the bank to find her standing four feet off to his left, watching him.

"I have a present for you," she said. "A thank-you for all your help today. Here." She held out a trout fly. "I tied this myself. It's a La Fontaine Emerger, my version of a black caddis."

"Why, thank you, Lew. I'm not sure what I did to deserve this. . . ." Osborne reached for the trout fly.

"You did plenty, Doc. If it hadn't been for you and Ray, my investigation would still be at point zero. I'd be ridiculously late with the IDs, and most of the evidence at the sites, particularly that first one, would have been destroyed. You know that."

Yes, he did. A late afternoon thunderstorm blew away not only the humidity and the summer haze, but the cloudburst had pounded the ruts and footprints near the trestle back into the sand.

"I forgot to ask. Did your bug man make it in time?"

"Yes, thank you. If I hadn't called him when I did, we might have missed that, too. Told me he got maggot samples from both corpses, Sandy Herre and the Olson woman, and he ought to be able to establish time of death to the hour, if not closer. We did good today, Doc." She gave him a warm and wonderful grin.

So he was happy to accept the trout fly and relieved to see it was tied onto a healthy size-fourteen hook, large enough for him to be able to thread the tippet in easily, thanks to his bifocals. Any smaller, and he was likely to struggle for hours unless he put on his good reading glasses, which he hated to do. He was always afraid he might lose them in the river.

"Hold on, Doc." Lew reached for his tippet after he had twisted and looped a pretty good knot. "With these emergers hatching, I think you need to put a sinker on right about . . . here. . . ." Using her teeth, Lew clamped a tiny hunk of lead onto his tippet above the fly. "Then . . . I've got this great new trick. . . ."

She pulled a small disk from a pocket high up on her vest and opened it to pluck a gob of bright orange gunk, which she squeezed around his tippet about eighteen inches up from the fly and the sinker. "Hank showed me this, and I love it. Okay, try a false cast. Let's see how it works."

Osborne made an awkward move with his fly rod. Leader, tippet, and fly flapped in the air.

"What the hell is wrong with your leader?" Lew demanded. She grabbed at the line and checked it closely. "Oh, shoot, you've got one of those damn braided leaders. Now why are you using that? I hate those things."

One new leader and trout fly later, Osborne was finally in the river, casting into the pool he was directed to by Lew. "When the hatch is this thick," she said, "you want to isolate a fish and go after him, otherwise you're just practicing your casting." She watched him false, then roll cast. "Good, better. But you need to practice off your dock."

A sudden swirl hit the water by Osborne's fly, his rod bent, and Lew, who had just turned away, swung back around and crouched, crying, "Set the hook! Set the hook!" The rod flipped up, and she dropped to her knees in the water, frustration and laughter on her face. "Oh, God, Doc, you're so slow. You are *so slow!*"

The fish long gone, Osborne looked at Lew, sheepish and bewildered. "A grown man humbled by a twelve-inch fish. This is a tough sport."

"Next time," said Lew, "you want to tighten the line with a nice *even* pull. Okay, now I'm going to leave you alone. You work on mending your fly. Keep the rod tip parallel to the fly as you let it swing back, imitating the current." She lifted her rod and made an incredibly smooth, easy cast, demonstrating what she meant. Osborne watched in silence, then nodded.

She waded off to position herself near a pool about fifty feet away. The water around them burbled softly, making it easy to talk.

Concentrating on his form as he cast, then doing what he thought was mending the fly, Osborne decided to ask a question that had been nagging him ever since she invited him to fish earlier that day. "So how many boxes of flies does your friend Kendrickson carry when he fishes?" Osborne tried to sound casual.

Lew sent out a lovely cast. "You boys never grow up, do you. Always comparing."

"Not at all," lied Osborne. "I assume he knows a lot more than I do and is better prepared. Ties his own, huh?"

"Yep, he does. He runs that game preserve, y'know, so he gets a lot of his own supplies from the deer, elk, turkeys, even some more exotic birds. I'll have to ask him to show you his dead animal room. It's pret-ty amazing. Quite the professional setup."

"Nothing like an expert." Osborne flopped his fly and hoped to hell she didn't see.

"I didn't say *that*. His casting technique is sloppy. But he tries, you have to give him credit for trying."

"You didn't answer my question, Lew."

"Ten boxes."

"Ten?!"

"So he's a show-off. But we know that, don't we." Lew's tone was matter-of-fact. Osborne was acutely aware that she had once exhorted him to never enter a trout stream with more than one box of trout flies, albeit selected with care after observing the hatch or possible hatches.

Still, Osborne had to admit Hank sounded experienced if not expert. And experts like to fish with experts. Darn, he cursed again all the years he had let his fly-fishing equipment lie unused because Mary Lee resented the expense.

"Hank runs a game preserve, huh. Which one?"

Lew didn't answer the question. He watched her, body bent slightly forward from the hip, right arm high and in front, left arm stripping line. There was a time, when he was a young man, that Osborne had hoped to be an artist, sculpting, drawing. Reality changed his mind, the reality of mak-

ing a living. But he never lost his love for the grace of line,
how it could search and define in lovely ways.

That could explain one of the things he had grown to love
about Lew: the extraordinary economy of motion in her cast.
Watching her body arc against the water, shadowed in gold
by the setting sun, he was mesmerized. The woman was a
study in opposites: Feet planted on land, she was rock solid,
but put her in water, hand her a fly rod, and she became a
creature of air and elegance, a spinner of gossamer threads.

"I'm sorry, Doc. What did you say?" Lew reeled in a ten-
inch brookie.

"I asked which game preserve Kendrickson runs."

"Wildwood. It's just this side of Mincoqua, off Horse-
head Lake. He told me he wants to convert it from a game
preserve to a game farm and become a supplier to hobby
farmers. Said he hates the hunting side of the business. And
he's adding buffalo, which he plans to butcher and sell to
restaurants."

A sudden pull hit Osborne's line. "Lew!" This time he
braced himself, happy that he had stripped in enough line so
he could meet the force with an even pull. The rod tip bent.
"Lew! I got one."

"Set the hook. . . . Good, Doc. Play out some line. . . .
Good, great. Let it go, let it go . . . now!"

The trout danced hard, pulling his line through the riffles
and darting behind a boulder where he might shake off the
hook, but Osborne stayed with the fish. He could tell it was
good-sized. His heart pounded with excitement. Finally, he
lifted the glistening beauty from the water and slipped a
hand under to hold it gently for a brief time. He slipped the
hook out, then cupped the fish in both hands.

Lew had waded over to coach. Now she pulled a camera
from her vest pocket. "Kneel and look up at me, Doc. That's
a beautiful brown . . . at least fourteen inches. Smile."

Osborne grinned up, happy as a four-year-old with his
first bluegill. "This is the biggest trout I've ever caught,

Lew," he said as he guided the silvery fish back into the rushing stream.

Only later would he remember that Hank's catch the day before was almost twice the size. But even that couldn't diminish his joy. And grudgingly, he had to admit he now understood why Hank had barged in so rudely.

Twelve trout later—eight caught by Lew, including a twenty-two-inch brown she'd been after for two years, and four by Osborne—they were back at the truck stripping off their waders and boots. It was past nine, a darkening sky well on its way.

"A spec-tac-ular night," said Lew as she handed him an ice-cold ginger ale. She popped open a Leinenkugel's for herself.

"Yep," she said, "an absolutely spectacular night for trout, Doc. Life just doesn't get much better than this." She raised her beer can for a toast.

She took a long swig. "What a day."

"You can say that again. And tomorrow promises more of the same," said Doc. They looked at each other, tired but happy to be alive.

"So if you can pick up Gina Palmer at the airport for me," said Lew, confirming a plan she had presented earlier, "and bring her over to the office, I'll meet Phil Herre at his daughter's apartment at seven in the morning."

"Sandy worked at the phone company, didn't she?" asked Osborne.

"No. That's what's so interesting. She left six months ago. Her parents had just helped her buy a new computer so she could start her own bookkeeping business. According to her folks, she's been on the road from here to Rhinelander and beyond, meeting with potential customers. She wanted to specialize in the small business community, and she had a lot of good leads as a result of her five years with the phone company."

"So . . ." Osborne took a swig from his ginger ale and

swatted a mosquito simultaneously. "A lot of leads, I guess, huh?"

"Too many. Who knows how many people she talked to last week alone. But Phil said she was keeping notes on all her meetings in the computer. We're going over those tomorrow."

"Gina Palmer said she'll be bringing photos of Ashley's ex-boyfriend," said Osborne, "the one she's convinced is hiding up here somewhere."

"Thank goodness. I have no idea where to start with that one," said Lew. "We've only got ten thousand fortyish and nice-looking men between here and Minneapolis."

"Not to mention Isle Royale."

"Or Milwaukee."

"How did I get so busy, Doc?" Lew grinned at him. "I might have to cancel my Thursday breakfast with Hank."

"Now why would you be having breakfast with Hank?" Osborne asked without thinking. "Sorry, none of my business."

"We're on a committee for the Trout Unlimited banquet," said Lew. "But after today, I have to beg off, given the circumstances . . . though Hank is good at computers. He could come in handy."

"Isn't that nice," said Osborne. He kicked at the ground with the toe of his boot.

"Hank's amazing. He's catalogued every trout fly he's tied in the last two years. He trades on the Internet and has gotten ten, twenty dollars *each* for some of his flies."

"Hmm." Osborne set down his can. "Getting late, Lew. Ready to head back?"

"You betcha, Doc. But what a night, huh?"

As Osborne slid onto the hard seat beside her, he decided not to mention that he was developing an acute allergy to Hank Kendrickson. And now the guy had a way to muscle in on the investigation. Great.

•　　•　　•

Thirty minutes later, Osborne pulled into his own driveway. He parked, entered the house, and let Mike out for an evening run. Walking back toward the kitchen, he paused in front of a mirror hanging in the hallway. He scrutinized his face. Did he look his sixty-three years? Did he look ten to fifteen years older than Hank?

The early-summer tan gave him a healthy glow beneath his full head of silver black hair, if he had to say so himself. His daughters told him he looked distinguished, and he wanted to believe them. The high cheekbones inherited from his Meteis grandmother kept wrinkles to a minimum. And yet his life was there in the lines around his eyes and mouth. The pains, the pleasures, the responsibilities, the years of loneliness in his marriage, things done . . . and not done. Osborne turned away and shrugged. At least it was an honest face.

The phone rang suddenly. He glanced at his watch. Nearly ten. Had to be family.

"Hi, hon," he said, expecting the voice of Erin.

" 'Hon' yourself," said Ray. "I got a big problem, Doc. Got a minute? I'm coming up."

"Good news or bad news?"

"Oh . . . good news. It's good news, Doc."

Osborne set down the phone. He wasn't stupid. The tone in Ray's voice was not happy. Whatever it was, it was not good news.

twelve

"No human being, however great, or powerful, was ever so free as a fish."

John Ruskin

The water was black and still around the dock as Osborne rocked gently in his old chair. Ray sat in the green plastic Adirondack that he had carried up with him.

"Twenty-two bucks at Wal-Mart," he said, ambling toward Osborne's dock with the chair held high. Osborne watched as he plopped the chair down, angled it just so, stood up, turned around, and stuck out his flat butt to ease all six feet five inches down onto the chair, slowly. Very slowly.

Osborne looked out into the night and waited. Ray's strategy for dealing with complications in his personal life was identical to his strategy for landing a wary, wise trophy muskie: slow, methodical, exploratory casts leavened with patience. Hours, days, and weeks of casting. Tonight's pace signaled something was up, all right. Something serious.

"Did you hear the one about the nut who screws and bolts?"

"Five times, you razzbonya. Most recently yesterday morning at McDonald's. Everyone you know has heard it five times, Ray." Osborne kept his voice brisk, hoping to speed up the process. A faint whiff of whiskey on the night air worried him.

"Jeez, really? I must be losing it. . . . Anything new on Sandy Herre?" Ray stalled.

"Nothing. How did the gun work?"

"Fine. She loves it. We're shooting skeet Thursday. She's

bringing her friend along. Guy's got a thirty-six-thousand-dollar Rigby twelve-gauge side-by-side. I tell ya, Doc, this shotgun thing is outta control." Ray's voice was flat. He wasn't thinking shotguns.

Osborne said nothing. He waited, his eyes growing adjusted to the darkness, good enough for him to see his neighbor's profile a few feet away. Suddenly Ray shifted forward in his chair, bracing his elbows on his knees and looking away from his friend.

"I had a call from Elise tonight. She's flying in tomorrow."

"Wonderful," said Osborne with a determined lack of enthusiasm. How many times had he listened to Ray talk about the woman who had stolen his heart in high school and held it hostage ever since? The pretty girl with the almond eyes who left Loon Lake for the big city and a career as a fashion model, followed by a career as the trophy wife of a series of ever-older rich men. The current husband paid well: Twice recently Elise had arrived in a private jet to see her mother. And when she came, she always managed a visit with Ray: just long enough to lure him in, keep him circling.

Osborne didn't like Elise. He didn't like her when she was a spoiled teenager with a fast red convertible—the kind of car he could never afford for his own daughters—and rotten teeth from too much candy, gum, and Coca-Cola. And he didn't like her now. He didn't trust her. Not from the day she broke an appointment and swore to her mother that Osborne's office had made the mistake. Osborne had charged for the visit anyway. When Elise's mother called up, angry with the bill, Osborne clarified the situation: "I don't need you or your daughter as patients of mine any longer. Do I make myself clear?"

As far as Osborne was concerned, the etchings of rot on Elise's molars were more telling than the calculated perfect smile. But Ray knew and loved a different Elise. "Her face is as breathtaking as a forget-me-not," he would say, comparing her to the exquisite blue flower that sprang up in tiny, perfect arcs along the lakeshore. Osborne was tired of hearing it.

"That woman is no reason to fall off the wagon, my friend. I sure as hell hope—"

"Nope. This is not her fault."

"Al-l-l righty, then. You must have a good reason. You *better* have a good reason, because I am not in the mood for an all-night intervention." Osborne sighed. He was tired and cranky, and he couldn't help it.

"Ray, we've been here too many times before, you and me. And I'm sorry if I seem rude, but Lew's asked me to meet a flight at eight-thirty tomorrow morning . . . but, well . . ." Osborne threw his hands up in frustration. He wanted to be rested and alert when he met Gina Palmer, and he felt guilty about that. But he just didn't have the time to waste tonight, especially if it had anything to do with Elise.

"Elise may be on the same flight, Doc."

"Slumming it, is she? What happened to the private plane?"

Ray ignored the sarcasm in Osborne's voice. "She's bringing someone this time."

"I'm afraid to ask. Her husband? No, wait. Her *next* husband."

"My son."

The words hung in the still air. Osborne wasn't sure he had heard right.

"Your son." He repeated Ray's words, hoping he'd heard wrong.

"Yes."

"You never told me you had a son."

"I didn't know until this afternoon."

"Ray . . . how could you not know such a thing?"

"That's what I thought, Doc. So after she called, I went up to see her mother at the nursing home. The old lady's still got her wits, y'know. She said it's true."

"Oh come on, she's always believed anything her daughter says. You know that."

Ray ignored him. "I guess . . . I guess what happened was Elise got pregnant the end of our senior year. Then, in the fall, we both went off to different schools. I thought so, anyway. But it turns out her family sent her to a place in Minneapolis where she had the baby. They kept it a secret. Elise's older sister and her husband wanted to adopt the baby. They raised the boy. Then, last year, Elise's sister was divorced, the boy was having problems, and Elise decided she wanted her—our—son back. She says he's a good-looking boy."

"Oh." Osborne remembered a phrase his daughter Erin had used, referring to problems she was encountering as a president of the Loon Lake School Board. "So, parenthood as a fashion statement?"

"C'mon, Doc, Elise isn't that bad."

"Ray." Osborne sat forward, halting his rocking chair. "I find it impossible to believe you would not have known about this years ago. How did she keep it a secret when you two were kids, for heaven's sake?"

"She told me she didn't even know until she was three months along. Then her parents made her swear to keep it quiet. I believe her. You know her father hated the sight of me."

Of course he did, thought Osborne. He and that wretched mother of hers had big plans for their lovely little girl. Elise was raised to marry well, a plan that most certainly excluded local boys. They weren't paying the bills for Northwestern University just to see her return to Loon Lake.

"Does the boy know Elise is his natural mother?"

"Now he does. And Elise told him I'm his birth father. But the kid's kinda screwed up, Doc. She's handing him off to me. She thinks maybe some time on the lake, away from friends who are a bad influence . . . maybe that'll make a difference. Anyway, I don't have a choice. He's coming."

Osborne stared at Ray's shadow in silence.

"You've got to be kidding."

"I wish I was. They're on an early United flight tomorrow morning. Could be the same one you're meeting, I guess.

"Jeez," was all Osborne could muster. "Exactly what kind of problems is this kid having, Ray?"

"The usual. Drugs, alcohol, too many Cheez-Its. I'll know more when he gets here. Elise said he won't listen to her. He's run away a couple times. He's rowdy, arrogant."

"And you're supposed to be a good influence? You've never grown up yourself, Ray," said Osborne, grinning. "I'm having a hard time imagining how this is going to work."

"Yeah," said Ray, his voice lightening, "me, too. Pretty goofy, huh?"

The two men sat in silence. A fish slurped somewhere off in the blackness. A loon sent out a haunting cry.

"You never know, he might like it here," Osborne said finally.

Ray nodded, then turned his head sideways to look at Osborne. "Doc, there's something I've always wanted to ask you. . . ."

"Shoot." Osborne hoped to hell he wasn't going to ask him how to raise children.

"Why *did* you stay married to Mary Lee?"

That was a bullet out of the blue. Osborne turned away from his friend to stare into the velvet blackness. Tiny pinpoints of light stood out on the far shore. A cloud cover overhead shut out the stars. Osborne paused before he spoke. "I've never discussed this with anyone, Ray, you know that. Not even myself, I guess. I don't want to talk about it."

Ray waited.

"Okay . . . I'll talk about it on one condition: You promise not to touch that bottle again."

A long, long wait. The water was silent. No voices whispered in the tall pines guarding the shore behind them.

"Okey-doke." Osborne heard a rustling and saw the

outline of an arm arc overhead. A soft plop and the pint bottle sank into the weed bed ten yards out from the dock.

"I like to think I'm an honorable man," said Osborne. "I keep my promises. It's as simple as that. My generation, Ray, whether it was the Depression or the wars or growing up Irish Catholic, I don't know . . . We weren't raised to feel we had the choices you have."

"Even though you were miserable."

"Being happy wasn't the issue. Being responsible was."

" 'All men lead lives of quiet desperation'?"

"Something along that line. Who said that, anyway, Thoreau? G. K. Chesterton?"

"David Letterman."

"Baloney."

"You were happy being unhappy."

"No. I had no alternatives, Ray. I made my living here, I had children to raise. Loon Lake has been my home since I was a young man. I could never see changing one thing without changing everything. Why are you asking me this tonight?"

"I'm trying to figure out how I messed up, Doc. I mean, what the hell do I think I'm doing? I fish, I dig graves, and now some poor kid finds out he's got me for a father. I feel . . . I feel . . . I have nothing to offer this boy, Doc." Despair edged his voice like a tear down a cheek. "Now, someone like you, someone who has always done the right thing—"

"The right thing? Hold on. Let me finish what I was saying," said Osborne. "I kept my promises, all right, but it was the easy way out. I wasn't fair to Mary Lee those last years. To be married to her and to feel about her the way I did. I can tell you I was an honorable man, but I can't tell you that I am proud of that. Does keeping promises mean I never made a mistake? I don't think so. Strange as it may seem, I envy *you*, Ray. You live an honest life."

"O-o-h, I don't know about that," said Ray. "I've made promises. Lots of promises." He was leaning forward, right elbow on one knee, his chin cupped in his hand. Osborne figured he was thinking back to when he was eighteen on a warm summer night, promising Elise whatever it took to get what he wanted. "I've kept none. Not a one."

"Now that's not true," said Osborne. "You're being a little too hard on yourself, don't you think?"

"Name one I've kept."

"You promised me that if I stayed off the booze, you would show me your secret weed bed over on Dog Lake. And you did."

"That's true, I did, didn't I?"

"You've kept many promises, Ray. You're a good man."

"I'd like to be a good father. I'd like to not embarrass the kid, y'know?" Ray stood up and stretched. "Thanks, Doc. Time for bed. And no booze . . . I promise." He picked up his chair and started to walk north toward his own property. When he reached the path he could follow through the trees to his trailer, Osborne called out.

"Ray," he said softly, knowing his voice carried through the still air. Ray paused on the rise above him, his face hidden in the shadows. "I didn't keep *all* my promises. Look at Mallory."

"She's you through and through, Doc."

"She's having a hard time. That's my fault."

"C'mon, we all have to find our own way."

And then he was gone.

Osborne remained where he was, rocking. The loon called. Mourning. Once. Twice. And yet again. For the first time in a long time, Osborne felt at peace. He had no idea why.

The pockets were heavy in his old fishing pants. Osborne looked down in surprise. He hadn't seen these pants in years. Didn't Mary Lee throw these out? He pulled at the waistband to adjust the trousers. The weight was pulling them down.

Damn. What *did* he have in his pockets, anyway? Thrusting both hands deep, he yelped in surprise as something clamped hard on both sets of fingers, clamped and bit and kept on biting.

Screaming with pain, Osborne yanked both hands out.

The teeth in his pockets began chattering. The two mouths opening and closing in a fierce staccato, leaping against the fabric as though they could tear right through the pockets. Terrified that they might come at his eyes, at his face, Osborne struggled with his belt. He couldn't get it undone, he couldn't get the pants off! My God, they were biting through the fabric. He screamed.

He woke to a pitch-black room. Mike's anxious wet nose pushed against his shoulder. Osborne lay perfectly still, registering where he was. He was in his own bed, he wasn't wearing pants, no teeth were coming at him. He flexed his hands where they lay at his sides. They were free.

He shivered in the dark and sat up to reach for the quilt and the sheet that he had thrown off.

"It's okay, Mike," he whispered to the black Lab who now had a paw up on the pillow. "Go lie down. Be a good dog." Mike gave a quizzical cock of his head, turned, and loped back to his sheepskin pillow.

But even as Osborne dozed off, he could still feel where the teeth had seized his flesh.

thirteen

"Of course, folk fish for different reasons. There are enough aspects of angling to satisfy the aspirations of people remarkably unalike."

Maurice Wiggin

Gina Palmer flew down the stairs from the Northwest plane and pushed through the doors of the Rhinelander airport like a dragonfly in flight.

She was dressed all in black and quite tiny, though her slim figure was topped with a largish head. Her big eyes were startling in their intense blueness against luminous white skin. Or maybe it was just the intensity with which she stared as she headed in his direction. Osborne braced himself for a landing.

She headed toward where he stood behind the small cluster of people waiting just beyond the security door. "Dr. Osborne?" Her voice was deep and loud, the voice of a woman three times her size.

"How did you know?" he blurted.

"You look like a dentist," she said. "No, of course not." Her voice might be loud, but it was friendly. "Look around. How many older gentlemen do you see? You told me you were retired, right? And I was hoping you weren't that idiot over there with the fish on his head."

Osborne glanced around. She was right. The only other people in the tiny airport were a young couple greeting an elderly woman and two college boys, probably camp counselors, lining up a gaggle of youngsters that had been on Gina's flight.

"You're very observant," he said.

"Not really." She shifted a bulging black leather bag to another shoulder. "Years of reporting make it second nature. You rarely have more than fifteen seconds before the cops bump you from the crime scene, so you grow fast eyes."

"You have luggage?"

"I sure hope so," she said. "I wasn't expecting a puddle-jumper. They stuck my carry-on underneath and made me check my computer. Where will I—oops, I see it."

"Yep, right there." Osborne pointed to a metal bin, which was the top of a luggage carousel in the middle of the one-room airport. Next to the carousel, elevated on a wooden stand, was a plastic column housing a display of local real estate agents. At the moment, it was also supporting the right arm of Ray Pradt, who leaned against it as he sipped from a cup of hot coffee.

"My people are on United," he said, waving his cup to catch Osborne's eye. "Looks like they're a few minutes late."

"Ray, I'd like you to meet Gina Palmer," said Osborne as they walked toward the carousel. Before he could finish the introduction, Ray had curled the upper right corner of his lip and let go with a bird sound. The soft trill went on for several seconds before ending with a "tyeep." Then Ray set his cup down on top of the case and extended his right hand.

Osborne sighed. Ray's lack of appropriate behavior would drive him nuts someday. Here he was with a woman still grieving over the death of a close friend, and Ray had to make weird noises.

"Gina, this is Ray Pradt. He moonlights as a deputy for Chief Ferris when she needs us."

"Apparently he moonlights as a warbler as well." Gina kept a straight face.

"Nope. Robin," said Ray. "Spring song."

"Ray is one of our premier fishing and hunting guides." Osborne gave his buddy a dim eye as he hastened to correct Gina's first impression. "Excellent tracker. Best in the region. He's helping out on this case." He motioned to Ray to remove his hat, which he did, hiding it behind his back.

"I apologize," said Ray as he shook her hand. "I thought you were someone else. I realize this is a sad occasion—"

"Forget it," interrupted Gina. "We're all here to do something about it. That's what counts." Her clipped tone made it obvious she wanted nothing more said about Ashley Olson's death at the moment. If she was grieving, she was keeping it to herself.

Osborne checked his watch; Lew was expecting them in Wausau in one hour. He was surprised the luggage wasn't up yet. It only had to be carried a few hundred feet from the plane.

Suddenly, Gina flashed Ray a generous smile, looking him up and down. "How interesting; you're a fishing guide," she said, cocking her head. "Depending on how long I end up staying, maybe you'd have time to take me out?"

"I dunno," said Ray. "I'm not sure what my schedule is over the next few days. Doc here's darn good. Maybe he can take you out."

Osborne was stumped. This was the first time he hadn't known Ray to jump at the chance to take an attractive woman fishing. Brother, he *had* to be stressed over the kid's arrival.

Impatient with the delay on the luggage, Doc checked his watch again. Gina, on the other hand, was enjoying the attention of the two men. She crossed her arms and spread her feet apart as if to balance herself against the weight of her heavy leather bag. "I feel like I just walked into Banana Republic, you two. I don't think I've ever seen so much khaki. Is this like a local costume or something? Maybe I need to buy some if I want to fit in, huh?" She laughed. Her laugh was musical, bell tones moving up and down the treble scale, filling the small room. Ray grinned at her pleasure.

Osborne gave a soft chuckle. Again she was right. Almost every day of the summer he wore khaki. He owned exactly three pairs of good khaki pants and ten or more variations in shirts. Khaki was easy; it was formal enough for anything you ever had to do in Loon Lake, yet you were ready to fish on a moment's notice. Khaki was cool in the sun, warm in the breezes, and the shirtsleeves protected from mosquitoes.

Ray, too, was always in khaki, though today he had dressed with particular care. Like Osborne, he was wearing freshly laundered and pressed pants, khaki of course. But his shirt was one Osborne hadn't seen before: an expensive hemp fishing shirt, albeit khaki in color. Given his propensity to have walleyes embroidered across everything, including his underwear, today he was unusually sartorially restrained. Not a walleye was in sight. And for the moment, the stuffed trout was hidden behind his back.

Osborne was about to compliment him on this restraint when Gina, leaning to peer around Ray's lanky form, piped up, "So what's with that hat?"

"Ah, the hat . . ." Now this Ray could deal with. Anxiety-ridden or not, he could always talk about his hat. Pulling it out from behind his back, he placed the precious object carefully on his head, backed off from the plastic column, bent his knees to better see his reflection, and carefully set it at a jaunty angle. He looked from side to side, then gave it yet another slight adjustment. Finally, he straightened up and turned to look down into Gina's questioning eyes. "You've heard the famous saying, " 'A fish on a bonnet is worth ten on a plate?' "

"Yes, I have, and that's not how it goes," said Gina. "It's 'A *bird* on a bonnet—' "

"Oh, picky, picky," said Ray, obviously tickled. "Now how do you know that?"

"I'm a newspaper editor," said Gina. "I spend my life checking facts. Facts and phrases and anything else I don't believe. I'm very good at what I do, too."

"I'll bet you are." Something in Ray's tone made Osborne believe he might change his mind about taking this woman fishing.

Meanwhile, Osborne had noticed something was different about the hat. He was still trying to decide exactly what it was when Ray caught his eye.

"I made me a new one last night, Doc, a summer version. How do you like it?"

The new hat featured the same stuffed trout, but this specimen rode on a baseball cap instead of the usual leather hat with its fur-lined earflaps tucked up. The head and tail of the fish still protruded over Ray's ears, but he had replaced an antique muskie lure with a brilliant coral red walleye jigging spoon that was hooked across the breast of the fish. The jig, known locally as Ray's Jive Baby, was his own design and one he was hoping to patent. Ray referred to it fondly as his retirement account.

"This is your marketing dollar at work, I take it?" said Gina.

"You might say that," said Ray. "I'm known for my first impressions."

As legendary as Ray's hat was, Osborne, who had survived the adolescence of two daughters, wondered if Ray had any idea what effect he could have on an unsuspecting teenager. Osborne opened his mouth, then he closed it. Then he opened it again. He owed Ray. He would not let him go into dangerous territory unwarned.

"Do you really want to do this to a sixteen-year-old?"

Ray looked confused. "Why? What? I think I look pretty good, don't I?"

Osborne shrugged. He would say nothing more, especially in front of Gina. Maybe it was better the kid find out sooner rather than later, anyhow.

"Do you mind if I ask what you two are talking about?" said Gina.

Just as she spoke, the baggage carousel gave a great creaking sound and coughed up one piece of luggage. As she walked toward it, Ray waved. "Here's my flight, folks. See you later, Doc."

fourteen

"There is more to fishing than catching fish."
Attributed to Dame Juliana Berners, fifteenth century

Waiting off to the side while Gina made arrangements for a rental car she could pick up later, Osborne had a good view of Ray and the passengers alighting from the United Airlines flight, which had just landed. Six people made their way down the shaky metal stairway and toward the airport lobby. Elise was not among them.

Osborne was not surprised. It fit that she would send a young kid off alone to meet a strange man purported to be his father. She probably had a hair appointment she couldn't break. Once again, Osborne wondered how Ray could be so good-hearted and so fair with people, yet refuse to recognize when his generosity was not returned.

A tall, gangly teenager wearing long, baggy black shorts and a wrinkled oversize purple T-shirt that said "Byte Me" in orange pushed through the plate glass doors, and Osborne could see that Elise had arrived after all. She was all over the face of the kid. His features were raw. He had yet to grow into the heavy bones of his brow, his cheekbones, and his jaw, but his eyes were his mother's: dark, almond-shaped, and slightly tipped. And even as Osborne knew Elise as a tall, full-breasted woman, he wasn't surprised to see this kid was already a good six feet two, maybe six four even.

But what if his height came close to Ray's towering six feet five? Would he have the man's grace? Could he ever slip through a forest as silently as a deer? Move as swiftly to set a fishhook or dodge the death grip of a snapping turtle?

Would he inherit his father's eye for signs on the forest floor, his ear for the secrets in the wind?

If this was indeed the son of Elise and Ray, which would he most resemble? The one for whom wealth had nothing to do with money? Or the one for whom money was worth the sale of body and soul? Osborne rocked back and forth on his heels, hands deep in his pockets, as he watched the two men approach each other. He was certain Elise was lying. But how would Ray ever know? *We'll see*, thought Osborne. *We'll just see.*

Ray stepped forward to greet the boy, a friendly smile on his face and hands extended palms up as if he was offering a plate of his superb fried chicken. The kid mumbled something Osborne couldn't hear, holding tight with one hand to the strap of a backpack slung over one shoulder and to a small black briefcase hanging from his other arm. A polite expression was fixed on his face, betraying nothing he might be thinking about the man in front of him, the handsome bearded man with the fish on his head.

Ray stepped back to let the boy walk past, then laid a light hand on the kid's shoulder. The boy gave a quick, imperceptible shrug, and Ray dropped the hand. He looked about as if he had stumbled and wondered if anyone had seen him. He caught Osborne watching from where he stood just a few yards off.

"This way," he said to the boy with a hearty friendliness. "I want you to meet one of our neighbors and my good buddy, Doc Osborne. Doc's a retired dentist and a blow-your-socks-off muskie guy. He's got a fifty-three-incher in his living room you won't believe.

"Doc . . . Nick."

"Huh," said the kid, holding tight to his strap and his briefcase. Nick was obviously a city kid, pale and lightly pimpled. Osborne also counted six silver earrings, three in each ear. Jeez. Looked like Nick could give Ray a run for the money when it came to personal adornment.

"Welcome to the Northwoods, Nick," said Osborne. "I

think we'll be doing some muskie fishing together in the next few days. Isn't that right, Ray?"

"I was hoping to learn how to fly-fish," the boy said. "That's what my friends do." His tone made it clear he could care less about any other kind of fishing.

"Oh?" Ray looked surprised. More than a little disappointed. "Doc can maybe give you a few pointers. He's been trying his hand at it, haven't you, Doc?"

"You'll want to try both, son." Osborne jumped to rescue Ray. "One gets you on the lakes; the other gets you back into the backwoods on streams and small rivers."

"I just wanna fly-fish." The kid was obstinate and, in Osborne's opinion, not a little rude. Surprise. He was Elise's son.

Before anyone could say more, Gina Palmer popped up at Osborne's side exclaiming, "Say, is that a laptop you got there? What the hell size is that thing? That isn't that new IBM I heard about? I'm thinking about getting one. How's it working?"

Osborne and Ray backed up as if they'd been hit by a straight-line wind, tornado strength. *Rapid-fire* didn't begin to describe Gina's delivery; she was more intense than she had been on the phone the day before.

Nick's face underwent a transformation. Gone was the impassive, almost sullen scowl. A passionate, spirited expression took its place. "Yeah! My mom just got it for me. Gotta minute, I'll show ya. It's *real* cool."

Gina, her own much larger computer case slung across her back, motioned him over to a nearby rack of chairs. Nick sat down, set the briefcase on his bony knees, and unzipped it to pull out a flat black box. Osborne, knowing little about computers, glanced over at Ray, who knew even less and was standing there mute, a quizzical expression on his face as if he had no idea what to do next.

"Ray? You have an ISP, don't you?" The boy looked up from where he was banging on keys in a way that made sense to Gina. She was leaning over Nick's shoulder, her eyes fastened on his monitor.

"What?" asked Ray.

"No, son," said Osborne. "I'm afraid we still have a pretty antiquated phone system out in our area. My daughter tried to go on-line a couple weeks ago when she was visiting, and the phone company told her we can't get Internet service until they replace our party line. That's not for another couple months, I'm afraid."

The boy stared up at Ray. He looked like he was about to cry. "You mean you're not *wired?*"

"I'm plenty wired," said Ray.

"That's not what he means," said Osborne, weighting his words so Ray got the message. "The boy is serious."

"Is *anybody* wired up here?" Gina stood up, a look as stricken as the boy's on her face.

"Lew is, I think," said Osborne lamely. "She said they laid fiber optics out to her offices and the new jail."

"Who's Lew?" asked Gina.

"I'm sorry," said Osborne. "I should have said Chief Lewellyn Ferris, head of the Loon Lake Police Department. That's who we're meeting in Wausau to complete the ID. And . . ." Osborne looked at his watch. "We're almost half an hour late, I'm afraid."

Gina looked over at Ray. "Didn't you say you're a deputy? Maybe she'll let us plug in over there, huh?"

Nick looked up from his computer. A look of astonishment flooded into his face as he asked Ray, "You mean you're a cop?"

"No. I'm a guide," said Ray. "Fishing, hunting . . . I am not a cop. We'll talk about it later, okay? Now let's get the rest of your luggage."

"Nice kid," said Gina as they piled her luggage into the rental car and locked it up. "I'd like to get another look at that laptop of his."

"I'd like to know why he's wearing all the jewelry," said

Osborne. "He has something in his tongue, too. Did you see that? Good thing he doesn't wear braces. Damn thing would get hooked."

"C'mon, Doc, you're not into pierced body parts?" Gina chortled. "Don't worry about what you can see; it's what they've got *under* their clothes." As Gina climbed into Osborne's car for the drive to Wausau, he lowered the windows. The sun was bright with fluffy white clouds scudding across the brilliant blue sky. The air was heating up. It would be a nice drive.

Just then, Ray and Nick emerged from the front entrance of the airport lobby. Ray hoisted Nick's duffel onto his left shoulder and pointed the boy in the direction of his pickup, parked right across from Osborne's station wagon. The boy started toward the pickup, then stopped, looking up in amazement. Osborne leaned forward in his seat, curious to see what had caught his attention.

"Whoa," said Nick. "You guys got a lotta sky here." He stood there for a good fifteen seconds, taking it all in. Unaware Osborne was watching, he let a look of excitement slip over his features, but it vanished the minute he heard Ray's footsteps behind him.

Still, Osborne knew teenagers. *Maybe there's hope,* he thought. *Maybe I'm wrong; maybe the kid's got a little bit of Ray in him after all. We'll see.*

Meanwhile, Gina had leaned out her window to wave good-bye. Ray waved in return.

"Now watch this." Osborne lowered his voice and motioned to Gina to watch the proceedings across the way.

Ray tossed the duffel into the back of the beat-up blue pickup and opened the door on the driver's side of the truck. He stood there looking over at Nick. The leaping walleye hood ornament flashed silver in the sunshine. And the passenger door refused to give in to Nick's yanks on the handle.

"Oops, sorry," said Ray, "that door doesn't work. You gotta either climb through the window or go in on my side."

"For real?" Nick was taken aback.

"Yeah, I need to get it fixed," said Ray.

"What do most people do?" said Nick, his voice a little edgy.

"Go through the window."

With that the kid gave a shrug, swung his briefcase in first, then heaved himself up to wriggle through the generous opening. As he did so, Osborne heard Ray say loudly, "Gotta Wisconsin joke you can tell your buddies back in New York City.

"What's that?" Nick's voice was muffled.

"Whaddaya call cheese that isn't yours?"

"Nacho cheese," said Gina with a groan and a smile. "That is one joke. Does this go on all the time?"

"You betcha." Osborne gave the ignition a healthy twist.

fifteen

"There are matters beyond the knowledge of non-fishermen. . . . Forests . . . can insulate you against the woes of the world as completely as the widest water of an ocean voyage."

Frederic F. Van de Water, author

Leaving the airport, Osborne turned right onto Highway 8. He hadn't driven a quarter mile before he heard a siren. He looked up to see Lew's cruiser in his rearview mirror. He pulled over.

Lew jumped out of her car and ran up to his window. "Doc, thank goodness I caught you. Roger never did get the van back to Timber Lake. One of the lab guys came up at the crack of dawn this morning to do a preliminary. I tried to reach you at the airport. The victim is still in Loon Lake, so we can do the ID at Saint Mary's. Thank goodness, too. I did *not* want to take four hours to go all the way down to Wausau." She looked past Osborne. "Gina Palmer?"

"Yes. Are you Chief Ferris?"

"I sure am," said Lew, "and very glad I intercepted you two. Can you follow me back to Loon Lake, and we'll meet at the hospital? I'd like to get this over with as soon as possible."

"Me, too," said Gina.

Ashley Olson was no longer curled into a fetal position, nor was she in running clothes. Her body, naked and straight, had been reduced to a landscape of bumps under the morgue linen.

Earlier, while waiting for a hospital attendant to let them

in, Gina had spoken of her friend in such vivid detail that Lew and Osborne were able to understand the magnitude of her death. Gone was a vibrant, savvy woman who had pumped life into a new and respected marketing firm, holding her own easily among senior executives from major corporations. Gone was a woman, generous and kind to her friends and to those who worked for her.

The more good things were said, the more Osborne wondered what went wrong. If Gina knew her as a woman of vision who could build a management team as easily as she built a landmark mansion, then where did she make her strategic mistake? And why did she travel so far from her home—so secretly? What made her so determined to see someone who wanted to see her . . . dead?

A wave of sadness played across Gina's face as she pulled the sheet up and back, then layered it, fold on fold, across the waxen surface of her friend's naked abdomen. She looked down, studying the still form. Her professionalism showed; someone unaccustomed to violent death would have turned away.

The wounds were more obvious now that the crusty blood had been cleaned up. Osborne found them hard to look at, especially the slashing across the upper torso. He backed off to lean against the wall. Lew stood quietly behind Gina, moving with her as she moved around the body. In a low voice, she asked Gina to confirm that this was indeed Ashley Olson. Gina whispered an answer, then stood perfectly still, staring down in silence.

And as she stood there, her back straight, her head bowed slightly, a phrase from a Native American prayer for the dead ran through Osborne's mind: "Do not stand at my grave and cry. I am not there; I did not die." Nice phrase; not true.

Gina turned and gestured for Lew and Osborne to stand beside her. Her face was slick with silent tears. She pushed a few loose curls back from Ashley's forehead and then, touching her chin, tipped the dead woman's head slightly to the right to more fully expose the gaping wound left by an exiting bullet. Her face hardened, but she said nothing. Then, pointing to the slashes that crisscrossed Ashley's chest and sliced into the throat, Gina threw her hands up in an expression of futility. "This is hate," she said. "Fury."

She lowered the sheet further. She examined the left hand, then the right. "No cuts. She didn't even try to defend herself."

"I don't believe she had the opportunity." Lew spoke softly. "The preliminary lab report states she died instantly from the bullet with all this occurring later. We'll have a complete report in a day or so."

Gina nodded.

Lew had been watching Gina carefully as she studied the corpse. Now she placed a comforting hand on Gina's shoulder as she leaned forward. "Did you see these?" she said, pointing.

"No." Gina had to bend over to see the bite marks on each shoulder. She looked up, confused.

"Human bites," said Lew. "We found the same marks on another victim. Please keep this confidential, by the way."

Gina looked at her in surprise. "The other one . . . killed with a high-powered rifle?"

"Yes," said Lew.

"No." Gina shook her head angrily, the blue eyes sparking. "If you think Ashley was the victim of some random attack, some serial killer, I can assure you, I disagree. This . . . this slashing and cutting . . . I know that Michael Winston did this. I have proof that I'll show you when we leave here." She paused for a moment. "Did the other victim have slash marks like these?"

"No," said Lew. "Only the bite marks are similar . . . but they are in the same location on both victims."

Gina shook her head. "I don't know how or why that could happen, but I am convinced that if we can find Michael Winston, we'll have the man who killed Ashley."

She reached to pull up the sheet, then paused. She leaned forward like a parent over a sleeping child.

"And so we die before our own eyes," she whispered, bending to place a kiss on the shattered face. She laid the sheet down gently, then turned to Lew. Still whispering, she said, "I spoke to her lawyer and several close friends. When you release the body, I'll arrange for cremation, and I'll take Ashley home with me."

Lew held her arms out as if she expected Gina to weep, but Gina shook her head, straightened her shoulders, wiped at her cheeks, and walked briskly out of the small room, grim resolve, not grief, on her face.

sixteen

"Fishermen are born honest, but they get over it."
Ed Zern, *Field & Stream*

Hauling the wooden armchair across the oak floor in the sunny office, Gina planted herself in front of Lew's desk and slapped down a stack of the file folders.

"I brought you everything I've got. Except for any photos of Winston. Our paper has been converting all the paper files in the morgue onto disk, but very slowly, with society photos having the last priority, dammit. The ones I wanted, which are from four years ago, haven't been scanned in yet. But I am having them pulled and FedExed up here, hopefully by Friday. These are my own files."

Gina leaned forward, arms on her knees, a cup of black coffee in her right hand. Osborne noted once again what a striking woman she was. Quite slim in narrow-legged black slacks and a long-sleeved black shirt, Gina's porcelain face with its crystal-blue eyes looked carved from stone, an effect reinforced by the severe cut of her straight black hair. The hair, cut blunt to her lower jaw, framed the outline of her perfectly oval face. She was a tiny woman, he realized. Even her teeth were tiny. But her sex and her size hardly diminished her.

Osborne was amused to find that her direct, no-nonsense approach mirrored Lew's to a point. Lew's speech pattern, however, was quite the opposite of Gina's. Where the reporter ran on nonstop, scarcely taking a breath, Lew was a listener, always watching and succinct in her remarks.

Lew seemed to have warmed instantly to Gina, which was not her usual pattern with strangers. Not only had she shared the information on the bites, but she had handed over the preliminary report from the Wausau tech, saying, "Let me know if anything in here catches your eye."

The report, basically a listing of the tissue and fluid samples taken, along with the clothing and samples from the site, said nothing new except that the full report would be completed in forty-eight hours or slightly longer. Also included were copies of photos shot at the scene and in the small morgue. Nothing on it caught Osborne's eye, anyway.

"You're kidding. *Forty-eight hours?*" Gina was appalled.

"At least," said Lew. "Just think where I'd be if I didn't have Doc here to help me with a basic ID. Jeez, Doc, that reminds me. Do you know if Ray got to Timber Lodge before the rain last night? Roger said he canvassed the four homes in the half-mile radius around the site but found nothing. I was hoping Ray might have taken a look in those woods back there—"

"I doubt he had a chance, Lew. He didn't say anything and he's got a pretty full plate right now. But I'll see him this afternoon."

"How many people will be working on this case?" asked Gina.

Lew rocked back in her chair and snorted." This is a very small town and a very small police force. I have two full-time deputies, whom I *inherited*." She stressed her last word, underscoring her not-so-high opinion of Roger and his cohort.

As she spoke, Osborne sipped his coffee. It was just the right temperature and tasted great. In fact, life was great. Nothing beat sitting here, listening to Lew, seeing her smile, watching her eyes darken in thought. And he loved to hear her snort. Never in his life had he expected a woman to snort. *This is happiness, old man,* he told himself as he took another sip.

"Those two can't keep up with parking-meter fines, drunk drivers, and old ladies upset because their trash didn't get picked up," Lew was going on. "So when I have a serious problem, like these murders, I am very fortunate to get help from Dr. Osborne and—when I absolutely must—Ray Pradt." Her emphasis implied Ray was the last guy she called.

"Don't get me wrong." She looked at Gina. "Ray is the best tracker in the county, which is why I hope to hell he got out to Timber Lake. We know the killer's vehicle had to be back in there somewhere. If anyone can find a trace of it, it'll be Ray."

"So what's the problem?" asked Gina, sipping from her coffee. "I'm missing something here. Sounds to me like Ray should be working full-time for you. I don't mean to be critical, Chief, but I know what I look for when I hire an investigative reporter."

"Well . . ." Lew raised her eyebrows and glanced quickly at Osborne. "Ray maintains his own list of misdemeanors, which are well known to our Loon Lake community. It so happens I have to report to the mayor and the town board, and some of those folks give me trouble when I use Ray."

"What kind of misdemeanors?" Gina's rapid-fire delivery was beginning to sound normal.

"You've met Ray?"

"At the airport. Interesting man. Quite personable. I'd say he has some style issues, but otherwise he's okay."

"Style issues?" Lew's eyebrows went up.

"The fish chapeau is a bit much." Gina chuckled.

"Personable, huh." Lew looked at Gina. "He's too personable. Guy refuses to grow up, Gina. At least once a season, somebody nabs him on the Flowage astral-traveling. I don't know how he finds the stuff, but he does. And poaching. In Ray's world the natural universe belongs to everyone. He has no respect for private land."

"This is not murder one," said Gina. "Though I can see he's not going to get the Republican nomination for president."

"It's an *irritation*," said Lew. "Every time I need his help, I have to prostrate myself before all these nincompoops.

Ah . . ." Lew waved her hand in disgust. "I shouldn't get into it. I get my way in the end and Ray makes a few bucks. Everyone wins in the long run, I guess. But . . ." Lew waggled a finger at Gina, "watch the *personable*. This is a warning."

"I hear you." Gina gave Lew a broad grin, and Lew grinned back. Osborne, watching the two women, was confused. Then it dawned on him. Without even being there, Lew knew Ray would have an interest in Gina. Or was it vice versa? He'd have to keep his eyes open. Jeez, how did Ray do it?

"So Ray Pradt makes a living as a fishing guide?"

"And he digs graves on the side," said Lew, "in the heat of the summer when the fish aren't biting."

"And the dead of the winter," said Osborne. "Sorry. Poor choice of words, but Christmas is Ray's busiest season for digging graves. Every year it's the same."

Gina's mouth hung open in disbelief. "C'mon."

"No, we're very serious," said Lew. "Strange as it may sound, that's another reason it works for me that Ray isn't a full-time cop. This is not the most affluent community, Gina. Because Ray's out there making a buck however he can— running a backhoe at the cemetery or shoveling the library roof in the winter—he's connected. He knows everyone, he hears everything."

"I get the picture," said Gina. "He's your street source."

Lew nodded. "That's one way to put it."

"The mayor and the town board are good people," said Osborne, "but they forget that the Northwoods is also home to folks who don't identify their whereabouts with a fire number—"

"Or a mailbox decorated with pine trees," said Lew. Osborne threw her a look. He had one of those.

"Or an income tax return?" said Gina.

Lew sat back in her chair. "Does that answer your question on who I've got to work this case?" said Lew.

"It makes me think you won't mind my two cents," said Gina.

"Not at all," said Lew. "Not at all." She shook her head as she waved a ballpoint pen over the notepad in front of her. "Tell me everything you can about Ashley and her friend, Mr. Winston, but don't take it personally if I don't tell you everything or if I have to tell you to back off. Understood?"

"Tell me to back off, tell me to shut up, but let me tell you," Gina pointed her empty coffee cup at Lew, "we're gonna get this guy, and I'm gonna be there."

"Help yourself to more coffee," said Lew, pointing to a half-full pot on the small oak table to the side of her office door. "Gina, before we go any further, you said at the morgue that you have proof the ex-fiancé is involved. What kind of proof?"

"Never thought you'd ask," said Gina, standing up. She had slipped her hand into her purse while Lew was talking. Now she pulled out a long, cream-colored envelope addressed in script. She handed it to Lew before walking over to refill her coffee cup. "I found this in Ashley's desk drawer last night. My hunch is there were plane tickets included, too."

Lew pulled out a single sheet of expensive, buff-colored stationery, read the brief message, and handed it to Osborne.

"Dearest," read the letter, "You have no idea how important that moment of hearing your voice on the phone was to me. I still cannot believe how lucky I am that you found me. I can't wait to see you. I love you. I want to return everything—including my heart." The signature was a flourish that started with a large *M*.

Lew looked at Gina. "No date. What am I missing here?"

Gina waved her hand airily. "Check out the postage mark."

Lew looked at the front of the envelope, then handed it to Osborne. The postmark was Loon Lake, Wisconsin, dated two weeks ago. The postage was metered.

"That's right here," said Lew, a quizzical look in her eyes.

"I know. I checked the map. I figured you wouldn't have any problem getting your post office to check the number on that postage meter," said Gina. "That could be Michael Winston's big mistake."

Lew checked her watch. "The post office is closed for lunch."

At the expression of disbelief on Gina's face, Osborne jumped in. "This is a small town, Gina; our post office closes from eleven to two every day. They don't even open on Saturday."

Gina rolled her eyes as she reached for the first stack of file folders. "Okay, then. I'll run through this background quickly."

seventeen

"Regardless of what you may think of our penal system, the fact is that every man in jail is one less potential fisherman to clutter up your favorite pool or pond."

Ed Zern, *Field & Stream*

"These are my personal files." Gina separated her stack of manila folders into three precise piles on Lew's desk. The tab on each file was labeled in tiny script and not a sheet of paper poked out from a folder

They reminded Osborne of his own organized, detailed dental records. Settling back in the other wooden armchair, he caught Lew's eye. She was impressed, too. That didn't surprise him, having witnessed Lew's meticulous sorting of her trout flies and muskie lures.

"By the way," he said to Lew as they waited for Gina, who had reached into her briefcase to pull out her notebook computer, "looks like a cold front moving in tonight. Why don't we try for muskie off my dock? Just give it an hour. Still haven't tried that Striker of yours."

"Not a bad idea," said Lew. "I'll be ready to soothe the old brain, and the streams are getting a little warm for trout. But I doubt I can make it before seven. I've got a ton of paperwork on Sandy Herre that I just haven't had time to finish up. Is seven too late?"

"No-o-o. Heck, it's light till eight-thirty. Tell you what, Lew. I've got a few venison chops in the freezer," said Osborne. "We'll fish for an hour or so, then I'll throw those on the grill."

Lew looked pleased. "I'll see if I can scare up some dessert."

Jeez. Osborne resisted pinching himself. The day was getting better by the minute.

"Okay, I'm ready," said Gina, making eye contact with both of them as she sat down. "I want you to know why I'm so sure Michael Winston lured Ashley up here. I also think there may be something in this background that will help you find him. I don't know what that might be exactly, so I know I'm going to tell you more than you need to know—"

"Don't worry about that," said Lew. "You just talk, and we'll listen. I'll stop you when I have a question."

"Thank you," said Gina, her eyes determined. "This goes back about two years. I had decided to profile Michael Winston for reasons that included—but went beyond—my friendship with Ashley Olson.

"My initial urge to investigate the guy was basic reporter cynicism, the reason we all go into this business. As a senior editor on the business desk at the *Star*, I was hearing about him constantly and finding a lot of what I heard a little hard to believe, just too good to be true. He'd been in town only a year, but already he was everywhere. The business community couldn't get enough of him.

"First, he was Mr. Bigshot, worth sixty million bucks; then he was the new board member of the most prestigious bank in town, then he was chairman of the big horse show; *and then . . .*" Gina raised a finger significantly, "he was voted Kansas City's Bachelor of the Year. Need I say my feminine instincts kicked in?

"To back up for a second: Before Winston arrived on the scene, I wrote a similar profile on Ashley Olson and the extraordinary success of her start-up. We hit it off during the interviews. Later, she wanted help writing a book about her business, and I started coaching her through that process. That's how we met and became good friends."

"So you and Ashley were personal friends before Michael Winston came on the scene?" said Lew.

"Very much so. We would have lunch or dinner a couple times a month. We belonged to the same gym, so we would work out or play tennis together. We were both single women in our mid-thirties with high-stress careers. We were on the same wavelength. Know what I mean?"

Lew and Osborne nodded.

"So if one or the other of us wasn't seeing someone, it was fun to do something together. I think Ashley liked me because I was very different from her other friends, who were mostly wealthy society or business types. And she had a good sense of humor, which I got a kick out of.

"But what she didn't have was any sense when it came to men. I mean *any*. She dated the biggest jerks. I told her that, too. Many times!"

Gina sat back in her chair, crossed her legs, and started kicking her top leg furiously. "She went out with a guy who was in the Kansas City mob for a while. I told her she was crazy. Stark raving mad."

"And?" Lew said.

"He found someone else, I'm not sure. But that's why her sister came to me. I told Doc on the phone yesterday that her younger sister, Chris, was a copy editor at the *Star*. Very good, too. She came to me right after Ashley started seeing Winston. Before this, in fact, she and I had talked a couple times about Ashley's bad taste in guys. We kidded around about it."

Gina looked at Lew and Osborne. "Let's be real here. Most women I know, and, I'll bet, most women you know, have poor judgment about men. They cut guys wa-a-y too much slack. Chris had criticized Ashley's beaus before, but Michael Winston had her very, very worried. She was absolutely convinced he was after Ashley only for her money. And access. Through Ashley, he was meeting a lot of heavy hitters.

"I'll never forget the morning Chris came to me, either. Because as well as I thought I knew Ashley, she had never told me about her cancer and the surgery."

"Doc mentioned that," said Lew. "She had breast cancer, double mastectomies and re-construction, right?"

"Yes, very unusual for a woman in her early twenties. Chris said the experience had been so traumatic that there were times when Chris worried Ashley might commit suicide. But the surgery was a success. They got everything, and her reconstruction was very natural. Like I said earlier, Ashley and I worked out together, and I never noticed a thing.

"But you have to know Ashley. She was very into appearance and style. Small like me and always on a fierce diet, she was extremely self-conscious about her calves. They were a little thick for her build. You could tell she had had acne as a kid, too. So even though she knew how to make herself up very well and she dressed beautifully, I think the cancer left her with a severe self-image problem. A problem Winston would have capitalized on . . . expertly."

"So she was attractive but no glamour girl," said Lew, "financially successful, very bright, but not the most self-confident woman."

"Exactly. That's why she was so flattered when Winston hit on her. Every other woman he had dated was drop dead gorgeous . . . trophy bimbos."

"Did you ever talk to one of them?" asked Lew.

"Yes, I did. Only one, but she told me something very interesting. She said that her dates with Winston were strictly for show. He wanted her on his arm during a social gathering, but when no one was around, he sent her home or back to the hotel room—alone. No sex, no romance. Quite the opposite of what he did with Ashley.

"Chris told me that he came on to Ashley during a plane flight. Apparently, someone who knew them both had introduced them in the airport club at La Guardia in New York, then Winston got his seat changed so he could sit next to her on the flight back to Kansas City. Chris said they got off the plane, went to the hotel at the airport, and spent the night together."

"Really," said Lew. "Was Ashley—"

"No," said Gina. "She wasn't."

"Then he's quite the charmer."

"Yes, he is," said Gina. "Intensely charming. Murderously charming. You can understand how Chris would find it disturbing that he could get to Ashley so easily. I was pretty damn taken aback myself. And it's not like I haven't been around."

"Did . . . do you find Winston attractive?" Lew asked.

Gina paused for a long moment. "He's interesting. I told Doc he's a mild-looking man, probably wears lifts to give him height, but pleasant to look at. He has a way, when he is focused on someone, of being . . . endearing. An odd word, I know. But when he wants to, he can be seductively sweet and attentive . . . if you are his target, that is. And, of course, let's not underestimate the charm of sixty million bucks." Gina shrugged.

"Right," said Lew.

"But if you're not the target, he's a blank," said Gina. "I don't know any other way to put it."

"Did he come on to you?"

"Never. And I saw him at a number of cocktail parties before he hooked up with Ashley, so there was opportunity. In fact, I made it a point to introduce myself. He didn't even see me. I wasn't even a blip on the radar screen. It was like talking to a brick wall."

"That's unusual for you, isn't it?"

"Well . . . yeah . . . it is. I'm not an unattractive woman. Look at your friend Ray, he paid attention."

Lew laughed. "I wouldn't use Ray as an example. Not to hurt your feelings, Gina, but Ray loves women—all shapes and sizes."

"And they love him," said Osborne.

"In my experience, most men are like Ray," said Gina.

"Were you jealous?" Lew's voice was soft, forgiving.

Gina looked hard at Lew. "I wasn't jealous so much as I

was puzzled. I'm used to getting a second glance at least. That's why I listened to Chris, especially the money angle."

"So Chris put you on alert. . . ." Lew urged her to continue.

"Yes. Then, a couple months after we talked, she was killed in a car accident. Coincidentally, right about the time that Winston went to work for Ashley."

"How long ago was that?" asked Lew.

"Two and a half years ago. It still bugs the hell out of me—and I brought the file on it. I was on the city desk the night of the accident. I got a call from one of the EMTs at the scene. She's married to a reporter who works for the paper, so she recognized Chris from the copy desk. When she called that night, she told me something that's haunted me ever since."

"Describe the circumstances of Chris's death first," said Lew.

"Single-car accident. She hit a tree on the way home from work, about three in the morning. Some alcohol in her blood but not enough for a DUI. It was classified an accident, even though a number of her friends and colleagues, even Ashley, thought it might have been suicide."

"Why is that?"

"Chris was moody. The sisters were opposites. After she survived the cancer, Ashley was relentlessly upbeat, while Chris had a habit of getting down on herself. She was looking for another job at that time, too. She hated her boss."

Gina stood up suddenly to refill her coffee cup. Then, cup in one hand, the other thrust deep into her pants pocket, she paced as she talked. "Here's what the EMT told me. When they were cutting Chris out of the wreckage, the intern with the emergency team noticed that her arms were not broken."

"I assume she hit the tree pretty hard?" asked Osborne. "Other bones must have been broken."

"Yes. Actually, the car caught fire on impact, and she was badly burned, too. But the intern was confused by the condition of her arms. I talked to the intern, and he said Chris took the impact of the crash on her head and her entire lower body. Her arms, except for the burns, were okay. He said it was so unusual for her arms not to be broken that it made him think she was limp when the car struck the tree—that she was already unconscious. He tried to bring it up with the cops, but they wouldn't listen. As far as they were concerned, it was an accident, case closed."

"And Ashley thought it was suicide," said Lew.

"She was *convinced* Chris had committed suicide."

"I see," said Lew.

"I, of course, was sure she was killed. And so I talked my boss into a magazine story on Michael Winston. In my gut, I knew something was really wrong."

"Oh," said Lew, "so this was not a *short* newspaper article that you wrote."

"Oh no," said Gina. "The business section had already run at least half a dozen of those. No, I talked my managing editor into a good, long magazine piece. Something that would give me an excuse to really dig.

"And that's when things got interesting. I called Harvard to check on the business school degree and learned he had attended some two-week session, not the full program. He listed it on his résumé as a Harvard MBA. But, hey, just a venial sin. People do that all the time. Then I called the family business in Texas, and they flat-out refused to talk to me. That got me going. So I called a former colleague of mine who's a sportswriter for the Houston newspaper. As I told Doc yesterday, *pay dirt*. And here's that file.

"The sportswriter recognized the name instantly. He switched me upstairs to a special projects investigative reporter who had covered the stock fraud story. He just about fell out of his chair laughing when I told him Winston was saying he was worth sixty million dollars. But he sobered up when I told him I had a dear friend almost engaged to Winston. And he got real serious when I said she was wealthy. He went to the courthouse that afternoon and overnighted the divorce papers. My timing was impeccable. Winston had been in court down in Houston, six weeks earlier, swearing he was worth less than fifty thousand dollars and trying to weasel out of his marriage—he had a wife and three kids.

"Meanwhile, back up in Kansas City, word got out that I was working on the story. Somehow, someone—I don't know who—learned I was nosing around Winston, and they got in touch with the one guy who had something on him. I got a phone call in the middle of the night from that man. He told me that Winston had stolen his business, his wife, and tried to kill him."

Lew had been taking notes as Gina was talking. Now she raised her pen from the paper to look at Gina.

"Yes, attempted murder. The source said he had been the sole owner of a small commodity investment firm. His banker introduced him to Winston, who made him a good offer for half the company, probably with a line of credit from the idiot banker. Working with Winston, my source refinanced his end of the operation, taking on several million dollars in loans, which he put into the company. Six months later, he walks in one day and finds himself locked out of his office, locked out of his own business!

"It got worse. Winston was sleeping with the guy's wife, and she had helped him forge papers that put control of the company in Winston's hands.

"Then it got real nasty. My source decided to confront Winston. He went to his home—the wife had kicked him out—and as he's walking up the driveway, he sees a car headed right at him, Winston at the wheel. The source said he didn't believe Winston would actually hit him so he stood his ground. But the car kept coming, knocked him down, and ran over him. Broke both his legs."

"What did the police do?" asked Lew.

"My source never reported it. He told me he was so humiliated losing his business, losing his wife, he couldn't bear to have his business colleagues know what he let happen to him."

"And you believed him?" said Lew.

"The man wept, Chief Ferris. He was broken, he was distraught, he was deeply disturbed. Yes, I believed him. And it's why I believe Michael Winston is capable of killing Ashley."

"Why do you think Winston stopped at breaking his legs?" asked Osborne. "Why didn't he kill him?"

"Because he had a plan that wouldn't work if the guy was dead," said Gina. "This shows you how sick Winston is. After he left town, the commodity firm went belly up. When the financial statements were reviewed, whose signature was on the loans? The original owner. Who's holding the bag right now?"

"That gentleman doesn't sound very bright," said Osborne.

"No one looked bright after Winston left town," said Gina. "He is the consummate con man. Ingratiating, charming, a pathological liar: He is the perfect example of why a gifted con man is called an *artist.*"

Lew snorted. "I know exactly what you're talking about. Loon Lake may be tiny, but we are a microcosm of the world. We've got everything here. We have perverts, we have card sharks, and we certainly have con men. Actually," she winked at Doc, "we are very fortunate to have Ray on our side."

"Really?" said Gina. She looked intrigued. "Now that's interesting, because I happen to believe the only way to stop Michael Winston is to beat him at his own game. And I can guarantee you that when we find him, he will be running a scam of some kind. He always does. He has to. He's *driven* to con people."

"There's another side to that," said Lew. "People ask for it."

"Absolutely," said Gina. "Greed—and laziness—make it easy to dupe people. Think about it. He was indicted for fraud less than a thousand miles away, but no one checked his credentials. And he is very sly. Take Kansas City. Here's an old-fashioned town that is traditionally closed to outsiders. No one gets into monied society in that town unless they're born to it. But he did. Instantly. Ingratiated himself not because of *his* money but because he could make *you* lots of money.

"My hunch is that's how we'll find him up here. He's making money for somebody else, allegedly anyway. Someone powerful, someone networked."

Lew looked at Osborne. He shook his head. He couldn't think of anyone either.

"Gina," he said, "we don't have anyone like that up here. Loon Lake is hardly a finance capital of America."

"Casinos, maybe he's got a tie into casinos."

"I doubt it," said Lew. "The Native Americans operate close to the vest. Not too many outsiders get in."

"But that's exactly the point I made about Kansas City."

Lew shrugged and made a note on her pad. "Did you tell Ashley about the incident with his ex-partner?"

"No, the way things went over the next six months, I didn't think I had to. In a way, I thought I was saving her from being broken, too. I thought I could save her from further humiliation."

Gina sat down, crossed her legs, and swung the top one hard again. "I was so wrong."

eighteen

"The woods were made for the hunters of dreams,
The brooks for the fisher of song
To the hunters who hunt for the gunless game
The streams and woods belong."

Sam Walter Foss

"Did you know all this before your interview with Winston?" ask Lew.

"Yes, but I told no one. I wanted to be sure he wasn't tipped off before I could get to him. So I called his office and set up an interview and, of course, he loved it. He was thrilled to get the attention."

"Why? What did he have to gain from all this publicity?" asked Lew.

"Business. He had ownership of the commodity firm. He was selling himself as an investment expert: giving seminars, he even got himself on *Wall Street Week*. People were falling all over themselves to throw money at the man."

"And where is that money today?" said Lew.

"Gone. Every penny plus Ashley's half million. Went with him when he left town."

"You mean to tell us that people were investing large sums of money with this man, and no one checked on his credentials?" asked Osborne.

"They never do," said Gina. "The only people who ever check credentials are newspaper terriers like me . . . and people hate us for it. They hate us because we blow holes in their heroes. This is not a new story. Kansas City loved Michael Winston because he rode into town as the quintessential American male: self-made millionaire, handsome, a man's man. You know the type," said Gina. Then she sat up straight, flexed her biceps like a weight lifter and, lowering her voice, growled, "Me big game hunter."

"Is he a hunter?" asked Osborne.

"Not just a hunter, he is an expert marksman . . . or so he would brag. That really appealed to the good ol' boys because Kansas City is big on hunting . . . horses and hunting. At the time I started researching my story, the most sought-after social engagement in town was an invitation from Winston to join him in his private plane for elk hunting in Montana, pig hunting in the Carolinas, pheasant hunting in the Dakotas . . . or duck hunting in Eagle Nest, Wisconsin. And that, I think, is where he made the one misstep that will lead us to him."

Gina scraped her chair forward once again, crossed her arms over her chest and looked at them intently.

"Keep in mind that the event I'm about to describe takes place *before* our confrontation interview, okay? Winston has no idea I'm on to anything. And he's extremely solicitous, probably convinced he can con me into a flattering profile that will boost his image ever so much more. Rumors are floating that he'll be drafted to run for the U.S. Senate; everything is going his way."

"Got it," said Lew.

"It's a week before my interview, and Ashley and Michael invite me to a party they're giving, a Sunday brunch to celebrate Michael's affiliation with Ashley's company."

"Wait, what about his commodity firm?" asked Osborne, confused.

"Oh, he had that, too. And his real estate interests. *And* his personal investments. Remember, this is Superman we're talking about here. He would toss off any questions about how he juggled it all with comments like 'My people are running things' or 'Multitasking is my talent'' or 'I'm easily bored.' Fact was, he had no plans to be in Kansas City long-term and he was siphoning money out of those ventures as fast as he could.

"But back to the party. I'll never forget that morning. Ashley's home was still under construction, so they held the brunch at this horse farm north of Kansas City that Michael supposedly owned. Later, of course, I found out it was rented.

"As you approached the main house, which was perched at the top of a rise—" Gina gestured with her hands—"there was this long drive through a field covered with purple, pink, and bright-yellow wildflowers. Absolutely breathtaking. And the house was expensive. Lots of glass, lots of marble. Not exactly your Midwest farmhouse. Very impressive.

"We were greeted, about twenty of us, with champagne and caviar, and everyone milled around oohing and aahing over the antiques and the art and the horses. The usual status bullshit. The other guests were all business types with their wives. I was the only single woman there," said Gina. "I'm still not sure why Ashley included me, although there was a recently divorced lawyer, so maybe she was matchmaking.

"That went on for a while; then we were marshaled into the dining room, where we all sat down at this long, long rosewood table. That was funny. Someone commented on the table, and Winston said he spent thirty-two thousand dollars on the damn thing. Oh, and he said he got a deal. Can you imagine spending that kind of money on a dining room table for God's sake?"

"So we had this fancy breakfast, and after the entrée, the subject of hunting came up. Michael was taking Ashley hunting in Mexico—for white wing doves. This led to a discussion of expensive shotguns, and suddenly Michael had to show off his gun collection. So all the men—and me—got up from the table and headed downstairs."

"And you?" said Lew. "Do you shoot?"

"Yes," said Gina. "I'm originally from Upstate New York. My dad taught me how to hunt when I was a kid—

deer and grouse—but I haven't hunted in years. I am good with a pistol, though. And I just bought a new Smith & Wesson Airweight. I like having a gun around these days . . . for obvious reasons.

"Anyway, we trooped down the stairs to the basement, where Michael had a closet full of guns, *full* of guns. Shotguns, rifles, pistols. He must have had at least thirty, maybe forty guns down there. Old, new, beautiful guns.

"He started handing them around, which alarmed me a little because several of the men had no idea how to handle a gun. They were pointing them every which way. But that aside, it was clear to me Winston has a passion for guns. Just the way he stroked them. Do you know what I mean?"

"Yep, sure do," said Lew.

"So then, just to tease, I asked where his Uzis and his AK 47s were. This was just a joke, okay? But he gives me this look, turns right around, walks back into the closet, and I'll be damned if he doesn't walk out with an Uzi and hand it to me. Then he winked and said, 'Now don't tell Ashley.'"

"Were his friends impressed?" asked Lew.

"Oh, it was a manly moment. I'm sure he enjoyed the look on my face. It's one thing to own an illegal weapon, but to show it off like that? What arrogance."

"I see it all the time," said Lew. "So he left town with the money and the guns?"

"No. He took only the money. And that's how I think we can find him. Winston loves guns. He loves hunting. I cannot imagine him living up here without buying a gun. Make that plural—without buying *guns.*"

"Gina," said Lew, "do you have any concept of how many guns there are in the Northwoods?"

"I know, I know. But that's why I brought my computer. I was hoping you would let me run a database analysis of the ATF records for this region. All your gun dealers have to register sales, right?"

Lew groaned. "ATF: my nemesis," she said. "They've been on my back to update records for months."

"Bureau of Alcohol, Tobacco and Firearms?" asked Osborne. "What would you have to do with them, Lew?"

"They fund us to keep the gun registrations up to date in this region. I'm responsible for three counties," said Lew. "Six months ago, I agreed to take their money and try to fit it in. Saves them manpower. Gina, I don't see how this would work," said Lew. "Even if you're right, and Michael Winston is hiding up here, he has to be using another name, don't you think?"

"I have a way around that, Chief. I have database software that I can use to pinpoint certain patterns. The source information behind the patterns shows me where to start. I know it works. We use this constantly in our investigative reporting at the newspaper, like with arrest records, vehicle licenses, FAA data, that kind of thing. Federal and state databases are almost always available for this kind of analysis.

"Look, I'll show you what I mean," said Gina, pointing to the screen on her open laptop computer. "I brought an ATF database from Kansas City to demonstrate."

Osborne and Lew walked over to stand behind Gina. Her fingers moved swiftly over the keys. The information on the monitor was easy to read: a detailed description of guns sold, date of purchase, name of buyer, driver's license of buyer, name of dealer, and location of sale. She hit more keys, highlighting categories of information. "We customized the software ourselves," said Gina. "This is proprietary, but I have an okay to share it with you for the purpose of investigating this case."

"You're looking to see names of buyers?" asked Lew.

"Names of buyers and, just as helpful, names of dealers who are moving certain types of guns, or guns at certain prices, or I might see a pattern where a specific type of gun is being sold frequently, and I can check that frequency against the norm for recent months. Basically, I can enter any field I want in order to search the data from different angles.

"But assume I find a pattern in your records, Chief. Given that those photos of Winston should arrive tomorrow or the next day, I can show those to any dealer whose sales pattern is suspect. So even if he has changed his name, we may still have a way—"

"I see," said Lew. "Now I get it. That makes more sense. Except for one small problem, Gina."

"What's that?"

"The situation with our new system and staffing. As you might expect, this is one slow-moving bureaucracy up here. Even though the assignment and the money from the ATF to update the county files came in months ago, the installation of our new computer system was just completed. I didn't get an approval to hire an information services manager to run it for us until several weeks ago.

"We have someone starting July first, but I have waited on purchasing software for the system until that person is on board. In the meantime, I have templates from ATF for the data, and I have basic word processing and spreadsheet software, but I am afraid that's as much as I have right now.

"And I am simply not familiar enough with the system yet to know how to do what you are suggesting. Also, this is not a small job. I must have at least twenty-five gun dealers in my region—"

Gina raised her hand, a bright smile on her face. "Not to worry. That's why I'm here, Chief. We can copy my software onto your system and use it to look at the data you've got."

"But . . ." Lew shook her head helplessly, "I'm afraid that's what I don't have."

"You mean, if I call the dealers and they fax in recent sales, you don't have someone who can just type the data into the system?"

"No. I've got two switchboard operators and my deputies. That's all."

Gina looked perplexed. Then she shrugged. "Okay, what

do you figure, maybe a thousand records? I mean, the new law hasn't been in place that long, right?

"It's about that many," said Lew. "Maybe less, even."

"So I'll get started with the data. Do you need to get an approval from somewhere for me to work on your system?"

Lew thought for a moment before answering. "I see no problem with that."

"Good. That's good. But just so you know, I am likely to have one small hassle as I get started," said Gina. "I know from experience it will take some tweaking to get my software up and running on your system. I'll need to connect with somebody who has some basic programming skills and can help me work out the bugs. That'll take a few hours, no more."

Lew raised her hands in a gesture of futility. "Now we're back where we started. The tech guy doesn't get here for another two weeks."

"But you've got a PC system, right?"

"Right. We have six PCs and Internet access with T1 lines.

"What if I find the tech support *and* a few bucks to pay for their time. Got a problem with that?"

"No. But I have a miscellaneous account I can use for emergencies, Gina. You don't have to pay for it if it's reasonable."

Gina looked over at Osborne. "That kid at the airport today. Think he needs a summer job?"

"You mean Ray's son?" said Osborne.

"Ray's *what?*"

Osborne had to grin at the look on Lew's face. She was flabbergasted.

nineteen

"Muskie fishing can be compared to tracking a deer all day and seeing only some tracks. A muskie can be a gray ghost appearing as a shadow behind your lure only to fade and disappear, making you talk to yourself and wonder if you really saw something after all."

Ray Ostrom, bait dealer and muskie expert

It was after five when Osborne finally got home. He eased the two bags of groceries down onto the kitchen table, then reached into the tall wicker basket standing just inside the kitchen door.

"Sit!" he commanded Mike. The black Lab stopped bouncing and settled his butt on the floor, eyes eager with anticipation. "Now, what do I have to do to get Lew to look at me that way?" Osborne flipped the dog biscuit into Mike's mouth.

"Cook her a steak, light a candle, and touch the woman, for God's sake."

"Thank you, Mike. I knew that." Osborne got a kick out of ventriloquizing with his dog. Sometimes he surprised himself with the words he put in Mike's mouth. "I can do just fine with your first two instructions, but I'm not sure about that third step. I don't think she'd let me. Plus . . . I think I'm too old."

"Yep, too old."

"No, I'm not."

"Okay, you're not. You figure it out. I need to pee."

Osborne opened the door and followed the dog out into the fenced yard. The late afternoon sun was high and the air still warm but with a hint of humidity. The puffy white clouds that had scudded high against the sky all day drooped now, gray underbellies visible through the canopy of Norway pines that guarded Osborne's shoreline.

He studied the muted sky, happy with the threat of a good thunderstorm. Nothing titillated the big girls better than an active barometer. He could get lucky, this could be an excellent muskie night, even if they only got in a couple hours. Osborne almost skipped back to the house.

He checked the answering machine. The solitary message was from Mallory, canceling her visit. Her excuse was too much to do: "Dad, I have a project due in the environmental lab course and my time at Hazelden is going to make it tough to get everything done. Can we reschedule?"

The best part of the message was the word on Hazelden. He was relieved. She was sticking with it. Rehab was becoming a family tradition. He knew he was lucky to have been forced through it. When he and Erin encouraged Mallory after the divorce, he hadn't been sure she would listen. But she did. Every time she called, she sounded better. He jotted a note on the pad by the phone reminding himself to call Marlene and let her know Mallory would not be coming this weekend.

Back in the kitchen, he sorted quickly through his freezer. "Aha!" he exclaimed to the pheasant mounted on the wall when he located the package of venison chops. He laid it on the counter next to the two perfect Idaho potatoes he had selected at the grocery store. Alongside those was a plastic bag of freshly washed lettuces. He had been careful to follow Erin's instructions and avoid the homely iceberg heads. Still, unsure if he had made the right choice, he had stopped by his daughter's house on the way home.

"Looks fine, Dad," Erin had said with amused eyes. She would turn thirty this year, but to her dad she looked nineteen: tall and slender with long, straight, honey-blond hair. Today she wore it twisted into one thick braid that hung down over her left shoulder. As he stood there, displaying his selection of lettuces, she was distracted by Cody, who had just assaulted his older sisters with a squirt gun. The toddler giggled hysterically as his mother chased him round and round the big oak table in the dining room of their Victorian home.

"Sorry, Dad. This kid is driving us all nuts. What are you using for dressing, that same old bleu cheese gunk?"

"What's wrong with that?"

Erin collared Cody, grabbed the gun, and booted him out of the room. She opened her refrigerator and reached in. "Take this. Just in case. Give her a choice." She handed him a bottle of peppercorn-buttermilk dressing. Then Erin leaned back against the kitchen counter and crossed her arms. "Have you cooked for her before, Dad?"

"No."

"Well, if you want to cook for her again, you better do it right, doncha think?"

Osborne, studying the bottle of dressing, glanced up to find her watching him with a funny smile on her face. "Dad, seriously, do you mean to tell me after all the times you have fished with Chief Ferris, this is the first time—"

"She's a busy woman."

"Trust me, she's not that busy. You're such a wuss, Dad. Just . . . go for it, y'know."

"What are you talking about?" He tried to give her a stern look, but she slapped him on the shoulder and hooted with laughter.

Then her face settled into an attempt at a very serious look. Dropping her voice so his two granddaughters watching television in the next room couldn't hear, she leaned forward. "Dad, if you don't know it now, you never will."

"*What* are you talking about?" Osborne knew the moment he uttered the words he'd made a mistake.

"What do you mean, what am I talking about? Those are Mom's famous words. That's all she ever told me and Mallory about sex. 'If you don't know it now, you never will.' "

"Honestly, Erin, sometimes you're worse than your children."

"Da-a-d . . . . Go for it. I like Lew. Mallory likes Lew. We want you to—"

"This is embarrassing. We're just fishing buddies. And, um, there's a fella by the name of Hank Kendrickson who's been asking her out, too."

"No . . . for real, Dad? He's an interesting guy. I know I'd put him on my list if I were single."

"What?" Osborne was taken aback. "How do *you* know Hank Kendrickson?"

"He made a presentation to the school board several weeks ago. We're looking for ideas on how to better invest the endowment, and someone suggested Hank because he's been so successful in the stock market. I was impressed.

"You know, Dad." Erin crossed her arms and leaned back against the kitchen counter, a thoughtful look on her face. "There's a guy who is a good example of what attracts a woman. I mean, he's not drop-dead handsome, but he's got a shrewd look in his eye, a very nice smile . . . and he listens."

"He listens?"

"Yeah. Most men don't; they're always looking over your shoulder or their eyes space out while you're talking. Hank Kendrickson comes across as very smart and kinda sexy, if you ask me. Plain old charisma."

The look on Osborne's face must have been one of acute dismay, because Erin reached to hook her arm through his. "Hey, don't look so down, Dad. You're not a bad catch yourself, y'know."

"Oh sure. I'm ten years older and short sixty million bucks."

"That may be, but you are the best-looking man in Loon Lake."

"Easy for you to say, sweetheart."

"You are, Dad." She gave him a teasing look. "I have single friends who have asked me about you."

"They have?" His spirits lifted a tiny bit.

"Yes, they have. Don't you worry about Hank, even if he

does call Lew. I can tell from the look on her face she thinks you're very cool."

Osborne shook his head. "You're just saying that to make your old man feel better."

"No, I'm not! Oh, darn. I shouldn't have said anything. Now you're all worried. Listen, Dad, Lew would not be having dinner at your house—the two of you alone—if she wasn't interested. Trust me on this. I'm female. I know. Now get outta here and get cooking."

Erin pushed him toward the door. "Put a candle on the table, Dad. Okay? Placemats, napkins, silverware, and a *candle*. Promise?"

"I promise."

He knew she was smiling after him as he walked out the door. Driving home, Osborne wondered if he would ever make it through this passage in life. It isn't easy falling in love when you're sixty-three.

It was nearly seven when Osborne hurried down to the dock with his muskie rod and tackle box, anxious to set up so he and Lew could start casting the minute she arrived. The clouds were darker now; they would be lucky to get in an hour of fishing. Osborne counted four boats out on the lake, four sets of numnut fishermen willing to risk death by lightning because it upped the percentage for hooking a big one.

He heard voices and looked over to see Ray out on his own dock with Nick. Concentrating on helping the kid learn to cast, he wasn't aware Osborne was watching. Ray's voice carried easily, even though they were a good 150 feet away.

"Good . . . good," he heard Ray coach the boy. "All right, cast toward the horizon, that'll help you get that lure up and out. Better . . . You're getting the hang of it. No matter what anyone ever tells you, you stay with this overhead cast; don't sidearm it, okay? Watch that razzbonya in the boat over in that weed bed to the right. He's doing it wrong. He'll hook a nose before he gets a walleye. . . . Jeez!" Ray flinched at the sight of the fisherman's next cast. "Now that,

Nick, is what they mean when they say, 'Fishing is a jerk on one end of a line waiting for a jerk on the other.'"

"Yeah?" The kid's voice sounded petulant. "This is dumb. Look how shallow it is. I'll never catch anything doing this, Ray. Can I quit now?"

The boy lowered his rod and turned to the man standing beside him. One look at the two of them, and Osborne recognized a familiar scene: He'd been there. As clearly as he saw the slouch in the boy's back, he could see the look of defiance on Mallory's sixteen-year-old face. A look she had turned on him every time he had tried to help or correct or be a good father. He finally gave up. Let her learn on her own. Maybe they always have to. The day did come that she walked into his house, asked for advice and actually listened to what he had to say. But that was six months ago. She was thirty-three years old. He sure hoped Ray wasn't in for such a long haul.

"So how come we aren't out in a boat like those guys?" he heard Nick complain again.

"Boater today, floater tomorrow," said Ray breezily. "Look, I'll put you in a boat when you have more control over your cast. Nothing is more ignominious than going into the lake after your fish."

"This is dumb," said the boy, giving his rod a halfhearted sweep. The lure landed about thirty feet away, just short of the weed bed fronting Ray's dock. He reeled in and as the lure neared the dock, Ray prompted, "Good, keep it steady, now remember what I told you about that figure eight, swirl it, swirl it—"

"Yow!" Nick screamed and backed up. Forgetting where he was, he stepped back so far he went right off the dock and into the water. Hitting flat on his back, he went under and came up sputtering. Staggering and flailing, he stood up in water just above his knees.

"Holy shit, what was that?"

"A small northern," said Ray calmly, picking up the rod that Nick had dropped on the dock.

"That was a monster," said the kid. He was scrambling up on the dock as if he thought the thing was after him.

"I've been trying to tell you, Nick. Fishing is a challenging sport." The dry tone in Ray's voice told Osborne he was tickled to death that a fish had struck at the lure. "Nice looking fish, huh? Tough to clean, but good eating. Up here we call that fish the wolf of the north."

"I believe it," said Nick. "Whoa."

"Small potatoes. A muskie is ten times that size. We call her the shark of the north, queen of the freshwater fish. This is what I've been trying to tell you, Nick, you haven't fished until you've fought a muskie. That's when *you* get hooked."

The boy stood dripping and shivering as water streamed from his shorts. The slouch was gone.

"A muskie is *ten times* as big as that one?" He was awestruck. "But that thing was huge. The mouth, the teeth!" Osborne was delighted. The kid had obviously gotten a full frontal view of the arcing fish.

"You betcha. You'll get used to it."

"Where's my rod? Did I catch that thing?"

"Nope. That's what we call a strike. And if you *see* the fish, but it doesn't strike your lure, we call it a follow."

"So how do I catch it?"

"That's the next lesson. I'll teach you how to set the hook . . . but we need to get you a towel and some dry clothes."

"No, no, I'm fine. So I really can catch a big fish just standing right here?"

"That's why I bought this place. That weed bed, this whole lake, is rich with trophy muskie. But the muskie is a wise and wary fish. We may know they're out there, but we can't see them in this dark water."

"Can they see us?"

"Oh yeah, and they are always watching. Y'know, Nick, men have paid me a thousand bucks a day to help them hook one of those magnificent fish. I can never guarantee success, because even I never know for sure what's under the sur-

face. What I can guarantee is the thrill when they hook one.
It thrills the soul, Nick. The soul. Life just doesn't get any
better."

"I'll tell you one thing," said Nick, "I'm never gonna
swim in this lake. Not with those things in here."

At that, Ray threw his head back and laughed. He
laughed and laughed. "They won't hurt you, Nick. Don't
worry about that."

The boy reached for the rod. "Let me cast just a couple
more times, then I'll go up, okay?"

Osborne could tell from his tone that Nick was both
frightened and happy and close to being hooked on fishing.
Not that he would admit it, at least for a while. And it
crossed Osborne's mind as he watched Nick's casts that seeing a youngster raise their first big fish was almost as good
as watching them take their first step. Both are moves that
can take you out into the world and lead to great happiness.

"Doc!"

Startled, Osborne swung around, tripping over the tackle
box at his feet. "Oops! Don't fall into the boat lift." Lew
grabbed him by the arms. She held on, too; she didn't let go.
"Steady there. I'm sorry if I frightened you."

"I didn't hear you coming," said Osborne. "I was concentrating on the fishing lesson Ray was giving young Nick over
there." They looked over to see Ray and Nick staring at them.
Osborne was suddenly aware he was standing so close to Lew
that with her still holding on to him, they must appear to be
embracing. Taking his heart in his hands or maybe it was
Erin's advice, Osborne decided he liked the image. Ray
would razz him anyway. So he took his own hands and placed
them at Lew's waist. He was very pleased to find the pose
seemed incredibly natural.

"Now I'm very steady, Lew," he smiled down at her.
"Thanks."

"You're welcome," she said looking up at him with a
pleased smile as she took her hands away. Osborne let his
linger just a moment longer. He resisted the impulse to pull

her closer. Something told him she might not resist if he did. A happy calmness settled over him. *Not yet,* he thought to himself, *not quite yet.*

Lew had changed from her uniform into a pair of dark-green fishing shorts and a burgundy T-shirt. As she stepped away from him, Osborne touched her right arm just below the elbow with his finger. It was the spot where her skin changed from a warm brown to a much paler shade. "Fishing tan, huh?"

Osborne felt an instant charge of electricity as his hand grazed her arm. Again, she didn't move away. It was almost as if she lingered, even enjoyed being so close to him.

"Where's your gear?" he asked, his voice low so he wouldn't break the spell.

"Right there." She pointed back to the front of the dock. She walked over and knelt to pick up her rod and open her tackle box. She turned to him with a lure in her hand. "I was planning to fish with my Bobbie tonight, Doc, but I don't think it's right for this lake. And I've got an ounce weight in front of the bait, too."

"That'll drop way too deep, Lew. Now you know why I like the Mud Puppy. This lake is so shallow, I use a surface lure in most places."

"I can see that. I didn't think you could get a big fish in two and a half feet of water. How deep does this lake get, anyway?"

"Twelve, fourteen feet."

"Jeez, that is shallow. Good structure?"

"Excellent structure. We've got a long sand bar that runs across that southern end." Osborne pointed in the direction of the sand bar. "And a very rocky bottom with some huge boulders, most of them marked. You'll see three, four fishing boats anchored around those locations almost every morning. But that weed bed in front of Ray's dock is one of the best places to hook a muskie on this entire chain. I've seen some forty-five to fifty-inchers taken out of here. Lew, I thought you fished this lake the year you won the Hodag

Muskie Tournament over in Rhinelander. Ray told me you got first place."

"Yep, but I was fishing Lake Thompson. I've never fished Loon Lake. This is a first."

And not your last, thought Osborne. *Not if I take Erin's advice.* And with that, he handed over his bright-orange mud puppy. "Give it a try, Lew." He didn't tell her she was the first fisherman he ever let use the prized lure.

"There's magic in this mud puppy," he said, "I've caught more than a dozen muskies with this lure over the last thirty years, including one that measured a whopping forty-seven inches."

Osborne watched her tie it on, his heart happy, his trophy for the evening not a fish at all but a lovely woman named Lew. The mud puppy was magic indeed; it worked in reverse!

twenty

"Muskie: the fish of 10,000 casts."

Anonymous

The storm was moving in fast. Lightning lacerated the western sky. Dense clouds silhouetted the tamarack spires on the far shore and masked the early evening sun. The temperature had dropped, too, from the low eighties to nearly sixty, a summer cold front.

Soon soft, warm pellets of rain began to drift toward them. Osborne lifted his face, letting them fall like a sweet shower against his eyelids and cheeks. He looked over at Lew. She had that unmistakable gleam in her eye that said she knew what he knew: This was exactly the kind of rainstorm that pulls lunker muskies—huge muskies—up to the surface. They *love* warmer water. They may hide deep, they may fight deep, but they love to tease the surface when air and water temperatures are colliding.

Ray's dock was empty. He and Nick had retreated into the trailer with the first raindrops. In fact, all the docks within sight were empty, and only two of the fishing boats remained. This was typical. Osborne had learned years ago that only a select few muskie fishermen would brave a thunderstorm. Actually, only a crazy few. But at the end of the season, if they were still alive, the storm guys would have seen a lot more muskies than the wimps. Ray usually fished storms. Osborne figured he must be trying to keep Nick happy; otherwise for sure he would be out.

Now the only sounds to be heard between the wind gusts were the soft whir of their casts, the burble of the lures spinning through the water, and the suck as the lures were swirled and lifted to be cast again.

Lew was comfortable in the silence between them as she always was. And Osborne marveled, as he always did, at how easy she was to be around. *Serene* was the word that came to mind as he launched a cast as smooth and long as any he had ever made in his fifty years of fishing. She made him feel serene.

"Give me erratic weather any day," said Lew ten minutes later as she let fly a long, long overhead cast that landed at the very edge of the high weed bed. "The minute that surface goes through a change, that's when I have my best luck. Now . . ." she paused as if making a point while teaching a class, "I don't mean to hurt your feelings, Doc, but I'm switching to a bucktail in five minutes if I don't have a follow or a strike on this lure."

"Okay, okay," said Osborne, shaking his head in mock disappointment. "You're just too set in your ways, Lew."

"Come on, Doc. I've fished muskie so long, I know in my bones what I need when I need it. And I'm not too set in my ways, okay? I am not an old lady, okay?"

She grinned at him. "Trust me, I'll try anything, so long as it's exciting." He wanted to think the grin she threw his way was seductive, but that was too much to hope for. Or was it?

Osborne looked away and changed the subject. "Hey, I tested when I walked down here tonight, and the water was right around sixty-four degrees." He laid his rod down and reached into his tackle box for a thermometer. He knelt down and thrust his arm into the water. "Holding," he said. "Perfect for the big girls."

"Speaking of girls . . . darn, I wish I had more on the Herre murder," said Lew. "Sandy's family is calling every few hours—"

"Lew, you know you're doing the best you can. Now stop thinking about it. You need a break."

"Yes, I do. Thanks, Doc." She grinned over at him.

• • •

The dusting of rain proved to be the front end of a downpour. Before they got soaked, Osborne and Lew reached into their respective tackle boxes for flat envelopes that unfolded into rain ponchos. Draped in vinyl, the fishing continued, the two anglers working parallel rhythms in silence: cast, reel, swirl, and cast.

"Wind just switched to northwest," said Osborne. The chop grew rougher.

"Any wind's a good wind, west wind's the best wind," said Lew. She bent over to unhook the mud puppy and replace it with a hairy bucktail. "Now what I think . . ." she paused as she sent her lure skyward, ". . . is at this temperature, a muskie loves a fast retrieve. Sometimes I don't think I can reel in fast enough, y'know?"

Osborne stopped to watch her bucktail skitter along the surface, making gargling noises as it moved. "Yep," he said, "I agree. Ray tells me that noise turns 'em on. You put that together with the high weed bed and this warm water and—

"There! Lew, you got a follow."

Feet apart, Lew bent her knees slightly to brace herself as she swirled the lure along the edge of the dock.

"Get ready for a fight, Doc. It's a big one."

A long, black shadow followed the lure just below the choppy surface, close enough so they could see it through the dark, tannin-stained water. Osborne's heart beat faster. The fish was a good forty-five inches long, and it had a huge head. "She's a monster," he said softly. He held his breath.

Could Lew handle it? No other freshwater fish fights as hard as a muskie. A fish this big would test her strength and her skill. More fishermen lose a muskie *after* it's hooked than before. As Osborne watched, he remembered Ray's words to a boatful of clients: "The muskie is just plain brilliant, fellas. That fish can throw a lure and snap a line like no one of you bass fishermen would ever believe.

"Dammit," said Lew with a snort as the fish swirled suddenly and disappeared. "She invites me to the party, then she leaves. Damn. These fish are just plain mean, Doc. Why do I fish these suckers, anyway? I can catch a mess of walleye or bass for all this time and effort."

"You know why you fish 'em."

She looked at him with a sly smile. "Of course I know. I'm just disappointed. God, I'd love a big one like that in my net. Have you raised her before?"

"No-o-o," said Osborne. "I would remember that one. I swear that fish had a thirty-pound head on it."

"Yep, I think so. Well, it was a thrill to see her. Hey, Doc." Lew looked over at him as she checked her line for nicks. "I'm sure glad we're doing this. I get so wrapped up in my fly-fishing, I forget what a challenge it is to fish muskie."

"Shark of the north," said Osborne, repeating one of his favorite phrases.

"Funny," said Lew. "Big muskies are always females, but we insist on calling 'em *king* or *big boy* or *big guy*. Now, why do you think that is?"

"What do they say about a tough woman?" said Osborne. "She's got balls."

"You consider that a virtue?"

Osborne looked over to find her eyes were fixed on his. Waiting, teasing.

His heart moved. Even though they were standing there exposed, with rough water at their feet and the wind and the rain lashing at their faces, he felt like he was in an intimate space, a very intimate space.

It wasn't until the lightning split the sky directly over-head that the two remaining fishing boats finally pulled anchor to buzz for the safety of the public landing directly across the lake.

Lew, as resolute as Osborne in the accelerating gusts, re-fused to quit until her casts were blown back and the light-ning had become a serious hazard. Only then did they nod in agreement, unhook their lures, grab all their tackle, and hurry up the stone stairway toward shelter.

• • •

The heat of the day lingered in the house, making all the rooms feel cozy. Osborne was pleased. He couldn't have prayed for a better evening to entertain Lew. In spite of her long day, she looked relaxed and happy, the quintessential fisherman, satisfied to have seen a big one, whatever the outcome.

They puttered in the kitchen together while the summer storm pulled out all stops, drumming on the roof and filling the house with the wonderful fragrance of moist pine needles.

"Excellent taste, Doc," said Lew on opening the refrigerator after volunteering to assemble the salad. "I *love* this peppercorn-buttermilk dressing. It's the only one I use."

The venison chops cooperated, too, searing and broiling to perfection on the grill outside the kitchen door. Osborne was forever thankful he'd taken the time one summer to extend the roof out over the small patio so he could grill in bad weather. Mary Lee had argued against it, saying the new roofline would destroy the integrity of the architect's design, but he had persisted. After all, he was the one who always got stuck grilling outdoors.

The final detail was the potatoes. They emerged from the oven perfect, flaky and white under a fat pat of yellow butter.

The setting sun broke through the clouds long enough to send shimmers of violet across the dark lake just as Osborne pulled out a chair for Lew. He had set the small, round table on the porch, using a tablecloth that he'd bought Mary Lee for her birthday one year. She had tried to return it, as she did most of his gifts, and was disgruntled when she learned she couldn't because he had purchased it on sale. She never did use it.

Just as well, thought Osborne as he pulled it from the drawer. He liked it: a thick, creamy cotton weave with a border of dark-green firs, and napkins to match. His forest-green earthenware, a Christmas gift from Mallory, looked quite handsome on it, too. And candles, of course. He had set out the two sterling silver candlesticks with the beeswax candles that usually decorated his piano. Simple in design, the candlesticks were tall with flat, round bases. They had belonged to his mother.

"Where on earth did you get this butter? It's real!" said Lew.

"Erin gave me that," said Osborne. "She buys it from the Mennonite farm in Starks . . . non-USDA approved but absolutely delicious. She gets eggs there, too."

"I didn't think you could buy butter like this anymore," said Lew, savoring her potato. Then she looked up from her dinner and focused her alert, good-natured eyes on his. "Now, Doc, what is this malarkey about Ray having a son?"

The candles had burned less than an inch, the venison chops were half eaten and Osborne's recounting of Ray's dilemma had just ended when he heard a knock on the kitchen door.

"Who could that be?" Osborne jumped up from the table, napkin in hand, and started through the living room entry only to see Ray coming toward him in sections. From a certain angle, Ray's six feet five inches appeared to be structured in five separately movable parts. The kneecaps and the lower torso always struck Osborne as entering a room ten minutes before the rest of Ray's body. Tonight was no exception. Only tonight, Ray's happy-go-lucky grin and his stuffed trout hat—the usual toppers to the five-part symphony of movement—were missing. Ray was distressed.

"Sorry to interrupt, Doc, but Nick's driving me nuts. I need help. Can I talk to you for a minute?"

"Come on in," said Doc, trying to sound pleasant. In fact, he was thinking, *Dammit*. He reminded himself that he owed Ray. He would always owe Ray.

twenty-one

"A jerk on one end of a line, waiting for a jerk on the other."

Classic folk definition of fishing

"**Oh**, Chief, sorry. I didn't know you were here," said Ray, ducking through the doorway as he walked onto the porch. If he noticed the candlelight and the intimate dinner, he said nothing.

"Sit down, sit down," said Osborne, pulling another chair up to the table. "What's up?"

With a heavy sigh, Ray dropped into the chair. "I'm stuck, Doc. Nick's mother signed him up for summer school, which starts tomorrow, and I have no way to get him there. I've got that woman from the Dairyman's that I'm supposed to take out shooting clays with her new boyfriend, and I can't reach her to reschedule. Is there any chance you could drop him off for me?"

"I don't see why not. What time?"

"Eight . . . and could you pick him up at noon? Just bring him back here. He'll be all right on his own, doncha think?"

"Oh, he'll be fine. I'll be around, or I'll let him know where I am if he needs anything," said Osborne, relieved it was such a small favor. "Where is he right now? I'd like Lew to meet him."

A look of unhappy resignation came over Ray's face. "He's taking the telephone apart. He's trying to wire in or whatever the hell it is those computer kids do. I'll tell ya, that kid is pret-ty darn unhappy with the phone situation. He's been going on about staying in touch with his friends and all this stuff he has to do on the Internet. I had to tell him our phone lines won't be replaced until—"

"You two and your damn party line," said Lew. "Doc, I thought you told me you were being switched over this month."

"August we get the new lines," said Osborne.

It had been a ten-year struggle. Ever since he and Mary Lee had built off Loon Lake Road they had been restricted to the antique phone line maintained by the locally owned phone company. The company had refused to lay any new lines until every customer agreed to the increase in billing that would result.

Three elderly sisters, each living in separate homes, had refused, holding the remaining twenty-four households hostage to rotary dial phones and a party line system. Osborne wasn't sure if the old biddies were against the modest increase in their bills or if they didn't want to give up their opportunity to eavesdrop. He suspected the latter. But two of the three had passed away over the last year. The surviving sister had agreed to an update in the system only when she was told that she couldn't have a personal safety alarm installed unless she had the new telephone cable. Grudgingly, she caved in. Plans were already in place to celebrate at the annual Loon Lake Association Fourth of July picnic.

"Why don't I put the boy in touch with Hank Kendrickson?" said Lew. "He does something with computers at the game preserve. Maybe he can help—"

"I have an idea," interrupted Osborne, desperate to put the kabbosh on Hank. "Joel Frahm's son is good with computers. He's been computerizing dental records for Joel. And, you know, I think he's Nick's age, or close."

"Joel Frahm . . . Why does that name sound familiar?" asked Lew.

"He's the dentist who bought my practice when I retired three years ago," said Osborne. "I'll give him a call right now," he said, jumping up from his chair and hurrying into the kitchen to find the phone book.

Joel answered immediately. Osborne explained that one of his neighbors had a teenager visiting from New York City who needed advice on a computer snafu. Could Joel's son help out? To Osborne's surprise and relief, Joel was immediately agreeable.

"Paul," he said, treating Osborne with the deference he had accorded him since they first met, "Carl has a part-time job working evenings. I'm due to pick him up in about twenty minutes. Would you like us to stop by your place on our way home?"

Osborne winked at Ray, who had followed him into the kitchen. "That would be terrific, Joel. See you in half an hour then."

"*Carl* Frahm?" Lew raised her eyebrows as Osborne walked onto the porch with his good news. "That's why the name rang a bell. That's the kid they call Zenner, isn't it?"

"I don't know. Why?"

"Just wondering," she said. The look on her face generated a swift glance between the two men. Did she know something they didn't?

"What?" said Ray. "Is he trouble?"

Lew looked at him with a twinkle in her eye. "No more'n you were at that age. He's okay, Zenner. But if I were you, Ray, if those two hit it off . . ." She raised an eyebrow. "Keep an eye out."

"What are you getting at?" said Ray.

"How old is Nick?" she countered.

"Sixteen."

"All I'm saying is be wary. You haven't been a parent, Ray. Your instincts aren't honed. If Nick had grown up here, you would know that the combination of summertime, adolescence, and genetic patterning—"

"Come on, Lew—" Ray started to protest.

"Okay, okay, all kidding aside." Lew waved her hands and gave Ray a sympathetic smile. "Zenner, Nick, whoever. These kids are bright, their hormones are raging, and they've all got that look in their eye. I expect trouble from boys that age, but it is rarely something serious: beer, a little pot, girl-friends with orange hair and black lipstick. You know what I'm saying, Ray.

"Add to that the fact that this is your busy season. You've got your guiding, graves to dig, leeches to trap. Think about it. You won't be here every minute for this kid, you can't be."

Lew stood to pick up her plate and Osborne's. She looked down at Ray. "I've raised teenagers, Doc's raised teenagers, and somehow your parents survived you. Call it karma, my friend." With a wink, she disappeared through the doorway.

"Welcome to the club, Ray," said Osborne with a smile and a lift of his glass. "Do you want to call Nick and tell him to head on over?"

"I did, Doc. I told him to come up when he reached total frustration. He'll be by."

"I didn't think you would want him around Kendrickson after what you told me last fall," said Osborne, hoping Lew was out of earshot.

"You better believe I don't," said Ray, "That goombah. Guiding him once was enough, let me tell you."

"You guided Hank?" said Lew, coming back into the room. "I didn't know that. How did it go?"

"Well . . ." said Ray, crossing his legs, relaxing back into his chair, and making a tent with his fingers, a classic signal that he was about to launch what the locals called a "Ray tale."

Mutual expressions of alarm crossed the faces of Lew and Osborne. They knew better than anyone that Ray, if allowed to run loose, could turn a two-minute story into a full-hour ramble, interesting enough but so detailed and lengthy that any audience would scream for closure.

Ray caught their look. "Don't worry, I'll keep it short," he said. "Mr. K.—known to me and my buddies as Mr. Answer Man—called up one day last fall and said he wanted me to help him find some trophy walleyes. Said he had an important client he wanted to impress. Now, as you may recall, we had a lot of rain last October."

"I remember," said Osborne. "Ground was saturated, and we had flood warnings in some areas."

"Thank you, Doc." Ray nodded. "He was a little authoritative on the phone, y'know. Made it clear my boat wasn't going to be anywhere near good enough for his party, so we would have to take his boat. Use his rods, et cetera, et cetera. Basically, all he wanted from me were the damn fish. Heck, I didn't argue, five hundred a day is five hundred a day.

"So I get up to Boulder Junction where he has this big honking-new bass boat. He's waiting, he's got this blond with him. The boat is rigged with every gadget, including six rods, and Mr. K. is so duded up, I'm hoping he doesn't go overboard. He weighed more than the anchor.

"The next thing I know is our man talks big but has no idea what he's doing. He didn't know a jig from a spoon. He turned white when I pulled out the leeches. But we're still okay. Five hundred bucks, remember; I'm workin' hard to make him look good.

"So I lay out a plan." Ray gestured with his hands. "We fish the Flowage, guaranteed fish. But, no, he's got a better idea. He wants to fish Anderson Lake. I told him that's a poor walleye lake. I named two more close by that would be much better, but he wouldn't hear of it. When we get to Anderson, the lake is in full bloom, and it's hotter 'n heck. I offered to go out for an hour and if there was no action we could try later. No extra charge, I'd take them out that night and guarantee fish.

"He won't hear it, he's sure this'll work. I realize at this point, he doesn't want a guide, he wants a lackey. He wants some poor jerk to take orders, put the leech on the line and tell those damn fish to bite. But, what the hey, I'm still thinkin' five hundred a day, I can do that. Meanwhile, I'm getting looks from this blond, and I'm hoping to hell that she doesn't become too obvious, you know what I mean?"

"And you're ignoring her, right, Ray?" Lew's dark eyes were quite amused.

"I am," said Ray. "Well . . . you know. Kind of. Very attractive woman. So we try a few spots where the structure looks good. Hank doesn't get a bite. I, unfortunately, boat five fish. And, unfortunately, the blond is impressed. Hank gets nothing. He makes me switch sides of the boat. Still no luck. Fact is, he can give orders until he turns blue, but the guy is not an experienced bait fisherman. So he misses every gol' darn fish. And I could see he wasn't going to take any instruction in front of the little woman.

"All of a sudden, he decides that the leeches I have him using are all wrong. Has to have minnows. What'd I tell ya? *Mr. Answer Man.* So off we go back to the landing, buy some minnows, and we head back to the same darn lake. We go back to the same hole, he puts the minnow on and, don-cha know, *he hooks a weed.* Insists it's a fish. She thinks it's a fish. I said, 'That's not a fish.' Meanwhile, he has his drag set too loose, so it keeps giving and he keeps working this imaginary fish."

Ray grinned ear to ear. "He fought . . . that . . . weed for fifteen minutes. Fifteen minutes! Thank God, the darn thing came loose finally. Now he says it's all my fault he lost his fish. I worked the boat all wrong. Well, I have my pride, not to mention my reputation—"

"Not to mention the blond watching," offered Osborne.

"True. So I showed him his minnow. Not a mark on it, hale and hearty. Still, he insisted it was a fish. Okay, I drop the subject.

"Now our blond friend has to visit the lady's room. ASAP. Can't wait to return to the landing. I'm looking for a suitable spot, but we're way up on the north end of Anderson where it's all wetland and bogs. Remember, the ground is saturated to boot, right? This doesn't register with old Hank, he insists I beach the boat immediately so she can get off for a few minutes. I counsel against this but . . ." Ray raised his hands in a gesture of futility.

"So I pull up on a spot that looks promising, I get out and I test to see if it'll be safe. Before I take two steps, he's pulling her out of the boat. 'Hold on, folks,' I said, 'this is real treacherous in here.' But Mr. Answer Man has no use for that, doncha know. He makes some unkind remark and veers off to the right with the girl holding onto his hand, and before I can say a word, they're down. Up to their knees in muck . . . and *sinking*. Hank is bellowing and thrashing and sinking, sinking, sinking. . . ."

"Which you are enjoying," said Lew.

"Yes and no," said Ray. "I gotta pull the mother out. And he's wearing fifty pounds of bullshit fishing fashion. The blond is losing it, even though she was lucky enough to get a foothold on a boulder down in all that muck so she only went in up to her rib cage.

"It was not a happy scene. Took me three hours to work those two commodes out of there." Ray's face lit with glee as he said, "You shoulda seen 'em. Muck up to their ears—leeches, black flies, ticks—you name it.

"I ask you, what was that guy thinking? I tried to tell him where to walk, but no. He has to do it his way. When I finally get the two of them back to the boat landing, he yanks the blond out of the boat and starts in on me. Like screaming at me is going to make a difference."

Ray inhaled and settled his shoulders back. "I let him go on, didn't say anything. Just let him go on. Finally, he threw some bills at me. After I had my money, I told him that I would prefer he didn't call again."

"Poor sport," said Osborne.

"Are you kidding me?" said Ray, an irate look in his eye.

"Not you. Kendrickson," said Osborne, suddenly remembering something he wanted to ask Ray.

"Yeah? Well, that's not the end of the story." Ray, his legs crossed, plucked at a piece of lint on top of his left knee. "A few weeks later, I go into the Thirsty Whale with a couple of clients. There's Hank at the bar with some fellow I've never seen before. I was genial, I walked by, said hello, shook his hand. You know. My group goes over to a table, and we order sandwiches. I've got my back to Hank the whole time, so I can't prove anything, but when we get back to our boat, someone has broken all seven rods we had rigged up, ev-v-ery single one."

"That doesn't sound like Hank," said Lew. "He's always been a gentleman in the trout stream."

"You haven't seen him up to his armpits in muck. *And it's his own fault.*"

"True. But destructive behavior like destroying expensive fishing rods? That sounds more like kids, Ray. Were there any around?"

Ray thought for a minute. "Probably, it was a Saturday afternoon. . . . Okay, I'm sure you're right, Lew. It had to be kids but y'know, I just felt like it was the kind of thing that guy might do."

Osborne's phone rang suddenly. "Excuse me." He left the room, missing Lew's response to Ray's remark. The caller was Lucy.

"For you, Lew," said Osborne. He waited until he could hear her talking before he asked Ray in a low voice, "What's the deal with the Deerskin Dam? Hank followed Lew out to Timber Lodge yesterday to show her a picture of this huge trout he caught in the Deerskin. Somehow she knew he was lying."

"Did he say where he caught it on the Deerskin?"

"Yeah, south of the dam."

"No trout south of the dam, Doc, the water's too warm because it's so shallow. I harvest suckers out of there."

"That's interesting. Why would he lie about that?"

"He found a good hole, and he wants to keep it a secret. I don't tell everyone my best spots. You know that."

"Doc?" Lew stood in the doorway, her hands on her hips and her dark eyes darker. "Will you take this call, please? Lucy has patched through one of the Wausau boys with results on those bite marks."

"Sure." Osborne hurried back through the living room to the wall phone in the kitchen.

"Dr. Osborne," said the male voice on the other end. "Chief Ferris asked me to let you know. On the victims' shoulders? Those are the marks of human teeth all right, with some trauma to the skin and tissue, but no human made those marks. At least no living, breathing human."

"Run that by me again?" said Osborne.

"I mean I can find no bacteria in or around those bites. Not what I would expect to find from a human bite, anyway. The marks you saw can be wiped off—like washable tattoos."

"Same on both corpses?"

"Yes, sir, identical on both Sandra Herre and Ashley Olson . . . Dr. Osborne, *nothing living bit those women.*"

twenty-two

"There is certainly something in angling . . . that seems to produce a gentleness of spirit, and a pure serenity of mind."

Washington Irving

When Osborne returned to the porch, Lew gave him a quizzical look. "What do you make of that?"

"I'm not sure," said Osborne. "Let me think about it."

She turned to Ray. "I assume you surveyed that area around Timber Lodge and didn't find anything?"

"I'm sorry, Chief. I haven't had a chance. Tomorrow morning on my way to Boulder, I promise. I was tied up with Nick all day today."

"Oh . . . ." Lew was obviously disappointed. "Forget it . . . all the rain."

"No, the rain shouldn't make much difference," said Ray. "That's a fifty-year-old pine forest back in there. A thick carpet of pine needles, very little undergrowth, and a canopy that doesn't let much wind and rain in. If anyone was back in there, I'll know. I'll call in tomorrow morning if I find anything, okay?"

The back door rattled as he spoke. "I'll bet that's Nick. C'mon in," hollered Ray, tipping back in his chair.

The kid slouched through the doorway onto the porch, his hands thrust deep into the pockets of his baggy black shorts. His eyes peered out, sullen under bushy brown eyebrows and a wide forehead he hadn't yet grown into. Osborne could see the boy would be as tall and broad-shouldered as Ray someday, but right now he was all raw material. The soft lighting on the porch didn't help, either, pooling in his eyes to make his mood seem darker than it might have been. Osborne couldn't help thinking the kid cast a shadow over what had been a very pleasant evening so far.

"Hey," said Ray, his voice softer than usual, "phone didn't work, right?"

"Right." The word was clipped and full of blame as if Ray, and only Ray, was responsible for the acute dysfunction of the entire Loon Lake regional telephone system. Nick glanced at the adults without changing expression, then walked across the porch to plunk his frame down on a sofa.

"Have a seat," said Lew, after the fact but with a smile.

"Nick," said Ray hurriedly, "I'd like you to meet Lewellyn Ferris. She's our Loon Lake chief of police and an *excellent* fly-fisherman. Chief Ferris, Nick wants to learn how to fly-fish."

"You mean *fisherwoman.*" Nick had a real knack for making his opinion of Ray's intellect quite clear. Pulling himself up from the sofa with great effort and shuffling all his knees and elbows across the brief expanse of flooring, he made the effort to shake Lew's hand. His posture shouted, *Well, if I have to. . .* Osborne was bemused. In the space of less than five minutes, the boy had managed to be rude to both of Ray's good friends. His opinion of the kid was hardening into a firm dislike.

"No, I said exactly what I meant," said Ray. "She's a terrific *fisherman.*"

Nick shrugged, then shuffled back to plunk down again. He ignored Ray.

"Must be tough to be a cop when you don't even have a decent telephone," said the boy, making it obvious he found it hard just to be *alive* without the right phone line.

Lew laughed. "Loon Lake is a little weird, Nick. We have one foot in the past, one in the future, and nothing in between. I . . ." she leaned forward with a twinkle in her eye, ". . . happen to have a state-of-the-art communications setup in our new jail where my offices are. Computer network, fiber optics, the whole kit and kaboodle."

"Cool," said Nick, not totally uninterested. "Glad someone can go on-line around here. I'll be doing Pony Express all summer."

"No, you won't, kid," Ray jumped in. "Doc, here, has called a friend of his who might help you out."

"Yeah . . ." Nick's tone flattened out again. He was as impressed with Osborne as he was with Ray. "Instead of carrier pigeons you got carrier fish?"

"Funny," said Ray just as another knock was heard at the back door. Lew turned her head to smile at the wall. Osborne had to admit he was also amused by Ray's lack of appreciation of a bad joke from someone supposedly of his own genetic makeup.

"That's Joel," said Osborne, standing up to head back to the kitchen.

"You sit down, Doc," said Ray, jumping to his feet. "I'll let him in."

After Ray left the room, Lew sat back in her chair, put her hands in her pockets and regarded Nick with a straight-on stare. "I've got one thing to tell you, young man," she said. Her tone was pleasant but pointed. "Ray Pradt is very highly regarded in this town. Some would argue he's the best fishing guide in the region. And that's a talent, not a skill, Nick."

Nick shrugged and averted his eyes. "Yeah, well, he barely makes a living." Something in the boy's tone, a smug snottiness, stung Osborne. He heard Elise in the boy. And he hated it. Maybe he hated it because it jarred another memory: an echo of Mary Lee. Mary Lee, a master of condescension.

"True. But look at the living he makes," said Lew, her voice low and deliberate, nonthreatening. She was cutting this kid a lot more slack than Osborne ever would. "He reports only to Mother Nature. He reads the future in the wind and the water . . . a hell of a lot more accurately than you will ever get in a computer printout. And . . ." she hesitated for emphasis, "he can always walk away from bullshit."

Her language seemed to take the kid aback ever so slightly. At least he was listening.

"One other thing," said Lew. "You may think you've been sentenced to a summer in Podunk, USA, my friend. But don't underestimate Loon Lake. We may be tiny, but we got it all: the good and the bad. Whatever you find in the city, you will find here. But here you'll deal with it a hell of a lot sooner. I know because I see it."

Before Nick could respond, Ray had stepped back onto the porch with Joel and his son in tow. The father was a sandy-haired, mild-faced man not quite six feet tall. He had the pale skin and quiet manner true to someone who made their living sitting in one place all day. The boy didn't look like him at all. Dark and short like his mother, whom Osborne had only met once, Carl hunkered in behind his father with a slouch more pronounced than Nick's.

The boy looked like a bullfrog. His head was large and round; his eyes dark and brooding. The wide mouth drooped at the corners. Osborne watched to see if his eyelids would lower halfway and stay there. But they didn't. Like Nick, Carl walked with his hands thrust deep into the pockets of oversize shorts, though his shorts were deep purple in color. And, like Nick, his ears sported a half-dozen silver earrings.

Carl's eyes had brightened ever so slightly at the sight of Nick. Nick, who sat slumped on the sofa with the lamplight glinting off the hardware piercing *his* body.

Watching the two measure each other, Osborne recalled Gina's comment in the car that morning after meeting Nick and Ray: "I'm more concerned with what's pierced under his clothing," she had said. He repressed a smile at the thought of that remark.

But she had said something else after hearing Osborne's concern over whether Nick really was Ray's son: "You're probably not the only one wondering. Kids today know things they're not supposed to know, Doc. That one doesn't look stupid."

After introducing everyone around, Osborne offered some pop to the boys and a beer to Joel. Starting toward the kitchen again, he paused in front of Nick. "Carl has a summer job working with computers—"

"On the net?" said Nick abruptly.

"'Course. Dad said you got a problem going on-line?"

"They got a crazy phone system out here. Something from the Middle Ages—a party line for God's sake. I never heard of such a thing. I'll bet Neil Diamond is big in this town, too, and I just got a new laptop—"

"Whaddya got?"

Nick described his equipment in terms unfamiliar to Osborne.

"Cool," said Carl, openly appreciative. "Can I take a look?"

"Sure. Come down to Ray's place," said Nick. "Is that okay, Ray?" A glimmer of manners suddenly surfaced in the kid.

"Absolutely," said Ray. "You boys have at it."

Nick leaped to his feet. It was the first energetic move Osborne had seen him make since he'd scrambled back up on the dock. "Where did you say you're working?"

"A game preserve the other side of Rhinelander. Guy named Kendrickson. Great stuff. I'll tell you about it."

"Follow me, guys," said Osborne. "I'll give you some 7UPs to take along."

The last thing he heard as the boys slammed out the back door was Carl saying to Nick, "Call me Zenner. No one calls me Carl."

"Dr. Frahm," said Lew as the adults pulled their chairs around to include Joel, "so Carl is working for Hank Kendrickson, huh?"

"He is," said Joel proudly. "Setting up his entire operation—debugged the software, built a database, right now he's designing a home page for the game preserve—and making twenty dollars an hour. He'll have a couple thousand in the bank for college by the end of the summer. If Nick is computer savvy, I'll bet Carl can get him hired on, too.

"Yep," said Joel proudly as he raised his beer mug in a toast to his absent son, "Kendrickson is darn lucky he found Carl. The kid loves computers, and he's honest about his hours. Once you get past E-mail, I don't think Hank has a clue about the stuff."

This time Lew half snorted, half laughed. "To hear him talk, *he's* the expert."

"Oh, well, Hank thinks he's an expert on everything, I guess," said Frahm gently, obviously unwilling to be too critical of a man paying his son some good money. "But Hank's too much the gentleman. Doesn't want to get his hands dirty. No-o-o, Hank talks the talk, but Carl does the work."

"How much time is he putting in?" said Lew.

"Most afternoons and some evenings. He has summer school in the mornings. English lit and an SAT prep course."

"Dr. Frahm, would you have a problem if I gave your son a little more work to do? I need some help with our new system at the jail. I have an emergency situation, a database that needs updating as soon as possible."

"What kind of database?" asked Frahm.

"ATF. I need to get our regional gun registrations up to date. Nick should be able to help out, too, though I haven't said anything to him yet."

"I think Carl would love it. Kid is big on guns. I bought him a beauty of a twelve-gauge for deer hunting. Sure, Chief, talk to him about it."

Then Frahm leaned forward as if he was telling a secret. "Anything to keep him from hanging out with that strange crew he got in with when we moved here. We've had some problems with the boy. I'm afraid Carl takes after me: more brains than muscle. He's just not into sports or the outdoors. He's smart, he's got a lot of energy, and the only thing that keeps him out of trouble is the computer. Thank God for the Internet."

"He seems a good kid," said Lew pleasantly.

"He *is* a good kid," said the father, not a little as if he was trying to convince himself. "Do you know the crowd I'm talking about?"

"Yes, I do. Interesting bunch. Not the in crowd, if you don't mind my honesty."

"So you are watching them?"

"Yes. But Dr. Frahm." Lew spoke gently. "I watch all the kids. It's hard to be a teenager in Loon Lake. I don't care what your sports are, if you love to hunt, if you watch TV all day, it is just damn hard to be sixteen in a town like this. I give 'em all a lot of leeway. And that crowd is no worse than any other."

"How many crowds are there?" asked Osborne.

"Too many," said Lew. And with that she diverted the conversation to talk of the new shoreline restrictions on summer cottages. Osborne watched her. He sensed a reason she didn't want to field any more questions about Carl's crowd.

Half an hour later, as the four adults walked down to Ray's trailer to check on the boys, Lew hung back with Osborne.

"Lucky Nick," said Lew.

"How so?"

"He'll learn to fish from the master."

"That's true, though I think he hardly appreciates it."

"He will someday."

"You think so? That kid is a handful. I'm glad you said what you did about Ray."

"He could use a few manners."

They walked in silence for a few paces, Osborne resisting the urge to put his arm around her waist.

"Doc," she said softly when she was sure she couldn't be heard, "I think I have a way to find out if Nick is really Ray's son."

"How so?"

"In our Child Support Division, we use DNA testing to determine paternity. Do it all the time—we have so many razzbonyas trying to avoid paying child support. All we need to do an STR, which is the name of the test, is a saliva sample."

"That's enough? But you need it from both parents, right? Elise would never consent, I'm sure."

"We can do it with just the father," said Lew. "We do it that way a fair amount. The STR targets the specific DNA we're interested in and the lab in Madison can have results in two days or less. The kicker is I have to have a saliva sample from both the child and the father. I've got Ray's saliva, Doc, but I need the boy's."

"How do you have Ray's?"

"That joint I confiscated off him last year? You and I both know Ray always rolled his own. That little puppy is in my evidence room, all bagged and filed with care. Hell, the Madison lab can get a few million cells off that if I ask 'em."

"What about consent? I hate to have Ray know we're doing this. Even though we should tell him," said Osborne.

"I have that, too," said Lew. "He signed a consent form for any kind of testing necessary the very first time you two helped me out. You've forgotten, Doc—you did, too. Those are on file.

"And while I don't need consent from a minor, I can skirt the requirements that I have parental consent if I believe the parents are not cooperating or being truthful."

"I see," said Osborne. "You have reason to believe Elise won't cooperate and Ray, thinking he is the natural father, is being suckered into a lie."

"Exactly. So I can have the test done without alerting Ray and Nick—*if* I can get a sample of Nick's saliva."

"Leave that to me," said Osborne. "I have an idea." He reached into his back pocket for his wallet. Opening it, he pulled out a charge card. "Expired." He waved it at Lew, keeping his voice low. "If I can get some of Nick's saliva on this, let it air dry and you keep it safe in an envelope—will that work?"

"Don't see why not," said Lew. "I just don't see how—"

"Wait and see," said Osborne. "I have my ways. What concerns me more is that we're doing this without Ray's knowledge . . . but I just don't trust Elise. I keep wondering what she's up to." He looked at Lew in alarm. "What if we're right? What if the STR indicates that Ray is not Nick's father?"

"We deal with that then," said Lew.

She kicked at some leaves as she walked with her hands thrust into her pockets. "You know, Doc, that's one thing I worry about with Ray. . . . He's too trusting. He wants to like people."

"You don't?"

"It's my job to question, Doc. I don't dislike people, I just don't accept everything they say, no matter how much I might like them." He could see her face in the final glow of the setting sun as she glanced at him. "Think how often we lie to *ourselves,* for God's sake."

twenty-three

"You can't catch a fish if you don't dare go where they are."

Norman Maclean

Ray's mobile home sat as close to the water's edge as the law would allow. Osborne suspected that it was even closer. Though Ray covered the marks left by the tires, every summer Osborne could detect the comfortable little trailer inching its way, week by week, to the shore. In the fall, he moved it back, out of the wind.

And why not? Old-timers in the Northwoods always said nothing was better for a good night's sleep than fresh air streaming through the windows of a sleeping loft in a boathouse cantilevered out over water. Such structures had been outlawed for years, however. But Ray, an outlaw at heart, was happy to risk a fine in return for the opportunity to sleep with the call of the loon in his dreams.

Osborne held the door open for Lew. Stepping into the well-lit interior, he could see that, as always, Ray's place was spacious and pristine. The living room held a plump, oversized, dark-blue corduroy sofa and matching recliner against cream walls with curtains to match. In one corner stood an old jukebox, Ray's pride and joy, and in the other, an antique wooden phone booth with a working rotary phone. Ray's two yellow labs, Ruff and Ready, were asleep on a hand-crocheted afghan that had been thrown across the sofa, leaving little room for humans.

The action was at the round oak table in the kitchen. The overhead light had been turned off, and Ray's colorful vinyl tablecloth, green and white plaid studded with cheery red apples, pushed back to expose the rich wood underneath. On the burnished hundred-year-old planks rested a slim black object, cover lifted and monitor alight with digital images dancing across the screen. Mesmerized by the screen were Nick and Carl.

"Hey." Nick looked up. "Zenner helped me finish installing my software. He got the sound working. You wanna see a really cool game?"

"I do," said Lew.

"Take my place," said Zenner. He stood up, eyes wide, face happy and hands outside his pockets. Osborne couldn't believe this was the same sullen teenager who had slouched into his kitchen less than an hour ago. Zenner headed for the living room. He stopped in front of the jukebox. Ray had plugged it in so that neon waves of color were traveling up and around the edges, making gurgling noises as they ran.

"Ohmygosh," said Zenner. "You got forty-fives in here, Mr. Pradt."

"Yep, collector's editions, some of them," said Ray, walking over to stand beside Zenner. Nothing made him happier than to talk about his record collection.

"You don't see forty-fives anymore," said Zenner. "My dad's got a few."

"Not like these. I got Elvis Presley, Roy Orbison, Del Shannon, Johnny Ray, Johnny Cash, Bo Diddley, Hank Williams, Patsy Cline. Whaddaya wanna hear?"

But even as he asked, Ray was punching buttons, setting up his own favorites. The raucous piano of Jerry Lee Lewis blasted through the trailer.

"Can you turn it down a notch?" hollered Lew from the kitchen table where Joel Frahm was hanging over her shoulder to watch Nick work his game. Ray reached behind the jukebox for the volume control, giving Zenner the opportunity he needed to move in quickly and make a few of his own choices.

Osborne wished he had a camera at the sight of Ray and Zenner, one shaking his head in time to the music, the latter bouncing on the balls of his feet. Zenner's flat-out exuberance caught the eye of his father who looked at Osborne with a pleased smile. Joel edged his way over to Osborne and leaned to whisper in his ear, "This was a good idea, Dr. Osborne. I don't think I've seen my son so happy since we moved here." He looked at his watch. "I know it's getting late. . . ."

As if she heard him, Lew looked up. "Doc, I need to get going. What time is it?"

"Ten o'clock," shouted Osborne over the music, reaching past Lew to tap Nick's shoulder. "Excuse me, son, would you mind standing up for a minute?"

Nick gave him an odd look but shoved his chair back and stood, looking at Osborne.

"Just as I thought," said Osborne. "Step over here in the light from the kitchen sink, would you?" He held the expired credit card in his hand.

"I think you have the same exact overbite that Ray does . . . you might need some work on that. Do you mind?" Before Nick could hesitate, Osborne had tipped Nick's head from side to side, then, opening his mouth, pushed his lower jaw down by pressing the credit card against his tongue. He peered into the boy's mouth, looking from side to side while tipping the card each way. "No . . . I think you may be fine," he said after a long pause. He pulled the card out of Nick's mouth and turned to Joel who was watching the procedure— "Let's keep an eye on this boy, he may need some orthodontics if that jaw continues to grow."

Osborne gave Nick a friendly pat on the shoulder as the boy sat down again beside Lew.

"Doc? Did you say it was ten o'clock?" Lew stood up and walked toward Osborne.

Osborne motioned to the door, and they stepped outside. Joel followed. The three of them headed down toward the water, away from the blaring music. As they walked onto the dock, the music suddenly eased to a much lower volume.

The trailer door opened, and Ray stepped out. He ambled down to join them. As he neared, the music stopped.

"I showed Zenner how to turn it off," he said. "The boys are playing one last round on the computer." Even as he spoke, they could hear the two boys hooting and giggling.

"Say." Ray put a hand on Joel's shoulder. "I can't thank you enough for bringing your son out here tonight. He's just what Nick needs. How 'bout you and I take those boys fishing. You got plans late tomorrow afternoon?"

"Sounds good to me, Ray. Zenner's having a great time," said Joel, dropping the formal Carl. Osborne wondered if this was the first time he had used his son's nickname.

"Why do they call him Zenner?" asked Lew.

"When we first moved here, he told the kids at school he was a Zen Buddhist," said Joel.

"You're kidding," said Ray.

The dentist shot him a long look. "I wish I were, Ray. How would you like living with a hormone-riddled Zen Buddhist? Not what his mother and I asked for when he was born. Zenner is what the kids at Loon Lake High started calling him, and it's stuck."

"How do you practice Zen Buddhism in this neck of the woods, Joel?" asked Osborne.

"Oh, he's moved on from that," said Joel. "You'll need all the help you can get, Ray. I know you're younger than I am, but kids are different these days. Very different."

For a moment, everyone was quiet in the soft summer night, the lake a glassy black, the air fragrant with pine. Then Joel spoke, his voice low and mesmerizing, almost confessional, in a rhythm that no one seemed inclined to break.

"I don't know what to do," he said. "The kid is bright, he's creative, but he's just so goddamn goofy. A couple months after we got here, he developed a crush on some girl who was a Wicca. Do you know what that is?" Osborne could feel rather than see his eyes in the dark.

"A witch," said Lew. "A good witch. Pretty harmless, Dr.

Frahm. Quite a few of the girls at the high school are into that. Beats LSD."

"Well . . . okay," said Joel, "but the next thing his mother and I knew, he had books about vampires lying around his room. Now what's that all about?"

"That was last year," said Lew. "I think the vampire thing has died down."

"I can't believe we're standing here discussing vampires," said Osborne.

"You need to work for me full-time," said Lew. "That's the tip of the iceberg, Doc."

"I just wish the kid would be a goddamn soccer player . . . or an ice fisherman," said Joel. "Something normal."

"That reminds me," said Ray with a chuckle, "I guess I better let ol' Nick in on the fact I dig graves. Better he hear it from me than one of those razzbonyas in summer school."

"He doesn't know?" said Osborne.

"Not yet," said Ray. "My trailer, the leeches, my wax worms in the fridge . . . not to mention the phone situation. It's all been kind of a shock for the kid. Elise did not exactly prepare him." He stood at the end of the dock, staring up at a half-crescent moon. "I'll take him out in the boat tomorrow night. I'll explain it all to him then."

The adults headed back up toward the trailer, where the door stood ajar. Ray's kitchen window was open, and the boys' voices, interspersed with giggles, came through clearly. Lew was walking at the front of the group. A sudden burst of giggling from inside the trailer caused her to stop and listen. They all did. Osborne grinned in the dark. He was starting to feel a little better about Nick. Maybe the kid wasn't so bad after all.

"Yeah!" Nick's voice rang out. A brief silence and a few clicking sounds as if the computer were being turned off.

Then Zenner's voice. "Hey, man, so what's your thing? Are you a jock or what?"

"Nah. I'm just a bytehead."

"Me, too. And I'm into Goth."

"Oh yeah, I got friends into Goth."

"But you aren't?"

"Nah. Well . . . I just moved to my mom's. I don't know too many kids at my new school yet."

"You got vampires there?"

"Some. Pretty subset, y'know."

"Huh. You got a stepfather?"

"My mom's got a new boyfriend. He's on Wall Street. Makes twenty million a year." Nick's tone was one of obvious pride.

Zenner whistled. "Guess you won't be living in a house trailer for long."

"I gotta be here all summer. Bummer. My mom's boyfriend is younger than she is. She doesn't want him to meet me until she's got him signed, sealed, and delivered."

Jeez, thought Osborne, *what was it Gina had said? Kids today know more than they should. How right she is.*

"So what's Ray to you?" asked Zenner.

Osborne held his breath, acutely conscious of Ray standing right behind him.

"I guess he's my birth father," said Nick. "That's what she says anyway."

"Did you see the birth certificate?"

"No."

"I know how we can go on-line and find it."

That was enough. Lew made a sudden noise to alert the boys of their presence.

Ten minutes later, after the Frahms had departed, Lew, Osborne, and Ray walked slowly up the lane toward the main road. Osborne waited until he was sure he was out of earshot of the trailer. He wanted desperately to say something that would make it right for his friend.

"That was interesting, Ray."

"Yep," said Ray. "Well . . ." He sighed resignedly. "I guess if he's gotta be here all summer, then he may as well go home a decent muskie fisherman. That's all there is to it, Doc. That's the best I can do."

"We know folks who pay good money for that," said Lew.

"Yep. Good night, you two." Ray walked his loopy walk back toward the trailer, his shoulders drooping and his head down. After watching his friend for a moment, Osborne handed the saliva-marked credit card to Lew.

"At least we know what Elise is up to," said Osborne once they hit the road. His own drive was just 400 feet ahead.

"Are you surprised?"

"No. You wouldn't be, either, if you knew the woman."

They walked on, silence warm between them. Lew's little red fishing truck came into view, parked in the left-hand space in Osborne's driveway. Its shadow loomed like bad news. He hated to see her go.

"Got all your gear in the truck?"

"Yep. Thank you for a nice evening."

As he walked with her to the truck, she paused to open the plate over the gas tank and reach inside for her keys.

"Habit." She grinned. She reached for the handle on the driver's side door. The interior light flashed briefly, then she let the door swing closed enough for the light to go out. She turned to face him.

Osborne found himself standing close to her, closer than he ever had. Lew curled her right hand into a small fist and nudged at his arm with her knuckle. Though she was touching him lightly outside his clothing, the sensation was of a stroke significantly more intimate. He couldn't help moving closer. The moonlight was hazy but bright enough that he could find her eyes. Her gaze held his.

"*I* had a very nice evening," he said, wondering why he had to lose control of the English language. Surely he could think of something better to say than repeating her words. Still, she held his eyes with hers, her dark, deep eyes.

Suddenly she lifted her face to give him a quick, impulsive kiss on the lips. A kiss both short and long. A kiss that held for a moment that he would replay again and again. What happened after that was a blur. How she got into her truck he never knew, how he got back to his own house was a blank, too. But he sure knew where he was from that point on: sky high.

twenty-four

"The congeniality and tact and patience demanded by matrimony are great, but you need still more of each on a fishing trip."

Frederic F. Van de Water, author

Osborne woke to a gray, miserable day. The chop on the lake was the color of lead, and a stiff, damp wind chilled his bones as he walked onto the dock with a cup of coffee. One sip and he headed right back up to the house. This was not the morning to watch ducks and ruminate on life's modest pleasures. Scooting Mike along in front of him, he put the dog behind the fence and hurried back into the kitchen to warm up.

Poor Gina, he thought. *She must be freezing to death.* This was the kind of day the tourists curse: Up for sun and fun, they get winter in June. They would be all over Loon Lake today, crowding the gift shops for trinkets, shopping at Ralph's Sporting Goods for sweatshirts and rain gear, and packing into the Pub for egg salad sandwiches and chicken noodle soup. Yep, the kind of day to stay warm from the inside out.

A sleepy-eyed Nick literally fell out of the door of Ray's trailer when Osborne pulled up. At first he thought the kid hadn't even changed his clothes. The uniform was identical to the night before, though a closer scrutiny showed the actual items of clothing had changed. The shorts were still baggy and dark, but not black. The T-shirt was still oversized and chewed-looking but it was a different shade of purple. The Teva sandals were the same. But from where he was sitting in the passenger seat, the boy did not smell.

Nor did he talk other than to utter a few grunts in response to Osborne's attempt at social intercourse as they drove into town. *You're gonna have to shape up if you're gonna fish in my boat, Sonny,* Osborne found himself thinking. But a flash recall of Lew's sweet good-bye crowded any opinion of Nick out of his mind for the rest of the seven-minute ride into town.

The sky opened up as they neared the high school, the downpour clouding the view of the building. Nick sat a little straighter in the car as they neared, peering through the cloudburst at clusters of students hurrying along the sidewalk from the parking lot.

Was he relieved not to be dropped off by a battered blue truck with a leaping walleye on the hood and a sign under the grill spelling out in large letters the word Gravedigger? Probably, thought Osborne. Poor Ray.

As Nick prepared to unload his bony arms and legs from the front seat of the station wagon, they heard a shout. Zenner came loping toward them, his face beaming under the hood of a dark green rain poncho and looking for all the world like a satisfied frog perched under a wet leaf.

"Hey, man," said Nick, stepping into the rain. The relief and happiness was so obvious in his voice that Osborne felt ashamed of his critical attitude toward the kid. Here he was thinking Nick was being deliberately rude when it was more likely the boy had been worried as hell about walking into a strange school all by himself.

"I got you an interview out at the preserve," said Zenner, splashing as he jumped up and down in his huge sneakers. He leaned into the car to see Osborne. "Dr. Osborne, Dad gave me the car today. If it's okay with you, I'll take Nick to work with me and drop him off later."

"But if this is an interview, shouldn't I take him back to change or something?" said Osborne. The two boys looked at him like he was crazy.

"No," said Zenner. "This is fine. He's got the job, really. I told Mr. Kendrickson Nick knows plenty, and I can show him exactly what to do. So, if you think it's okay, I'll have him at Ray's place by five."

"Well . . . sure," said Osborne, "I don't see why not. You and Nick and your dad are fishing with Ray tonight, right?"

"Yeah," said Zenner, nodding enthusiastically. "My dad said he'll be there by five, too." By this point, Nick was nearly soaked through. Osborne waved the boys off with a smile.

Yep, he had to give the boy a break. After all, Osborne himself had spent a good many years thinking Ray Pradt was a numskull. You couldn't blame the kid for being a little leery of a guy with a fish on his head.

By the time Osborne reached the jail, he was humming. The nice thing about a gray day was seeing all the lights on inside homes and businesses. Even the new detention center looked warm and cozy from outside.

Lew gave him a bright smile and a wave when he finally located her in the large conference room down the hall from the probation offices. His heart lifted. She was sitting alongside Gina, whose eyes were riveted on her computer screen.

Gina gave a quick glance as he walked in. "Morning, Doc," she said. Her voice boomed at him, clipped but cheery. Tapping at her keyboard with a flourish, she grabbed her coffee cup and stood up to get a refill from the pot sitting on a hot plate against the far wall. Lew moved over to study the screen.

"You must have been at Ralph's when he opened this morning," said Osborne to Gina as they filled their coffee cups.

"How did you know?" She looked puzzled.

"That shirt."

"Oh." Gina looked down. She was wearing a navy blue sweatshirt with burgundy letters running across her chest that read, *Loon Lake: Excitement, Romance, and Live Bait.*

The sweatshirt, paired with close-fitting Levi's, made her look neat, trim, and tiny.

"Say," she said as she sat back down, warming her hands on her coffee cup, "I hear there's a prime piece of lakefront for sale down the road from you and Ray."

"The old Gilligan place," said Osborne. "That's a nice lot. Good shoreline, but the old cabin isn't worth much, Gina. Folks up here want something you can winterize. That's a teardown."

"It's got running water," grinned Gina. "And every excuse never to clean it."

"You can't be serious." Osborne pulled out a chair to sit down behind the two women. "Would you really buy a place up here? Gina, you've only been here twenty-four hours."

"I like Loon Lake." Gina swung around, coffee cup in hand, and crossed one foot over the opposite knee. "Had the best cheeseburger in the world at the Pub last night. I ended up at the bar, where I had a long talk with a very nice young real estate broker." Her eyes were sparkling, and Osborne could see she had had a very nice evening. "Even if I didn't get up here that often, lakefront property is a good investment, isn't it?"

"As good as the stock market," said Osborne. The Gilligan lot was to the immediate north of Ray's place. He wondered how much that might factor into Gina's interest.

"And the people here are so nice," she said. "Yesterday afternoon I stopped by Ralph's Sporting Goods. Everyone was so pleasant, even though I don't know beans about fishing. Then I went to dinner by myself and made all these new friends. Trust me, you cannot do this in Kansas City, much less New York or Chicago."

Osborne nodded thoughtfully. "You know . . ." He paused, looking down at his own coffee cup. "That's why I think we're going down a blind alley looking for your Michael Winston in *this* neck of the woods. Everyone in and around Loon Lake knows everyone. Someone as self-important as I assume he is, from everything you've told us about him, a man like that would stand out in this town."

"Maybe I haven't made myself clear," said Gina, waving her left hand impatiently. "That's exactly what he does so well. He doesn't stand out in the usual sense. He makes everyone he wants to impress feel like *they* stand out; he makes *you* feel special. The man excels at seducing the unsuspecting. That is his talent."

Osborne chewed on that. He looked at Lew. He wanted to tell her she looked drop-dead beautiful, but instead he said, "Anyone come to mind?"

"Ray Pradt," she said without hesitation. They all laughed.

"Frankly, no," she said. "Not a soul. But I do think Gina has a point with the gun trail. I am more than willing to give this a try. If nothing else, I'll have a handle on our local arsenals."

"Fighting words." Gina swung back around to her computer. "I have the ATF data all lined up and ready to go," she said. "It isn't as bad as I expected, either. The local records work fine on my software. If I can get those boys in here tomorrow or the next day to help me install it on Chief Ferris's system, I think we can debug enough to run the data before the weekend. I may get a good chunk of the data entry done today, even," she said.

"Chief Ferris!" Hank Kendrickson stood in the doorway. Osborne jumped in surprise, splashing his coffee, as the man's voice rang across the room. "Can I see you a minute?"

Osborne looked over at the stocky figure in the doorway. Fluorescent lighting was not kind to Hank. His cheekbones were blotched over the full beard, and his yellow gray hair looked like dirty straw. The red flannel shirt, chinos, and suspenders he was wearing also conspired to emphasize his shortness, which Osborne noted with satisfaction.

Lew stood up to walk toward him, then she stopped and turned back toward the table. "Hank—" She waved at Gina to come forward—"I'd like you to meet Gina Palmer from Kansas City. Gina is in town on a sad mission. She's a family friend of one of the murder victims, but she's also giving me a hand with our new computer system. She's quite the expert."

Gina stood up and walked over, extending her hand as Lew continued, "Gina, this is Hank Kendrickson. He runs the Wildwood Game Preserve, where the young Frahm boy is working. Hank, I should get Gina out to your place for a tour before she leaves town . . . show her your elk herd."

"How nice to meet you, Hank," said Gina, pumping his hand. "Chief Ferris said your game preserve is in the process of becoming one of the first E-commerce sites in the county. I sure hope you won't mind if I pull your site expert, Zenner, in to help us out for a day or so."

Hank opened his mouth, but nothing came out. Then he shook his head slightly, turned away, and coughed. He pounded at his chest with the opposite hand, then gave a weak look and in a tight, constrained voice said, "Excuse me, I got a frog in my throat. A lovely woman does it every time."

"Thank you," laughed Gina, "but that is hardly the effect I want to have. Can we get you a drink of water?"

"No, no, I'll be fine." He waved away the offer, but his voice remained high and tight. "You use Zenner as long as you need to, Chief." He coughed again. *"Anything* I can do to help. But I am in a bit of a hurry this morning. If we could . . ." He backed toward the doorway. "Chief . . . ah . . . do you have a minute?" Hank flushed a little, tripping over his words as he thumped his chest once more. It was obvious he wanted to speak to Lew in private, and he was trying to clear his throat in way that would not appall the group. Osborne did not feel sorry for him.

"Golly," said Gina, tipping her head as she stepped back to look at him, "did I meet you at the Pub last night? I feel like we've met before."

"Umm . . . not last night," said Hank. Now he had his handkerchief out and was wiping at his eyes and nose. The man's mounting discomfort and awkwardness paralleled Osborne's feeling of smugness.

"I had a Trout Unlimited meeting at Ralph's last night—to plan our sponsorship banquet. Lewellyn, we missed you." Again he coughed and hacked. Meanwhile, the familiar way in which he used Lew's name did not pass unnoticed by Osborne.

"That's it. I was there, too. At Ralph's, I mean," said Gina, going back to her chair. She beamed at everyone in the room. "Now that's what I love about a small town. Doesn't take long to get to know people. I mean, gee, this is so fun."

"So what is it exactly you folks are doing that you need Zenner's help?" Hank asked Lew.

Before Lew could answer, Gina piped up, "Oh, just a little R&D with databases. Research and development," she added at the puzzled look on Lew's face. Gina waved her hand dismissively toward her computer screen. "Nothing too fancy, but Zenner sounds like he has the skills to help me install some customized software so it will accommodate Chief Ferris's needs. Shouldn't take long. Feel free to sit in."

"Say, Hank," interrupted Lew, "you've met a lot of people since you've been up here. Ever run into a Michael Winston?"

Hank dropped his head in thought. "No . . . I know *Jim* Winston, runs the Cove Restaurant. Could that be one of his sons?"

"No, this would be an older man. Dark hair, medium height."

"Sorry," said Hank, "but I can check our T.U. membership list if you want."

"Wouldn't hurt," said Gina. "You know, Mr. Kendrickson, I would *love* to see your game preserve. Can the public just drive in? Are you open if I stay in town over the weekend?"

Oh no, groaned Osborne inwardly. *Not her, too.*

"Well, why don't you and Chief Ferris plan to come out and let me give you a private tour," said Hank, obsequious in his geniality. "Let me check our schedule, and I'll give you ladies a call later today. Is there somewhere you can be reached, Gina?"

"I'm staying at the Stone Lake Motel."

"Good. Maybe Sunday. Nice meeting you," said Hank with a wave to Gina. Then he reached for Lew's elbow and propelled her into the hallway. A proprietary gesture if ever Osborne had seen one. He was so irritated, he barely listened as Gina rattled on.

"I'm not sure he's real happy about my using Zenner, Doc," she said. "Now how do I know him. I don't think I saw him at the sports shop and I know it wasn't at the Pub . . . hmm . . . I hate it when I do that. It can be so embarrassing. You'd think in my work, I'd be perfect at remembering names and faces.

"Hmm . . . this really bothers me, Doc. Gee, something about him is so familiar. Shoot! And I know it wasn't at Ralph's. . . ."

She paused, suspending her fingers above her keyboard, then she braced her chin in her hand, leaning her elbow on the table. She studied the air in front of her as she tried to remember. "Maybe he was on my flight. . . . Do you ever do that, Doc? Happens to me all the time in Kansas City. I'll see a familiar face, and I can't place it. Then I feel bad because I think it's someone I should know. Of course, half the time it's someone I saw in my shrink's waiting room, a face I'm not supposed to remember.

"My most embarrassing moment is running into one of my married friends out with another woman," said Osborne, trying to be polite and still overhear what was being said in the hall.

"Oh, come on. That doesn't happen here in Loon Lake—"

"Actually, it's happened twice. And with people you would never expect."

Before Gina could respond, Lew walked back into the room, pausing in the doorway to look back down the hall.

"That man can be such a pain," she said through gritted

teeth. "Sorry, I thought I'd never get rid of him." She rolled her eyes.

"Uh-oh. And there I go inviting us out to his place. I'm sorry, I had no idea," said Gina. "If he calls, I'll go by myself. But," she scrunched her face and her shoulders as if wincing in pain, "he probably won't call me. It's pretty clear who he wants to see." She winked at Lew.

"He's a nice man but a bother," said Lew. "Now he's roped me into fly-fishing tomorrow night with some friends of his from Minneapolis. Business partners, I guess. I don't mind when I'm not busy, but the timing is bad right now." She leveled a look at Gina. "For the record, it's not a date, it's a civic thing."

"You mean civil," said Osborne.

"No, I mean civic, Doc. As the head of law enforcement here, I have to humor certain individuals, I have to attend certain social events. Comes with the job."

"So whenever he asks you, you have to go?" asked Gina, teasing.

"No. But today he backed me into a corner. He had already talked to Lucy and had her check my calendar."

"What an asshole," said Gina. "That is totally out of line."

"That's what I mean; he's a bother. But enough of this," said Lew, slapping a file folder down on the desk. "Here's the last set of ATF files."

"Chief!" a woman's voice called from the door just as Osborne took his last swallow of coffee. It was Lucy, the switchboard operator. "Ray Pradt is on the line. Has to talk to you right way."

"Oh, good. Can you put him through to the phone in here?" said Lew.

The look of frustration on Lew's face changed to anticipation as she listened to Ray. "Yep, yep, okay. And Ray? Thank you very much." She hung up. "Doc, do you have time to run out to Timber Lake Lodge with me? Ray found something. He left it in the lodge office for us."

"What is it?" said Gina. "Can you tell me?"

"Ashley's fanny pack with her cell phone and a small journal still in it," said Lew.

"Forget ATF," said Gina, "I'm coming with you. If that's all right?"

The fanny pack lay on Helen's desk. Osborne had three pairs of surgical gloves from his emergency dental kit, which he had learned to carry in the station wagon ever since working for Lew the first time. He handed a pair each to Lew and Gina.

Helen sat at the desk, a piece of paper in front of her. She looked at Lew. "Ray had to be somewhere, so he asked me to pass along some information. He said he'll call you later. He seemed to be in a real rush."

Lew nodded, so Helen continued. "He told me to tell you it looked like the pack had caught on a branch while the body was being carried along a deer trail out there. Here's a map he drew for you." She handed Lew the paper. "He marked the branch, too, so you can go in and study the site yourself. He said whoever dumped Ashley's body must not have seen it catch and rip off."

"So much for Roger's ability to survey a crime site," said Lew dryly.

"He told me to be sure to tell you not to be critical of your deputy. When he didn't find any tire marks off the circle back in there, he drove down to Gaber's Landing and put his boat in. He came in through the swamp to a ramp that cross-country skiers use. You know the one that runs along the south bank of the river? That's where he saw bloodstains leading to the deer trail. He said he had plenty of sign along the deer trail until it crossed an old logging road, where it became more difficult to read. But Ray said he found enough sign for you to be sure that's where the killer came in."

"Yep, I know the area," said Lew. "Damn! This is all my

fault. I told Roger to look for evidence of someone *driving* back in there. Why didn't I think of access by water? Dammit."

"Lew, don't be hard on yourself." Osborne put his hand on her shoulder. "Who besides Ray would ever think to track through a swamp? We don't even hunt back there."

"But that is what makes it infinitely logical, Doc. I have to blame myself. My job is to think like a killer."

"Am I the only one who wants to see what we have here?" said Gina, pulling on her set of gloves.

"Open it," said Lew. Gina unzipped the pouch and tipped it forward gingerly. Out slipped a tiny, expensive cell phone.

"I'll take that. Lucy can call the phone company and ask them to help us get a listing on any calls made." Lew set the phone to one side. A set of keys and one other object had slipped onto the desktop.

"Those are our house keys," said Helen. "We give each guest a set so they can let themselves in at their convenience."

"Yes!" said Gina, reaching for a small brown leather-bound book with deckle-edged pages. "I was hoping we would find this."

twenty-five

"Once an angler, always a fisherman. If we cannot have the best, we will take the least, and fish for min- nows if nothing better is to be had."

Theodore Gordon

Gina paged excitedly through the small volume. "I looked for this before I flew up here. I've been wondering what happened to it. Remember I told you Ashley had asked me for help writing a business book?"

"Yeah." Lew nodded.

"I started her out with instructions to keep a daily jour- nal. I told her to write like she was talking to someone. I wanted her to get comfortable in her own voice and not try so hard to be literary. You know what I mean?"

"Not exactly, but keep going," said Lew.

"So okay." Gina turned pages, scanning quickly. "Here's an entry from three weeks ago . . . here's about two weeks . . . here . . . I got it!" She read in silence as everyone in the room waited. "Oh my God," Gina said softly, "I forgot about his dog. Oh my God. . ." She flipped back a few pages in the diary. "I'll start here."

She looked up at the expectant faces in the room. "I for- got Winston had a dog. Apparently, when he left Kansas City, he took the dog with him. . . ." She paused to read. "Oh no . . . Ashley never told me she was doing this." Gina took a deep breath. "Here, I'll read you something she wrote al- most a month ago—"

"Take my chair." Helen jumped up. Gina sat down and set the book carefully in front of her, smoothing the pages back. Osborne edged in closer, standing so close to Lew he could feel her shoulders against his chest. She didn't move away.

Helen checked to be sure the door was closed. The room was absolutely quiet as Gina started to read in a soft, deliberate voice.

" 'I start my search today. Am I crazy? I heard Gina tell someone at dinner the other night that you can always find a fugitive with a dog because they forget to change the dog's name when they take them to a vet. I wonder if Michael will do that. That could be how I can find him. I'm going to try. I must find him. I have to. I have to know if he ever loved me. I must know. I cannot live without knowing.' "

"Next entry," said Gina.

"What are the dates on these?" asked Lew.

"May fourteenth and fifteenth, about a month ago."

" 'I started calling today. Called twelve vets around Savannah, where he hunts boar. No luck. Then I called the lodge in Montana, out where he hunts elk. They gave me names I'll try tomorrow. Oh, Eagle Nest, Wisconsin. I almost forgot; I'll try that, too.' "

"Next entry . . ."

" 'An incredible day. I still can't believe it. My first call to a vet in Rhinelander, Wisconsin, and I might have something. They said they had a yellow Lab with that name in for shots six months ago. I'm sending a letter up for them to forward to the owner. I hope and pray this is Michael.' "

"So that's how she found him," said Gina, looking up from the diary.

"What's the dog's name?" asked Lew. "I didn't hear you read that."

"She doesn't say."

"You don't know either?"

Gina shook her head. "No. I was never around Winston and his dog. I never heard Ashley say anything about the dog, either, except that he spent thousands getting it trained for bird hunting. Ashley was a cat person; she didn't tune in to dogs."

"Damn." Lew snapped her fingers. "If only we knew the dog's name, we'd have Winston."

"Let's call local vets for a list of everyone who owns a yellow Lab," said Gina.

"That's not as easy as it sounds," said Osborne. "This is dog country, and Labs are the most popular breed up here, especially yellows . . . and they all need shots. You're better off tracking the guns first, if you ask me. What about someone in Kansas City who hunted with him? They might remember the dog's name."

"You're right," said Gina. "I'll see what I can find out."

"Gina, keep reading," said Lew with an impatient wave of her hand.

"'Michael called today. Out of the blue, his voice on the phone. I couldn't believe it. He sounded like he was in the next room. His voice was so warm and gentle. It fills my heart. He said he was thrilled to get my letter, that I would never know how much it meant to him. He asked me to forgive the cruel things he said. My heart stopped. I could only whisper. He asked if he could call again. I said I didn't know, but of course I want him to. Oh my God, my God.'"

"The next entry is dated the next day," said Gina.

"'Again that voice. I couldn't wait to hear him again. I'm lost, I'm lost in this man. I have the whole world, but all I want is him. He is so gentle. He asked if I could forgive, and I said the time to forgive was past. I said forgiveness is the heart of my love for him. He asked me to keep these phone calls a secret until we know what we're doing. He wants to leave the past behind. He wants to start over with me somewhere far away. God, how I miss him. When I hang up the phone, my heart is so full. I know in my bones this is right.'"

Gina read on. Two more pages, three more days, then Winston made his move: "'Today Michael asked me to marry him. But he won't let me answer until we're together. He's sending me tickets to fly up tomorrow. He said he wants to surprise me, so he has reserved a suite for me at a little bed-and-breakfast. He'll have directions for me when I get there, I guess. He said he lives in a beautiful place with trout streams, eagle nests, and six different species of hawks. I can barely wait, it sounds so heavenly. He said it is very important to him to return the money he needed when he left. He invested it and will return every penny four times over. Silly man. I told him I don't want the money, it doesn't matter. He said it does matter, it proves he did not betray me. I have a surprise for him, too: a wedding band. As for the money, whatever he gives me, I'll give back.'"

Gina turned the page. Only a few lines remained. "'I'm here in this delicious B-&-B. My love has called and we'll be together in less than three hours. I'm so excited. I told him I have to go for a run to calm my nerves. He thought that was cute and gave me directions to a route he said I will love. Funny, life will be so different when I pick up this journal again. Oh God, how this man stops my heart.'"

"That's where it ends," said Gina. She closed the book and set it square in front of her. She looked up at Lew and Osborne, her eyes hard with hate. Osborne had always thought hate was something evil. But he was wrong. In this moment, it was honest, true, and deadly.

"Hell of a book," said Lew with a slight smile, as if to break the tension.

"She found her voice, that's for sure," said Osborne.

"Oh golly, what time *is* it?" Lew pulled her sleeve back to check her watch. "The funeral for Sandy Herre is at noon, and I really should be there."

"It's just eleven," said Osborne.

"Thank goodness. I have to change," said Lew. "Gina, I'll be back at the office by two. Can you be there?"

"Of course. Do you want me to take these items with me?"

"Thank you. Ask Lucy to call the phone company—"

"I'll do it if you like," said Gina. "It'll take me two seconds. We do this kind of thing all the time at the paper."

"Lew, why don't I attend the funeral with you?" said Osborne. "It's at Saint Mary's and the Herres were patients of mine. I was planning to go anyway."

"That would be nice, Doc." Lew smiled with relief. "There are bound to be questions from the family, and I hate having no answers."

Phil Herre was waiting at the entrance to the church. A clear blue sky had banished the gray morning. Plump billows of white scudded overhead. Sunshine, fragrant with lilac, flooded the steps leading into Saint Mary's Church. Though the loveliness of the day lifted Osborne's spirits, he felt it a gentle mockery of the grief in Phil's face.

As they entered the vestibule, Phil spotted them. He hurried over to Lew and Osborne, gesturing weakly toward the sunshine spilling through the doors still open behind them. "At least we'll be able to go to the cemetery in decent weather.

"Chief Ferris, is there any chance you can finish going through Sandy's apartment today?" he said. "Her sisters would like to help her mother and me with her things while they're here. They both have to leave tomorrow morning." His eyes were red and bleary. "It'll make things so much easier on my wife."

"Of course, Phil," said Lew, placing her hand on his arm. "I'm sorry that I didn't finish before this. And it won't take long. I want to check her desk one last time, and her car. As you know, the car was found near the crime scene, and I had it returned to her apartment complex. The Wausau lab checked it over and dusted for fingerprints, but I'd like to have a look myself."

"I understand," he said. "You sure have your hands full, don't you. So I was thinking, we have the funeral luncheon following Mass, then the interment. . . . Could I bring the girls over after that? Does that give you enough time?"

"It should," said Lew. "I'll go directly from here, Phil. You just come by when you're ready. You have a key in case I've finished?"

"Yes." He turned to walk away, then stopped. "Do you think there's any connection with that other shooting?"

"It's too soon to tell, Phil," said Lew gently.

He gave a deep sigh and shook his head, saying, "What is happening in this town?"

He glanced over to where his wife stood near the casket, her head bowed, her cheeks sunken with grief. Osborne's heart ached at the sight of their faces. He could not begin to imagine losing one of his daughters. Even though he knew today that his life with Mary Lee had been hard, her unexpected death had left a hole too large, a hole he tried to plug with booze, until he put his own life in jeopardy. Thank God for the courage of the living; thank God for Erin's willingness to force him into recovery.

Osborne reached to put his arm around Phil's shoulder. He gripped firmly, wanting Phil to know that he understood. Turning toward Osborne, Phil returned the embrace for a brief moment. Osborne felt rather than heard the hard sob. Phil turned his face away as he raised his head, a thankful pat on the arm his parting gesture.

Before he could return to the bier, a young woman broke from the group and walked over to them. Slipping a protective arm around her father's waist, she extended her hand to Lew.

"Chief Ferris," she said, "I'm Carolyn Gardner, Sandy's youngest sister." As she spoke, the priest, Father Vodicka, took his place in front of the casket. She glanced nervously in that direction before saying, "Did Dad tell you? I talked to Sandy the day before . . . the day . . . well, she told me how she was starting her own bookkeeping business, y'know?" The girl wiped at her eyes. "And she was so happy because she already had two clients. One had even asked her to be their business manager." Carolyn sniffled. The organist started to play. Carolyn looked at her father. "Dad, are we starting?"

"Not yet." Phil patted her hand. "Not until everyone is

seated. Keep talking, honey, I want Chief Ferris to hear this."

"Then she said she had a big meeting the next day that might lead to some really good business, and if she got that contract, we were going to take a trip to Hawaii together."

"Did she happen to say who that was?" asked Lew.

"No, she said she didn't want to say any more because she didn't want to jinx it."

"I'm going to be searching her desk again," said Lew. "But I didn't find any datebook or calendar the first time I looked."

"Did you check her computer? Sandy had everything computerized," said Carolyn. "She told me right after she landed her first client that she mail-ordered a new PC that would do everything except wash her dishes. I'll bet anything you'll find her schedule in her computer. I know that's what I do," said Carolyn.

She looked at her father, and her face nearly crumpled. "Sandy was so happy going out on her own. She said even if it cost her a ton of money right now, she would make it back fast. She had it all figured out. . . ." Carolyn slid into a soft sobbing. Her father pulled her close. "She . . . she was going to work half-days, so she could fish afternoons."

"I didn't know she fished," said Lew.

"Bass," sobbed Carolyn. "She fished smallmouth bass. They're good fighters, y'know," said Carolyn as she sobbed into her father's lapel. She raised her head and wiped at the tears on her face. "That place where you found her body? That was just a mile from Shepard Lake, where she loved to fish. One of her favorite spots. Did you know that?"

"No, I didn't," said Lew. "That's good to know. And thanks for the suggestion on checking her computer files, too. I've been planning to check through those this afternoon. If I have any questions, I'll call you at your folks'. If you think of anything more that Sandy may have said about her client meeting the next day, or anything about her clients, please call. Lucy Olson is usually on the switchboard, and she always knows how to reach me, Carolyn."

Lew laid her hand briefly on Carolyn's sleeve; then she and Osborne entered the church, selecting a pew toward the back. Bells chimed, and the pallbearers started down the aisle alongside the bier on which rested the closed casket.

Behind them walked the family. Carolyn and another sister, Julie, brought up the rear of the procession, one carrying a fishing rod, the other a tackle box. They walked past the bier, through the gate to the altar, and up the carpeted stairs to lay Sandy's beloved fishing gear in front of a spray of flowers. Then they stepped back to take their places in the family pew. As the organist's requiem filled the church, everyone stood.

Osborne was acutely aware of the woman standing to his right. Lew had chosen a simple, long-sleeved black blouse with a round neckline that tucked into a straight black linen skirt. A black leather belt emphasized her waist and flat stomach. She looked trim and tailored, her skin glowing against the black.

She glanced up, catching his gaze as they knelt for the Offertory. Her eyes were soft and calm. He had attended Mass at Saint Mary's for over thirty years and seldom had he felt so at home and at peace as he did right now.

twenty-six

*"I still don't know why I fish or why other men fish,
except that we like it and it makes us think and feel."*
Roderick L. Haig-Brown

Yanking the yellow police tape from the door, Lew
opened the door to Sandy Herre's apartment. Osborne followed her in. With a twist of a rod, she flipped open the
metallic shades covering a wide front window. The room
was stuffy, a faint doggy smell lingering in the air. The three
o'clock sun streaming in didn't help, either.

Lew pulled out the chair in front of the desk on which
rested Sandy's computer. Just as she went to sit down, the
phone rang, startling both of them. Lew picked up the receiver. It was Lucy.

"Oh!" Lew sounded surprised. "Well . . . good. Send
them over to the conference room where Gina is working.
No, wait. Have them check in with Human Resources over
in the courthouse first, Lucy. Call ahead, ask HR to have
them fill out applications for temporary positions. If there's
any problem, let them know I need those two on board to as-
sist with an urgent computer investigation. Got it? Thanks,
Lucy."

She looked at Osborne as she hung up. "Apparently
something came up out at the game preserve, and Hank did-
n't show to put the boys to work. They stopped by to get
started with the ATF database . . . oh, and I got our saliva
samples off to the lab in Madison." She gave Doc a significant look.

"How long until we know?" he said.

"Um . . . late tomorrow, I requested a 'rush'." Lew gave

a quick glance around the apartment. "Doc, I've gone through her desk, the bedroom, the bathroom, everything on the counters, in the drawers, *and* in her storage unit. I saved the computer for last."

Sitting down, Lew turned on the computer. The machine hummed as a colorful pattern filled the screen.

"Drats," said Lew. "I was afraid this would happen. I don't recognize these icons. I'm not like Gina; I don't know much beyond the word processing we use on our system. I can fool around here, but I don't want to screw anything up. Dammit."

"Any reason not to call Gina?" said Osborne. "We're only five minutes from your office. It'll be at least an hour before the boys can get to work, won't it?"

"That is not a bad idea," said Lew with relief as she picked up the phone.

Ten minutes later, Gina barreled into the room like a petite torpedo: small, dark, and dedicated to a target. Shoving a computer printout at Lew, she said, "Right after your call, I got a fax of Ashley's cell phone records for the last two weeks. All calls, except one, were made to people in Kansas City. The one local call—to a Loon Lake number—was made at three o'clock Monday afternoon. To Ralph's Sporting Goods. A ten-minute call, too.

"Now why would she do that?" Gina asked Lew and Osborne. Before they could say a word, she answered her own question. "I'll tell you why. The record shows she punched star-sixty-nine just before placing the call. Someone must have called her, and she was trying to find out where they had called from—"

"Huh," said Lew. "Looks like I better see Ralph when I'm finished here. But first things first. I have to let the family in here later this afternoon."

"Excuse me," said Osborne, "what's this star-sixty-nine you're talking about?"

"Doc, if you ever get decent phone service at your place,

you will be amazed at the services you can get," said Lew. "The world has passed you by. Star-sixty-nine allows you to check the last call made to your line, even if you don't answer."

"I've got another piece of news for you, too," said Gina, seating herself in the chair just vacated by Lew. "But I can see from the look on your face you've got an agenda. This can wait."

"No, no, please, tell me now," said Lew.

"You'll never guess who one of your major gun buyers is, according to the ATF data that I've input so far." Gina's fingers moved swiftly across Sandy Herre's keyboard. She looked hard at the screen, then she sat back.

"I can think of a dozen people," said Lew.

"Carl Frahm."

"You mean Joel, don't you?" countered Lew. "The father."

"No. I mean *young* Frahm—Zenner. He's purchased seventeen guns over the last six months, and that's in just one county. Shotguns mainly, a couple rifles. He's been buying at estate auctions. And I think it is very interesting that the records from those auctions date back only six months, which, I guess, is when your gun control laws changed. Roger told me the auctions did not have to register gun buyers before then, which means . . ." Gina's eyes scanned the screen in front of her.

"Which means who knows how many he's bought," Osborne filled in the blank.

"Now you see why gun registration is a hot topic in the Northwoods," said Lew. "Roger is right. Estate sales and gun shows have, until recently, always been places where anyone could purchase guns easily. No one likes the change, and that's why I have compliance problems."

"I have another question," said Osborne. "Where does a kid get that kind of money? *Seventeen guns?* You're talking thousands of dollars."

"Not only that, since when does a teenage boy need an arsenal?" asked Gina.

"Well, now wa-a-it a minute. We have a lot of gun collectors up here, Gina," said Osborne, surprising himself with a sudden urge to defend the youngster.

"At that age? You buy that many guns?" Gina shook her head. "I don't know, Doc. You make a good point about the money involved. When I showed the records to Roger, he noticed that several of the shotguns were quite expensive. The high-powered rifles weren't cheap either."

"Anything else before we get into this?" said Lew, clearly frustrated. "I'm running out of time here."

"No, no. Ready to roll," said Gina, studying the screen in front of her. She was quiet for a few moments, then she spoke. "This is a brand-new system, all right. . . . I see only four folders aside from all the software icons.

"File One—that's *my* number Chief—she has them marked by name. File One is for AVCO Plumbing and Heating. . . . Let's open that little puppy. . . . Okay, according to an activity report that she has in here, she met with them a week ago and . . . was working on a proposal to do their estimated and year-end taxes.

"File Two is for the Wildwood Game Preserve. . . . Again, a handy little activity report. . . They want her as a business manager to keep computerized records of their purchasing, sales, and track the investment portfolio."

"That would be Hank Kendrickson," said Lew.

"Oh," said Gina, "according to her notes, he has offered to pay her with stock options rather than a fee. Hey, that's interesting, huh?"

"He's giving her equity in his company?" said Lew. "That seems awfully generous."

"Hank Kendrickson is always generous when it comes to *ladies,*" said Osborne.

"Come on, Doc." Lew punched him in the arm. "Give the guy a break."

Gina dropped her hands from the keyboard suddenly and

turned to Lew. "You know what bothered me about that guy? I finally put my finger on it. He doesn't look at you when he talks to you. Is that just me or have you noticed it, too?"

"You're right," said Lew. "He refuses to hold your gaze. He's attentive. He listens, but in an odd way, he doesn't connect. I thought it was me. Like I intimidated him or made him nervous. So you noticed it, too. Huh. Maybe he has a problem with women."

"My opinion? It's a dominance thing," said Gina. "Happens to me a lot during confrontation interviews. The person who wants to control the conversation is the least likely to make eye contact. I hate people who do that. I don't hire them, I don't date them. If you want to be around me, you better look me in the eye."

She swung her chair to look at Osborne. "Do men notice things like that?"

"Don't ask me," said Osborne. "I don't spend a lot of time looking into other men's eyes—I particularly avoid Hank Kendrickson."

"Doc judges people by their teeth," said Lew with a chuckle.

"C'mon, Lew." Osborne felt silly. She was absolutely right, of course. That was something else he didn't like about Hank; his teeth didn't fit, something in the outline of his molars. Every time the man smiled that supercilious smile of his, Osborne was aware of a lack of symmetry. You'd think a man who could spend so much money on cars and boats could at least buy himself a mouth that didn't look like it belonged to someone else, for God's sake. It was a mean-spirited observation, Osborne knew, and one he had no plans to share.

"I've noticed Doc hasn't much use for Mr. Kendrickson," said Gina with a big grin. The two women shared a look. Osborne felt foolish.

"Okay, okay, enough about Hank," said Lew. "Let's get back to business here."

"Oho," said Gina, straightening up in her chair, "this third file is new and different."

"Why?" Lew leaned over to peer at the screen

"It's not labeled, for one thing . . . that's odd . . . but then again, maybe that's because this is boilerplate. . . ." Gina scrolled down and down and down. "Boilerplate for money transfers to a bank in Canada with instructions to move percentages on consecutive days to an account in the Cayman Islands."

She sat back to look up at Lew and Osborne. "In my line of work we call this money laundering. Couldn't be more obvious."

"Was Sandy doing that for someone?" asked Lew.

Gina scrutinized the screen. "Not from this computer—there are no figures entered. That doesn't mean it didn't happen from another location. Let's see. . . ." Gina looked around the desk. "She's got a floppy sitting in her zip drive. Let's take a look."

Gina pushed the floppy into the drive and waited. "It's identical to the third file on the hard drive. All she did was copy the boilerplate off the disk." Gina ejected the disk and scrutinized it. "No label, darn. I thought we might at least see some handwriting."

Then she pushed back her chair and crossed her arms. "You want to find whoever gave her that floppy disk. Money transfers out of the country are not standard bookkeeping procedure."

"I should get it fingerprinted."

"Wouldn't hurt, although you'll have me and Sandy Herre all over it."

Osborne stood behind the two women. The room was airing out slightly, thanks to a window Lew had opened earlier. "Would she have gotten it from one of these other clients?" he asked.

"Except that the way she has things organized, I would expect her to have it in one of their files if that were the case," said Gina. "But it's certainly a possibility.

"If you'd like, Chief, I have a very good source in Kansas City who is on the legal team for the NASD. With your permission, I would like to run this scenario by her and see if they have a watch on anything in this part of the country. They cover the entire Midwest so they may know something."

"NASD?"

"National Association of Securities Dealers."

"Why . . . how do securities figure into this?"

"Before his move to Kansas City, Michael Winston got nailed for penny stock fraud. My source, who is familiar with that case, said they got on to him through his money transfers to banks in the Caymans. I suspect that's what he did with the money from Ashley's company, too. Now, this route through Canada is different, but for me to see money going to a bank in the Caymans . . . I'm sure it's a long shot, but it rings too many bells not to check it out."

"Okay by me," said Lew. "Even if it's not Winston, I'd like to know who in Loon Lake is that financially sophisticated."

"No activity report in that third file?" said Osborne.

"No, nothing."

"Go back to the second file. Does it show when Sandy met with the game preserve?" asked Osborne.

"Let me check. . . . yes, three meetings, at their offices," said Gina, "with the last one scheduled for a week ago today. Ready for the fourth file?"

Lew nodded, checking her watch.

"Okay . . . she's doing the monthly books for Ralph's Sporting Goods. And some consulting . . . they want her to set up a new program to track inventory, sales, taxes, etc., and train the in-house person. The activity report looks real straightforward to me."

"Anything else on the desktop?" asked Lew.

"Her daily calendar. . ." Gina's fingers danced. "All right." She sat back and surveyed a list in front of her. "Sandy budgeted time at seven A.M. Monday and Wednesday mornings to update her activity reports. If she died Monday afternoon, that would explain why the details of her appointments and phone calls made after Monday morning were not entered. Otherwise, she had scheduled meetings next week with AVCO and with Wildwood."

"That helps explain this," said Lew, reaching for a manila folder, which stood upright in a stand beside the computer. "She has notes in here dated up to last Monday."

"Really," said Gina. Lew opened the folder. Three small squares of paper, obviously torn from the same note pad that rested beside the desk telephone, were neatly tucked one behind the other. Lew studied each.

"It looks to me like she took messages off her answering machine and was planning to call these people back," said Lew. "Two calls from Wildwood, one from Ralph's."

"No one else? I want to know who gave her that damn disk with the boilerplate," said Gina, squirming in her chair.

"Gina, how long will it take you to reach your source in Kansas City?" said Lew.

"I can call now, but chances are I'll end up leaving a message for her to return the call later."

"Please, as soon as you possibly can," said Lew. "Are we finished with the computer? I need to look at Sandy's car."

The car, which sat out in the exposed parking lot surrounding the modest apartment building, was a white Honda Accord. The backseat was covered with a blanket, which must have been the dog's favorite spot for riding. The front seat was clean, with only a few candy wrappers neatly stuffed into a trash bag that hung off the knob for the cigarette lighter. An empty coffee mug sat in the plastic holder to the driver's right.

Lew released the lever for the trunk.

It was empty except for one good-sized cardboard box, which had been opened, the flaps folded back. The boot of a pair of waders stuck out from the tissue paper wadded inside.

"Looks like a gift," said Lew as she lifted it from the trunk and set it down on the pavement. She stuffed the boot back in and folded the outside edges of the box over as if to close it.

A large white label was affixed to the front. Across the top in small print read the name of the Loon Lake merchant from whom the purchase had been made: Ralph's Sporting Goods. Beneath that, written in longhand with an elegant flourish, was one word: Ashley.

Ralph's Sporting Goods was nearly empty when Osborne and Lew walked in. But it was after four on a sunny day late in the week. Every tourist in the 300-lake region would be on the water, in the water, or near the water. No one shopped when the weather was this nice.

Osborne looked around for Ralph, but the expatriate Englishman was nowhere to be found. Instead, one of his young clerks, Stein Michaels, spotted them and hurried down from the second floor camping section. Stein was in his early twenties and somewhat of a local legend. A dedicated cross-country skier, he was the only Loon Lake resident to finish in the top twenty in Wisconsin's famed Birkebeiner, a ski marathon that is ranked one of the most difficult in the world. Over 10,000 compete, including skiers from twenty foreign countries and forty-six states, making Stein's accomplishment no small feat. Osborne knew Stein's father, a forest geneticist.

"Hey, Doc, Chief Ferris," he said, "what can I help you with?"

"We need to talk to Ralph," said Lew.

"I'm afraid he's down in Chicago at a trade show," said Stein. "He'll be back Monday. Is this about Sandy? Gosh, that's a terrible thing. She was working for Ralph, y'know."

"I understand that," said Lew. "Maybe you can answer a couple of questions for us, Stein. Were you were working Monday afternoon?"

"Yes, we all were. Monday is always a madhouse," he

said. "Everyone checks into their cabins on Sunday and crowds in here Monday for swimsuits, sunglasses, float tubes, fishing poles. You name it, every Monday, every summer, it's the same: crazy all day."

"Well, two women have been shot and killed, Stein," said Lew. "You know about Sandy. The other victim was a woman named Ashley Olson. Does the name ring a bell?"

"Y'know, it does. . . ."

"She called here Monday afternoon around three o'clock. Apparently someone had placed a call to her from here, and she was able to trace the call back—"

"Right!" said Stein. "I took that call. But, I mean, I checked with everyone on the floor and no one working here had called her. We had a ton of people in the place, and you can see we've got phones on all the counters. I told her anyone could place a local call easily. But no one on the staff called her, that's for sure. I remember, Chief, because she seemed kind of hyper or something. She wouldn't take no for an answer. She made me check with everyone. And I had a customer waiting. Jeez, so that's the woman who was killed?"

"This box has her name on it, and it's obviously from here," said Lew, setting the box she had been holding under her arm on the counter. "A pair of women's waders."

Stein opened the box that had been in Sandy Herre's trunk. He pulled out the waders, looked at the tag, then poked through the tissue paper in the box. "Oh yeah, these are top of the line, too. No receipt. Did you find one?"

"No."

"What about the tag?" asked Osborne. "Does that help?"

"No," said Stein. "It's just a price tag."

"Do you remember seeing the box here in the store?" asked Lew.

"I work upstairs in camping equipment," said Stein. "This would be from down on this level. I'll ask around, Chief, but I'll be surprised if anyone will remember. We just do too much business on Mondays."

"Maybe we should ask Ralph. He works behind the main counter," suggested Osborne.

"He wasn't here Monday," said Stein. "That was part of the problem. He had a toothache and an emergency root canal."

Lew looked defeated. "Okay. Last question: Does the handwriting on the label look familiar? Is that Ralph's? Yours?"

"It's not Ralph's, that's for sure," said Stein. "And it's not mine. I've worked here three summers, Chief. That just doesn't look familiar to me. But you should ask Ralph when he gets back."

"Was it all regular staff working Monday, except for Ralph?"

"Sort of. Sandy Herre was here. She always worked with the bookkeeper on Mondays. And we had a couple T.U. guys volunteer to help out when Ralph had to leave."

"Who was that?"

"Well . . . I know I saw Bruce Palmery and Jerry Gibson. I'll bet there were a couple other guys, too. They didn't run the cash register, but they helped answer questions and keep an eye out for any shoplifting. We have a real problem with that when this place is crowded. I was so crazy upstairs, I didn't see everything."

"So you didn't see anything, and Ralph was gone. Anyone else I might talk to?"

"Shirley worked this floor. She's in tomorrow morning."

"But not today."

"We're closing in half an hour. You could try her at home."

"Oops." Osborne looked at his watch. "I've got to get out to my place, Lew. I'm supposed to meet Ray, Joel Frahm, and the boys at five for some fishing. But I'll stay if you need me to."

"No, heck, Doc, you go ahead. This is going nowhere." At the look on Stein's face, Lew's tone softened. "Thanks, Stein. Will you call me if you think of anything? I'll be working late tonight. And if Ralph calls in, ask him to give me a ring right away, will you?"

"Sure, Chief, but I'll tell ya Monday was a crazy, crazy day."

"Yes," said Lew, "it was."

twenty-seven

"In the religion of fishing, a cast is a prayer. As a devout angler, I try to do as much praying as possible."
Dr. Paul Quinnet

Osborne was shocked to look out his kitchen window and see Ray's beat-up truck swing into the drive with a forty-thousand-dollar Triton boat hitched on the back.

"Boys, life just changed," he said, heading out the back door with Nick and Zenner close behind. Joel Frahm's white Grand Wagoneer pulled in alongside Ray and the boat. All four converged on the boat at the same time.

"Holy cow, Ray," said Osborne. "Where the heck did you get this?"

"Marina asked me to try it out tonight. They're thinking of raffling one of these off during the Hodag Muskie Festival, but they want to be sure it's as good as the rep says it is."

"This sucker must be twenty feet long," said Joel. He passed an admiring hand along the side of the boat. "I heard these hulls are molded, laminated, and painted, all in one stage, no wood either; this is one hundred percent man-made composite material. Longest-lasting hulls on the market."

"No one knows composite material better than a tooth doctor," said Ray with a big smile on his face. "I got twenty-*one* feet of fishing heaven in this baby, doncha know."

"And a laser locator?" Zenner bounced excitedly.

"Could have, but I didn't want to take the time to have it installed," said Ray. Zenner's face fell. "*I'm* the laser locator, you goombah," he kidded the boy.

Joel threw his son a significant look. "Count your blessings," he said.

"Hey, Zenner and Nick, you two get up there." Ray waved the boys into the boat. He stood alongside, cradling Osborne's Browning in his arms as he waited for the boys to clamber in.

"Zenner," demanded Ray, "whaddaya see up there?"

"Looks like a muscle car," said the kid. "Wow, padded bucket seats." He lifted lids around the perimeter of the boat. "Jeez Louise, Dad. These livewells . . . they're huge!"

"This is more boat than most of us need," said Ray to Osborne and Joel. "You won't believe they got beverage coolers, plenty of room for fishing gear. Three times what I got on my boat. I'm trying to talk the marina into letting me use one of these for guiding and give me a commission on every one I sell."

"What's a livewell?" asked Nick.

"That's like a tank full of water where you keep your fish after you catch it," said Zenner, opening one to show him.

Nick's eyes widened. "You mean we might catch a fish this big?"

"Hope springs eternal," said Ray, "gives guys a chance to exaggerate the size of their catch just like they exaggerate—"

"You must have had a good day," Osborne interrupted before Ray moved into a series of tasteless jokes that Joel might not appreciate.

"I did, I certainly did," said Ray. "Wonderful day. Client was very happy, gave me a very nice bonus and, Doc, they love your gun. Made me an offer of five grand for it."

"Not for sale," said Osborne, taking his precious shotgun from Ray's hands. A sudden thought crossed his mind, and he looked over at the boys who were messing around in the Triton. "Zenner, you like guns. You want to take a look at this Belgian Browning side-by-side of mine?"

"What?" Zenner gave him a distracted look from where he was poking around in the boat. "Why?"

"Well . . . aren't you interested in guns?"

"Huh? Sure, they're okay, I guess. Can I look at it later?"

"I told Dr. Osborne you liked guns," said Joel, embarrassed by Zenner's dismissal of Osborne's offer.

"That was last year, Dad, this year I'm into computers, remember?"

"Never mind," said Osborne, puzzled. This was the kid who bought seventeen guns at estate auctions? "I'll put the gun away. Ray, what's the plan?"

"Meet you down at your dock in ten minutes," said Ray. "Hey, boys, out! I'll put the boat in water down at my place. You two go get your gear and come with me. Joel?"

"I've got beer and chips," said Joel.

"I've got O'Doul's, root beer for the boys," said Ray, "and some humdinger potato salad and cold chicken straight from the good nuns at Saint Mary's. Payback for bluegills."

"Well, thank you, Ray. Looks like you've got it all under control," said Osborne. Ray must have had a good day. He hadn't seen him so relaxed and happy since Nick arrived.

"You're as welcome as the flowers," said Ray, waving from the window of his truck as he swung through the drive onto the road. "See you shortly, Shirley."

As they lowered themselves into the boat, Osborne looked up. The June blue of the sky was speckled with clouds overhead and bordered with a solid gray wall to the south. "Could be some weather later?" he said to no one in particular. He hoped so. He was in the mood for some serious fishing.

"I like the clearance on this baby," shouted Ray as they hummed over Loon Lake. The water was glassy, a silver blue with streaks of peach rippling ahead of the narrow breezes. As the boat entered the shadows of the trees outlining the western shore, the peach disappeared, leaving the surface scaled deep blue and edged with silver, camouflaging the creatures lurking below. Ray turned the boat due west, and Osborne shielded his eyes, dazzled by the diamonds dusting the trail toward the evening sun.

Five minutes later Ray throttled down the motor. He let the boat idle as he stood, flashlight in hand, gazing down. They were close to the western shore. Pine spires loomed beneath them, etched in black and green against the opaque silence of the surface. "Now, Nick," said Ray, "if you come out alone one of these days, what you want to find is the end of this weed bed—not the edge but the end—got that?"

Nick listened and watched. "Why is this water so dark?"

"Tannin from the pines. That's good," said Ray. "Fish have no eyelids, and light turns them off. They like to hide near sandbars and rock piles or under logs—what we call *structure*. You have to fish structure on a lot of the clear lakes up here. But Loon Lake is nice and dark, so they stay a little closer to the surface. . . . Ah, here we are."

Ray threw out the anchor while Osborne and Joel sorted through their tackle. Nick sat in front of Osborne, struggling with his rod and lure and yelping each time he hooked a finger.

Ray moved over to sit down by Nick. "Did you hear the one about the nut who screws and bolts?"

Nick groaned as he gave up and handed his rod over to Ray. "You told that one yesterday."

"Welcome to the club, Nick," said Osborne from the rear of the boat. Ray was his old self at last. The world was good. Osborne cast for the setting sun.

"Isn't this boat nice," said Ray, moving back to his bucket seat at the wheel. "Look how steady it is. Doc, I want to show you the clearance on the outboard. You could take this mother up to Lost Lake if you wanted to."

"I doubt that, Ray," said Osborne.

"Holy shit!" shouted Nick.

Joel Frahm was rearing back, a fish leaping, twisting high in the air.

"Eh, small muskie," said Ray.

"That was a huge fish," said Nick, still stunned.

Ray smiled at the look on the kid's face. "See? This is what I've been trying to tell you. You put that line out on water, and anything can happen." Joel struggled with the fish as the boys watched.

"Nick, did you see how Dr. Frahm set that hook? That was superb." Nick nodded, not taking his eyes off the battle. "Now you see what I mean?" said Ray, pleased with the look on Nick's face, "When you got a fish on the line, you forget the rest of the world."

"This is *so* exciting." Nick's fascination was infectious.

"Damn right." Ray put his feet up on the side of the boat and crossed his arms, a big, happy grin on his face.

Finally, Joel pulled the muskie alongside the boat and deftly popped the hook, letting it swim away. "Just a small one," he grinned. "But fun. A good sign. We might raise something really big tonight, boys." Osborne saw him turn away with a pleased look on his face: Ray had made him look good in front of his son. No doubt about it, Ray had just made himself another friend for life.

Ray got Nick set up and watched him cast. "*With* the wind, Nick," he said gently, taking the boy's rod from his hands to unsnarl a huge wind knot that hung from the reel. "My fault, I should have said something sooner. Here, use my rod. You have to watch the breezes tonight. Read the water, see? See that breeze coming at you?

"Whoa, Zenner." Ray stepped back. "You got a follow— good-sized, too. Watch . . . watch Zenner, Nick. If that fish strikes, you'll see it hit with a pop, then *pound*. Nothing like it." The exuberance in Ray's voice was catching.

"Where? Where? I don't see anything," said Nick. The aloof teenager who had arrived at the Rhinelander airport one day ago had disappeared. In his place was a kid with all the enthusiasm of a five-year-old with his first cane pole. Osborne smiled and cast. Things might work out after all.

The night was lovely but the muskies wary. Joel's small one and Zenner's follow were all they saw during the first hour. The cloud bank with its threat of weather dissipated. Finally, Ray called a halt to the casting. He handed out paper plates, sodas, and the cold chicken. Munching happily as the

Triton rocked them gently on the water, they ate in peaceful silence. Two fishing boats came by, slowed as the occupants studied the big Triton, then waved and sped on.

"Ray, don't you ever get tired of fishing?" asked Zenner, talking with his mouth full of potato salad.

"This is my church," said Ray, wiping his fingers on a paper napkin after devouring two drumsticks. He stuck his long legs out in front of him and twisted the cap off an O'Doul's. "I made a trade with the Good Lord three years ago. If he would let me fish every day I wanted to, then I promised to leave a stringer of bluegills once a week at the convent and once a week for some old folks. Now, Zenner, you ask why do I do that?

"For me, fishing is an art form. Observe the cast, the retrieve, setting the hook. . . ." With the two front fingers of his right hand, Ray pulled at his beard, thinking. Then he pointed with his index finger. "And the filleting. Yep, fishing is an art form."

That seemed to be as much as he wanted to say on the subject. It was enough for Osborne. No one else urged him to say more. They just sat and chewed in the gently rocking boat.

"I've never heard it be so quiet," said Nick, looking around him. Two other boats could be seen, anchored at a distance.

"We put a bounty on jet skiers," said Ray. "That keeps the noise down."

"Really?"

"No, but we should. Strawberry moon up there tonight, our first full moon of June," he said apropos of nothing in particular. Then he reached for a bag of homemade chocolate chip cookies. He passed it around.

Osborne took a bite of his. It tasted wonderful . . . like the lake, like the breeze over the water, like the wind in the pines. He took another bite. • • •

"Tomorrow I'll show you how to use my Aluma Craft," said Ray to Nick as he held out a paper sack for everyone to dump their paper plates. "I need the big boat for guiding, but you and Zenner can take the other one out whenever you want."

Nick nodded, happy with the thought. Every trace of chicken, potato salad, and cookies had disappeared. The crew in the boat seemed all of the same mind: sated, drowsy, and ready to call it a day.

As the boat flew back across the lake, Ray put on the lights and swung to the north. "Anyone in a rush?" he asked. "I have to return this tomorrow, and I'd like to show Doc how good the clearance is on this boat."

"Fine with me," said Joel, twisting the cap off a beer. Zenner and Nick giggled at some private joke and settled into bucket seats for the ride. The boat moved soundlessly through the channel at the north end of Loon Lake, then turned into the bog, heading for the brook that marked the entrance to Lost Lake.

"I'm not sure I want to go all the way up there tonight," said Osborne.

"Hell, no, I just want to go up past the bog," said Ray. "You know how shallow this gets close to shore." He was right about clearance. The boat was built to ride well in the shallows. And it handled magnificently.

Ray put the outboard into reverse and started to back out. As he neared the brook, the lights from the boat threw shadows against the massive boulder marking the entrance, shadows that gave it a slightly different appearance from when the harsh light of midday sun flattened ridges and curves.

The boat moved slowly past the landmark as Osborne, fully relaxed in the padded luxury of the Triton's bucket seat, studied the patterns thrown by the lights. The boat had such exceptional clearance that Ray was able to steer close to the big boulder, so close that it looked less like a solitary rock than the wall of a cliff.

Osborne tensed in his chair. A cliff wall. That rock was

the backdrop in the photo of Hank Kendrickson and his trophy brown trout, the trout he had insisted he caught in the Deerskin. He didn't catch that fish in the Deerskin. He caught it right here, near the entrance to Lost Lake.

Now why would he lie about that?

twenty-eight

"When God created the earth, he made two-thirds of it water and only one-third of it land. It seems only natural that two-thirds of one's time should be spent fishing."

Anonymous

Ray was able to maneuver the big boat alongside Osborne's dock with time to spare before the sun dropped below the horizon. Osborne rose slowly to his feet, moving in the slow motion of the satisfied fisherman to unload his gear. For fifty years, he had moved this way whenever the fishing had been good. Tonight the fishing had been excellent: no fish, but that didn't matter. It had been a fine time on the water.

Ray, Joel, even Zenner and Nick, moved as languidly as he did, each in the unspoken acknowledgment that shore time was very different from lake time, and no one wanted to let go.

"Hey, Doc?" A man's voice called down from the top of the flagstone stairway. Osborne peered up at the silhouetted form.

"Yeah," he answered. The voice sounded familiar. "Is that you, Roger?"

"Yes. Is Ray Pradt down there?"

"As present as I'm ever gonna be," shouted Ray up the hill. "Hold on, we'll be right up." And so the five of them trooped up, rods, tackle boxes, minnow pail, and picnic hamper in hand. Osborne tripped a switch on the dock, and small knee-high lamps came on to light their way up the rock stairway.

Roger waited in silence. He had retreated to the patio outside Osborne's back door. His cruiser was in the drive, the signal flashing. Osborne's heart started to pound. Lew! He ran suddenly, letting his tackle box bang against his knees, "What's wrong? Is someone hurt?"

"Dead," said Roger flatly. "Ray, you're under arrest."

Everyone stopped moving and stared at Roger.

"Who's dead?" asked Osborne, afraid to hear the answer.

"We don't know who they are," said Roger, "but they were killed at the shooting range. Dwayne Rodd saw you with 'em, Ray. What the hell happened?"

"What do you mean, what happened?" said Ray. "I had a client and her friend out shooting clays. I left 'em there at four-thirty. Are you saying that my client is dead?"

"I saw her myself," said Roger. "I called the paramedics and they tried to resuscitate, but they were hammered at short range."

"Wha—! I had nothing to do with it," said Ray. "You're trying to arrest me for murder?"

"Where's your head, Roger?" said Osborne. "Does Lew know about this?"

"Can't find her."

"What do you mean, you can't find her?"

"I mean I can't find her. She told Lucy she was taking that woman from Chicago to dinner at the Pub, but the Pub is closed for cleaning tonight. They aren't there."

"Jeez, man, there are only four restaurants in Loon Lake. Did you check them out?"

"Yes, I did. No sign of her. Doc, I have a job to do. Can I ask Ray a question?"

"Shoot," said Ray. Osborne rolled his eyes. This was not a time for jokes; that much was clear from the expression on Roger's face.

"Did you fire a gun this afternoon?"

"Of course. I was demonstrating, I was teaching. Yes, I fired a gun." Ray's voice was soft and deliberate.

"And where is that gun?"

"In my cabinet," said Osborne. "It's my side-by-side."

"I'm sorry, I have to ask you to give me the gun," said Roger.

"No one is touching that gun until I talk to Lew," said Osborne. He was so furious, he could feel himself vibrating. "Roger, you stay right there. I'll call Lucy and have her patch me through. This is ridiculous—you can be sued for false arrest, you know."

Osborne marched into his kitchen and yanked the kitchen phone off the hook. He dialed the switchboard and got Jennifer instead of Lucy. "Jennifer, please patch me through to Lew right away," said Osborne.

"We don't know where she is," said Jennifer. "Did Roger find Ray?"

"Okay, patch me to Lucy at home."

"She's playing bingo somewhere on the res," said Jennifer. "I left a message with her granddaughter, though. If you see Roger, will you tell him Wausau is sending a tech . . . should be here in half an hour."

Osborne slammed down the phone. He went to the gun case and grabbed the Browning. As he passed through the back porch, he picked up the padded case for the gun and slipped the shotgun inside. Then he walked outside. Joel and the two boys stood silently in the driveway. Ray was already seated in the cruiser with Roger. At least he was in the front seat and not handcuffed in the back, noted Osborne with some relief. He walked up to the car. He opened the rear door and laid the gun carefully inside.

"Roger, this gun is very important to me. I trust you will take good care of it, please. My prints are all over it, too. Why don't you arrest me as well?"

"Doc, I'm sure this will all be cleared up by morning. But you have to see it from my side. Ray was there with a gun, the gun has been fired, two people are dead. I have strict guidelines I have to follow in situations like this. Without Lew, I have to follow those orders. What would you do?"

"For chrissakes, Roger. You know damn well Ray Pradt

is not capable of such an act. Now you've gone and had him arrested for a crime we all know he didn't commit . . . and you've done it in front of his son and his good friends."

"Might as well be in front of all Loon Lake," added Joel from where he stood in the shadows, his arm across Nick's shoulders.

Roger shrugged. "Department procedure. I'm sorry, fellas."

"Doc," Ray leaned across Roger, "could Nick stay with you tonight?"

"Of course. Don't you worry about it, Ray. I'm going to give Gary Paulson a call, too. You need a lawyer."

The magic of the evening was gone. Joel and Zenner loaded their two cars in silence. When the Frahms were ready to leave, Joel lifted one hand in a silent wave. Zenner spoke a few words to Nick, which Osborne couldn't hear. Whatever it was, the boys seemed to agree on it. Then Nick walked down to Ray's trailer to drop off his gear and get a toothbrush.

He wasn't gone long. When he returned, he had such a stricken look on his face that Osborne decided to break one of his long-standing rules: "Nick, would you like a drink? I have beer, gin, some good bourbon."

The offer caught Nick off guard. A look of embarrassment crossed with confusion crept over his face, "I thought . . . Ray said you were recovering—"

"I am," said Osborne. "But when you're a recovering alcoholic, you don't have a horror of alcohol, you have a horror of yourself and alcohol. Alcohol—as all good fishermen know—has its virtues. I shouldn't offer it to you, I know. You're a minor. But the way this evening is going, I need some vicarious relief. This is one of those times when the best you can do is pour yourself a drink and think it all over."

"Oh." Nick puzzled that one. "Well . . . what are you gonna have?"

"I would love a gin martini, but I will have a glass of milk."

"I'll take the beer—if that's okay?"

"Good. We deserve it. There's beer in the refrigerator on the back porch. Choose what you want."

His drink in one hand, a lawn chair in the other, Osborne led the way down to the dock. He took the rocker and handed the lawn chair to Nick. Seated, they drank in mutual silence, looking up at the stars. No phone rang up in the house, no cars drove down the road. The night was so still, Osborne could hear Nick swallow. The boy finished his beer and excused himself to get ready for bed.

While he was in the bathroom, Osborne changed the sheets in Mallory's room. Then, after making sure Nick was comfortable, he left another message on Lew's home phone. Where the hell was she? He called the switchboard for the umpteenth time. Not a word from Lew. Meanwhile, Ray was enjoying the comforts of the new jail, according to Jennifer. She also said that the Wausau tech would say only that a shotgun was definitely the murder weapon. He would not check out Osborne's gun until morning.

Nick went into the bedroom shortly after eleven. Osborne, anxiety clutching his chest, tried to do the same, but he lay in bed with his eyes wide open. He must have fallen asleep at some point because the phone, when it rang, sounded very far away. He struggled up through sleep to answer groggily.

The clock radio at his bedside indicated it was nearly two in the morning. "Doc?" Lew's voice was sharp with urgency.

"Where are you?" He leaned on one elbow.

"I'm at the jail. I've been here since midnight," she said. "Ray's cleared. I'm driving him out to your place in a few minutes. I've got your gun, too. Doc, I am so sorry. This would never have happened if I had been here—"

"Where were you? I tried you at home and I tried the

switchboard until, jeez, eleven-thirty. Where did you go after we left Ralph's?"

"Back to Sandy Herre's to check everything over once more before letting the family in. By the way, Ralph called right after I got back from the store. He knew nothing more than Stein—never saw the box either. But he's checking with the guys from T.U. for me. He thinks one of them might have handled it because they were helping out in the fly-fishing department.

"I didn't get out of Sandy's place until after six. Then Gina and I drove up to the Bear Claw in Land O'Lakes. On the way back, we stopped for a nightcap at the Old Stag. I had no idea no one knew how to reach me. I was sure I told Lucy where we were going and gave her Gina's cell phone number since we had Gina's rental car. I didn't call in until eleven. That's when I got the news about Ray."

"Thank God you're all right, Lew. I've been so worried. So what's the deal? How did you clear Ray?"

"We had a suicide over in Manitowish. The ex-husband of Ray's client, that woman. Her ex followed her up here, stalked her and the new boyfriend from the airport to the resort, and followed them to the shooting range. He hid in the woods until Ray left."

"How do you know all this?"

"He left a note." She gave a heavy sigh. "I should be fired."

"No, Lew. For heaven's sake, you have to be able to take time off. Lucy is the problem. She should have told Jennifer where you could be reached, at least given her the phone number."

"Yeah, well, Lucy should know better, but how often do we have this kind of thing happening? Roger is the one I need to have a come-to-Jesus with. That man, I tell ya, Doc, I gotta move his retirement up. This was absurd tonight." She dropped her voice. "Ray could file a lawsuit, y'know."

"You know he wouldn't do that, Lew. Is he doing okay?"

"Oh, sure, he had all our guests in stitches," said Lew, a

chuckle softening her voice. "They can't wait for him to come back."

Osborne hung up, relieved. Ray was cleared, and his gun was on its way home. And he liked the way Lew was beginning to confide in him. All was not lost after all. Smiling ruefully, he cracked open the door to the bedroom where Nick was sleeping and peered in.

The boy was sprawled diagonally across the bed, which was a standard double and way too short for him. The evening had stayed warm even with the windows wide open, and Nick had thrown off the light quilt that Osborne had given him. He was sleeping in his jockey underwear.

Osborne tiptoed into the room and bent to wake him gently. But as he leaned over Nick, a mark on the boy's shoulder caught his eye. Osborne stared, pulling his hand back in horror. He looked at the other shoulder.

Moonlight spilling in the window etched the outline of human teeth. The bite marks on Nick's shoulders were identical to the ones Osborne had seen on the two dead women. Not similar, identical. It is impossible to duplicate the five surfaces of a tooth. Even without a microscope he could see enough of the elongated upper right incisor to know it would be a perfect match.

He hauled the boy into the kitchen and slammed him down into a chair, turning the rheostat for the light fixture so high that Nick ducked to cover his eyes.

"What's going on?" Osborne shouted.

"I don't know what you're talking about," the boy stammered. "What's wrong?"

"What the hell is *this?*" Osborne pointed to Nick's left shoulder.

The boy turned and looked down at himself drowsily.

"Oh, that, that's nothing."

Osborne couldn't say a word for a brief moment. Anger pounded in his ears. He hadn't been so angry since Mary

Lee threw his prized forty-nine-inch mounted muskie in the trash while he was away at a dental convention. He took a deep breath.

"Nick, two women have been murdered this week in Loon Lake. We've kept it a secret that both victims had strange tattoos resembling bite marks on their bodies, in the exact same place and identical to the bite marks on your shoulders. Now you tell me—"

"It's a Zenner thing," said Nick, the sleep gone and a look of fear in his eyes. "It's nothing, Dr. Osborne, just, y'know, vampire stuff."

"No, I don't know," said Osborne. "You tell me. What the hell does 'vampire stuff' mean? Zenner goes around killing women?"

"Oh, God, no," cried Nick. "These tattoos? He makes them from casts he gets out of his dad's office. He makes them for his friends."

"I still don't understand." Osborne pulled a chair out and sat down.

"Up at the high school," said Nick, taking a deep breath, "just like my school out East, you have all these different groups. Like some kids are jocks, some are preppies and some . . . well, kids like me, we're into Goth, see. Some are still into vampires. That's old, though. Vampires were big last year at my school. But they're still kind of big around here, I guess. Zenner used to be in that group, and he made up these tattoos for them.

"Anyway . . ." Nick was calming now that Osborne seemed a little more under control. "When I was out at Wildwood this morning with Zenner, we were fooling around while we waited for Mr. Kendrickson. That's how I got these. You can't hurt anyone with ink, Doctor Osborne. Zenner just presses the cast onto an ink pad and then on you. Real easy."

"I see." Osborne considered all the ramifications of what Nick said. "I don't think you should see more of Zenner."

"Oh, come on, he's a good guy."

"I'm not so sure about that. In fact, I'm not sure that kid isn't one sick cookie."

A darkness crept into Nick's eyes. "So what's wrong with being a vampire? Beats digging graves for a living."

"If that's a slam at Ray, you're way out of line, kid."

"If I . . . if I . . . ." Nick jumped to his feet, his eyes fierce. Then something caught and he folded in on himself; crossing his arms he grabbed at his shoulders, shuddering. It took a minute for Osborne to realize the boy was sobbing.

"Oh my God, come on, Nick." Osborne felt helpless. "We'll figure it out."

But the boy lost control, his breath wracking deep in his chest. He sank onto the chair and doubled over. Osborne put a hand on his shoulder gently.

"Hey, son, I'm sorry. I shouldn't have been so hard."

"I—I just want . . . I have to have something real in my life," Nick sobbed. "I don't have anything." He looked up at Osborne, tears pouring down his face. "I thought—the woman I thought was my mother—turns out she isn't. She's like all screwed up from the divorce and stuff. I guess Elise is really my mom, but I know she doesn't really want me. Now Ray, he's up for murder. All I want is something real in my life—"

"Nick," said Osborne, his voice firm and urgent, "I woke you up to tell you Ray's okay. He's cleared of the charges. They caught the killer."

The boy looked up at Osborne just as the back door opened and Ray walked in. He stood in the doorway to the kitchen, a look of amazement on his face at the sight of Osborne and Nick, both in their underwear, both obviously distressed.

Soundlessly, Ray held the Browning out toward Osborne.

Osborne stood up to reach for the gun. "We were just talking," he said as he walked, gun in hand, to stand behind Nick, who was wiping his face with his hands. Osborne laid a hand on the boy's shoulder. "It doesn't get more real than this, kid. Really, it doesn't."

Osborne looked at Ray. "Sit down," he said. "Let me put the gun in the cabinet. We need to talk. Lew's gone?"

"Yep. She'll call you in the morning."

"Nick, tell Ray what you told me about those bite marks on your shoulders. We need to settle on some things before we all try to get some sleep."

Nick nodded. Osborne handed him a Kleenex. He wiped at his eyes and blew his nose. "I'm glad you're okay," he said to Ray.

Ray nodded and sank into the chair next to Nick. His eyes were as grave as Osborne had ever seen them.

twenty-nine

"Ratty! Please, I want to row, now!"
"Not yet my young friend . . . wait till you've had a few lessons. It's not so easy as it looks."
                    Mole and Water Rat, *The Wind in the Willows*

A lukewarm, half-full mug of coffee in his left hand, Osborne banged twice on the screen door to Ray's trailer early the next morning. It was two minutes before seven. He peered in. Nick, sitting with his back to the door and hunched over the kitchen table, turned around. Ray, caught in the act of slurping his own coffee, waved Osborne in.

"You two look as bleary as I do," said Osborne. Half grins greeted him. It was clear they all felt equally unsettled. As if to mock the anxiety level in the little trailer, the morning was sunny, light, and delicious with the aroma of frying bacon.

"Pancakes?" said Ray, managing to make his offer sound like a grunt. From the dirty dishes crowding the counter, it was obvious breakfast had been served.

"No, thanks," said Osborne. "I'm surprised you can eat." He had barely managed to choke down a bowl of dry cereal and skim milk. Even then, he ate only because he knew he was already on his way to consuming too much caffeine.

"How's that coffee?" He thrust his cup toward Ray, who reached back for the pot sitting in the coffeemaker.

"Jeez, I hate this," said Osborne. "I couldn't sleep I'm so worried about this whole situation. Do you think Joel has any idea what his kid is up to?"

It had crossed Osborne's mind that if Zenner was as troubled as it appeared he might be, the family might have to leave Loon Lake. That would put Joel in a very tough financial bind. Somewhere around five A.M., Osborne decided he would be willing to step back into the dental practice if it meant easing a tragic situation facing the parents. He would certainly do the same if the boy were killed in a car accident. This could be worse.

"Nick," said Ray, his voice weary as he poured, "tell the good dentist what's new and exciting in your life this morning."

"Zenner called a few minutes ago." Nick pushed his fork at a half-eaten pancake on his plate. "He wants me to skip school and go out to Wildwood with him. He said Mr. Kendrickson has a lot of work he has to have done today, and I could help out. He'll pay us overtime."

"I want him to go," said Ray as he set the coffeepot back on the burner. He clicked off the coffeemaker. "I want him to get Zenner to talk about those guns."

"Ray," said Osborne, "you're not serious. Not only does Zenner have some serious questions to answer on those bite marks, but this is a kid who's been stockpiling shotguns and high-powered rifles . . . rifles like the ones used to kill two women."

"Doc, with no bullets to trace, how can you be sure Zenner's guns are anything like the ones used? You don't know that."

"You're right," said Osborne, "but I don't like the connection with the bite marks, even if they are tattoos. I told you that at four this morning, and I'm telling you again."

Ray looked at Nick and Nick looked at Osborne.

"I think it's a good idea," said Nick firmly. "I don't believe what you guys are saying about Zenner. You're wrong, and I'm gonna prove it." The look on his face convinced Osborne that he was indeed Ray's son: To be that obstinate in the face of logic required a passion born of blood, not intellect.

"No." Osborne made his opposition unequivocal. "Lew will never stand for it."

"Lew won't know," said Ray. He raised a hand as Osborne opened his mouth to protest. "Listen to me, Doc. I'm with Nick. Something is w-a-a-y out of kilter here. We have got to hear Zenner's side of all this before we blow the whistle. It's one thing for me to sit in the clink; some folks expect it. But a young kid like Zenner? Jeez, just being suspected of something as horrible as these murders . . . that could affect his reputation for life. You know it will hit the papers statewide, not to mention TV. . . ."

Before Osborne could say a word, Ray continued. "So here's the plan. . . ."

Osborne stared at the tabletop, listening even as he knew it was the last thing he should be doing.

Ray caught the look on his face and shook a finger at his friend. "Now you hear this out before you say a word, Doc. It's a good, safe plan. Nick will go out to Wildwood with Zenner. He's picking him up in about fifteen minutes. They'll get there right around eight. At nine-thirty, you and I will drop in on the boys. That's when you and I have a little talk with the Z-man about the bite marks. By that time, Nick will have checked out this gun situation."

"I'm afraid to ask how you plan to do *that,*" said Osborne, giving Nick a dim eye. "If you ask me, you two are suffering from sleep deprivation."

"I can do it easy," said Nick. He spoke with a firm confidence that surprised Osborne. "We're always giving each other advice about computers, so I'll just change the subject to guns. I'll bring it up real casual, like now that I know I like to fish, the next thing I want to try is deer hunting, maybe bird hunting. I'll ask Zenner what guns he uses and if he would teach me how to shoot."

"Yeah," said Ray. "Then he'll ask Zenner why he likes certain guns, etc., etc., and will he show Nick a couple? Just like you and me, Doc."

"Well . . ." Osborne had to admit it did sound like a typical Northwoods conversation. "Throw in bow hunting,

Nick. If you ask about bows, then he won't think you're too focused on guns."

"Great idea," said Ray. "I like that. So, Doc, what we do then—when we know the story behind these guns—that's when we go to Lew. Maybe even with Zenner along. See, I think we'll find out he's been buying for his dad or a friend of his dad's. Maybe some collector who doesn't want everyone to know what he's looking for. That kind of thing. So now we'll have an explanation, and we're basically doing the job she's asked us to do."

Osborne relaxed slightly. This was sounding a little more controlled than it had appeared at first. Still, it bothered him. The fact remained that Zenner's name was on a lot of guns. And it was the high-powered rifles more than the shotguns that made him wonder.

"So, Doc," continued Ray persuasively, "all we're really doing is letting Nick skip a couple hours of school, help out on a computer project, and try to get his friend to talk about his hunting—"

"Cut the crap, Ray," said Osborne. "We're still talking a hell of a risk here. On the one hand what you say makes perfect sense, but you're assuming Zenner is innocent. What if the boy is a nut? A maniac? We don't know that he didn't murder those two women. And not knowing anything for sure, we are putting Nick at risk." Osborne looked hard at the one man he would trust with his own life. "Ray, you really think this is wise?"

"He's not a killer," said Nick. "I know he's not."

"You've only known Zenner for a couple of days, Nick," said Osborne, exasperated. "And you're a city kid. You have no idea—"

"I'm with Nick," Ray jumped in. "Zenner's innocent. I can tell by looking the kid in the eye, Doc. He's not a killer. He might be a little weird, but he's not full of hate, he's not twisted. Nick would have spotted that in the first five minutes. He's a city kid, all right." Ray pounded his hand heartily on Nick's right shoulder. "This boy's got street smarts." Nick sat up a little straighter.

Osborne let his eyes rest on the two men. He wasn't stupid; he knew what was at stake here.

"You win." Osborne threw up his hands. "But the only reason I'm agreeing is because I know Lew is swamped. Too much has happened in the last couple days, and I know she needs all the help she can get. Even so, I'll agree on one condition: Nick gets only two hours with Zenner, and we *must* tell Lew everything by noon today."

"I have no problem with that," said Ray. "All I'm asking is that Nick has a chance to talk to Zenner first."

thirty

Inspired by the beauty of trout, Franz Schubert composed the "Trout Quintet."

The parking lot at the new jail was clogged with vehicles of all sizes. Taking up at least six parking spaces were two trailers whose equipment and cables were strewn every which way. After five minutes of circling the lot in Ray's truck, they decided to park half on the lawn and risk a ticket. Otherwise, they would have to park over a block away.

"More construction?" said Ray. Closer inspection showed the two trailers belonged to television crews from out of town. "Oho," said Ray. "In that case. . ." He paused to look in the side mirror of his truck. Carefully, he set his fish hat on his head, then tipped it ever so slightly to the left, giving it a particularly jaunty angle. He saw the look Osborne gave him. "Hey, you never know, Doc. Letterman has to retire someday."

Striding through the automatic doors into the anteroom for the county offices, they were brought to a complete halt by the crowd in the lobby. The place was packed with people Osborne had never seen before. They all looked to be about Erin's age, around thirty or so. Osborne and Ray pushed their way through to the glass panel in front of the receptionist's desk. Recognizing them with a frantic smile, she buzzed open the door that led to the police department.

Lew's office was down at the end of the hall. Another cluster of young adults was milling right in front of her door, their video cameras, lights, and cables festooning the hallway. Osborne and Ray ducked into a room off to their right, where Lucy sat at the switchboard.

She was a hefty woman, the type who always ordered more at the all-you-can-eat fish fry. Shoulder-length auburn curls framed her generous cheeks and added to a general effect of impressive size. But big as she was, her heart was bigger. It took a lot to upset Lucy. Nor did she make many mistakes. For as much grief as she had caused the night before, Osborne knew it would be hard for Lew to stay angry at such a good-hearted, energetic soul who could balance a steady stream of incoming complaints with consummate ease.

And she thrived on social contact, which was reflected in the impish twinkle to her eye and her own admission that she was an inveterate busybody, the reason she gave for refusing to retire: "The day I stop talking is the day I die." The bustle of this particular morning suited her just fine. Her cheeks were flushed and her eyes happy.

"*Dateline* is here," she announced on spotting Osborne and Ray. She shoved the headphone off one ear. "*And CBS Evening News*. Do you believe it? They all flew into Wausau this morning. Got those vans from Channel Nine. Ray, that woman you were guiding? Her dead boyfriend was some big time builder from Chicago . . . real famous and rich. When Dick Richards over at the paper called the news in to AP last night, the newspapers and television reporters started calling here. They even called Lew at home . . . five o'clock this morning!"

"Lucy, you owe me an apology," said Ray gently.

Lucy dropped her eyes. "Yes, I do. I am so sorry, Ray. I completely forgot to leave the number where Lew could be reached. She gave it to me; it was my fault. You would never have been incarcerated if they had been able to reach her. I know, and I apologize. Chief Ferris sent Roger over to the *Loon Lake News* first thing this morning to be sure you won't be listed in the daily police report." She raised her eyebrows, obviously hoping the lack of press would offset the insult. "She told him he was fired if he didn't stop that at least. That man is on a real short leash right now, doncha know."

"He better be," said Osborne, still irritated with Roger's performance.

"Oops! Got a call." Lucy's eyes widened as her switchboard lit up. "Oh, gosh, excuse me. I guess you two need to see the chief?"

"Just checking in," said Osborne. "She's expecting us—"

"I don't know, Doc, the TV people are setting up to tape her, but let me call back there and see what the story is."

Lucy rang Lew's office. "Chief, Doc and Ray are here. . . . Sure, okay." Lucy waved them down the hall. "Excuse me. . . ." Lucy took a moment to concentrate on one call coming in and another going out. Then she shoved the headphone off one ear again. "I'm sorry. Chief's been trying to reach that Gina person. I keep redialing but no answer. You two go on in."

Lew was on the phone when Ray and Osborne were finally able to push through the crowd outside her door and slip into her office. One TV crew was wrapping while another set up. Lew motioned for Ray and Osborne to come in and sit down.

"People, people," she said to a group of three, one woman and two cameramen, who appeared to be doing their best to move around every piece of furniture in her office. "You will just have to wait a few more minutes. I run a police department here, and right now I have a meeting that has to take place."

"But we have a deadline to meet for the five o'clock news," said the woman, not a little belligerent. Skinny in tight black jeans and square-faced under a black baseball cap crammed over straight blond hair, she tried to wave Osborne and Ray away with the clipboard in her hand. Her eyes went to Ray's head. "Wait—" She thrust her face at him. "Hey, you're Ray Pradt. I need you next."

"Me? Why me?"

"You were there, just before they were shot, right? We

need to do an interview. Do you always wear that hat? Were you wearing it yesterday? This is great. God, you'll be great B-roll." She stepped back to gaze at Ray's full six feet five inches in amazement. Osborne couldn't get over it; the woman talked faster than Gina.

"Ray, shut that door," said Lew from her desk. Her voice was loud and firm and had absolutely no effect on the blond now blocking the doorway with her hips and shoulders.

"This afternoon, okay?" said Ray, obviously flattered. "Can't do it right now." He pushed the door against the woman's body. As Lew rose threateningly from her chair, the producer got the message and stepped back. The door shut with a slam, and Lew sat down heavily. She looked like she hadn't had much sleep either.

"I've been trying Gina at the motel. She isn't answering. I don't know if she's sleeping in or if she's out for breakfast somewhere. The front desk said her car is still there—"

"I'll bet she's out with that real estate broker," said Osborne. "He would have picked her up, y'know."

"I figured that. I tried calling the realty office, but no one's answering. Must be the monthly Kiwanis breakfast. But this package came for her this morning, and I'm anxious to see what we got."

"Go ahead and open it," said Osborne. "She got it for *you,* didn't she?"

"O-o-h, I hate to do that," said Lew. "Common courtesy means I should wait for her to open her own Federal Express package. But it is from her newspaper, and I'll bet you anything, it's photos of that Michael Winston." Lew picked up the large, flat envelope and tapped it on her desk as if considering ripping it open right then. "Oh heck." She set it back down. "I have that damn taping. If Gina isn't here by the time that's finished, I'll go ahead and open this."

Just then the phone rang and Lew picked it up. "Oh, okay, Lucy, put her through." She listened for a minute or two, then said, "Excuse me, before you go any further, let me say something. I have two deputies here in my office, and I'd like to put you on speakerphone so they can hear, too. Also, I want to switch this call onto a line that will be taped. Do you have a problem with that?"

The caller seemed to have no problems with either request. Lew put the call on hold and notified Lucy that she wanted one of the emergency lines that automatically tape incoming calls.

Lew covered the mouth of the receiver. "This is Gina's source from NASD. She can't reach her either and wants to leave a message for her with me. It sounds very interesting."

"Good morning." A woman's voice suddenly filled the room. "I'm Nora Daniels with the NASD."

"Good morning," said Ray and Osborne together.

"I got Gina Palmer's message yesterday," she continued. "I have some information for her, but since I'll be in meetings all day today, I hope you don't mind if we talk instead."

"Not at all," said Lew.

"I had my assistant touch base with our surveillance team for your region late yesterday afternoon," she said. "They examined any activity of note between Detroit and Minneapolis and from Quebec down to Chicago, the grid that includes your region.

"They saw no evidence of penny stock activity per se, but something else did crop up. A situation they have been monitoring for a while. Someone in your area has been spoofing stocks at irregular intervals over the last three months. The activity is coming from a series of different phone numbers, all within a hundred fifty–mile radius of Rhinelander, Wisconsin, which, I believe, includes your community."

"That's correct," said Lew.

"Late last night—and this may not be the first time it happened but it's the first time we caught it—a series of electronic money transfers were made to a Canadian financial institution. We have not been able to track the transfers beyond that point. We're waiting on cooperation from the Canadian authorities, which may or may not be forthcoming. Because Canada is notoriously lax on monitoring this type of activity, I won't be surprised to see more balances leave the continent before we can take action.

"We are also frustrated by the fact that our techs have not been able to track the source of the transfers. Whoever designed the operation knows how to work the Internet in such a way that the originating sites leave no electronic footprints. At least, none we've been able to track yet. We will find it eventually, but it may take another twelve to twenty-four hours. At least we're onto it, thanks to Gina. The amounts are so small that we might never have flagged the transfers if she hadn't asked us to run an electronic sweep."

"So it's not that much money?" asked Lew.

"Well, each transfer is just under ten thousand dollars," said Daniels. "But the transfers are occurring every two minutes from different accounts. It adds up. The same process may be repeated from Canada to wherever the money is going. Again, we aren't likely to have caught this for another few months even, certainly not before enough money would have been moved to make someone very happy. Happy and tax-free, which is my concern."

"What's spoofing?" asked Osborne. "I've never heard that term."

"Spoofing is a manipulation of stock prices by a trader who places sizable orders to buy at a high price on electronic trading systems, then withdraws them seconds later. This lures on-line traders who think they have spotted a buying wave and can sell at a high. However, by the time they do that, our spoofer has already withdrawn the high bid and is selling. The shares will soon fall.

"Spoofing is a serious problem these days, because the high-speed electronic networks make it easy for a pretender to place orders anonymously and cancel immediately with no consequences. It used to be, in the days before on-line trading, that you had to keep your bids and offers available for at least ten seconds. Spoofing is not illegal, by the way. At least not yet.

"We're putting legislation into place soon that will curb

this activity, but, please understand, whoever is doing this is not liable for prosecution."

"But you think the spoofing and the money transfers are linked?" asked Lew.

"That's what I have to thank Gina for," said Daniels. "She told me there are a limited number of servers in your region, and she asked me to see if our computers could pick up any patterns. The spoofing and the transfers are moving through the same server."

"Any other identifiers?" asked Lew.

"Like I said, we're working on it. Same old story: We're understaffed, and we've got our hands full with this type of activity."

"What can we do to help out?" asked Lew.

"Not much. The ball's in our court. If you will share this information with Gina, I would appreciate it. Tell her I'll try to reach her this evening."

"Certainly," said Lew. She hung up, then buzzed Lucy. "Any word from Gina?"

Her face fell at the answer. "Oh, well." She looked at her watch. "It's only nine. I know, I know, tell the producer I'll be ready in two minutes." She hung up.

"Gina is making an offer on the Gilligan property, I'll bet you anything," said Osborne.

Lew stood up and looked at her watch. "Would you two do me a big favor and see what you can find out about Zenner Frahm and those gun purchases? I meant to take care of that first thing this morning and now—"

"You took the words right out of our mouths," said Ray.

"I did?" Lew looked surprised. "Well, good. Just so you know, Gina installed her software on our system, but the boys had just a few minutes to help with the debugging last night. Barely a start. She's a little frustrated because nothing will run, so it could be a couple days before we can work with it here. By the time it's up and running, the data should be ready, too. One of the gals from the county assessor's office said she could do data entry for us in the evenings.

"These registrations under Zenner's name? I'm real worried. During dinner last night, Gina and I worked over the printout she ran on her computer for Oneida County. It's right there on paper: Carl Frahm has purchased twenty-one firearms—rifles, shotguns, and handguns—all purchased under his name and driver's license. Here's a copy of the printout." She handed a stack of wide, flat pages to Osborne. He flipped through the pages quickly as Ray leaned over his shoulder. "I'll tell you, I am not comfortable leaving Hank Kendrickson in the dark on this."

"I agree, Lew," said Osborne, "but Ray and I both feel bringing the boy in as a suspect isn't fair to him unless we have hard evidence. He'll be haunted all his life if we're wrong."

"I know," said Lew. "Too bad we couldn't find a bullet to give us a better reading on the rifles used on our two victims."

"Not even a cartridge," said Ray. "Like I said, they were shot elsewhere and dumped, Lew. If we can find the site of the shootings, we'll have a decent chance of finding a bullet."

"And until then, I have no way of knowing what gun was used. Not even the type. Golly, try explaining *that* to Georgia Herre! People just don't understand: This is Loon Lake, not TV.

"That reminds me." Lew shuffled through papers on the desk. "I had a fax in from Bob Marlett this morning. His maggot analysis showed the time of death for Sandy Herre was approximately six P.M. Monday. Ashley Olson's was four-thirty the same afternoon." She sat back in her chair. "What he can't tell me is *when* they were dropped where we found them, however."

"Still," said Osborne, "the fact that Sandy died after Ashley and that she had that box with Ashley's name on it in her car tells me they knew someone in common."

"Yes, absolutely." Lew rocked in her chair. "I just wish Sandy had been dressed for work. What I don't understand is why she was in a halter top. If it weren't for that, I would put money on the killer being someone related to her new business. Except for the bite marks . . . those give me pause."

Osborne bit his tongue. Ray studied the printout.

"Both victims were wearing casual clothes, weren't they?" mulled Osborne. "One for running and one for——"

"Fishing," said Ray. "Sandy looked to me like she was going fishing." Lew and Osborne studied him thoughtfully. Ray was still scanning the printout. "What's this circled down here?" he asked, pointing to a red circle on the first page.

"Oh, one of Zenner's firearm purchases, an early one, had a different driver's license number listed. Gina is checking it against the DOT database this morning. I'll let you know what she finds."

Osborne stood up. "We'll get out of your hair, Lew. Zenner is working out at Wildwood this morning——"

"Yeah, we thought we might amble in for a little chat about deer hunting," said Ray.

Lew looked at them. "The boy could be dangerous. You be careful, you two. And if you see Hank, tell him I am very sorry, but I have to cancel our fishing plans for tonight. If he looks offended, tell him I am up to my ears, exhausted, but maybe we can go early next week." She rolled her eyes. "If you don't tell him next week works, he'll be calling me this morning. So please, do me a favor, okay?"

"Don't you worry, Lew. I'll take care of it," said Osborne, standing up and heading toward the door. He paused, his hand on the doorknob. "By the way, I have one question. Was it really necessary for Roger to lock Ray up last night? I mean, did he have to be behind bars? Couldn't he have waited here in your office or, you know, been treated in a way that was a little less embarrassing? I'm not saying Roger didn't have to keep him under surveillance given the circumstances, but really, Lew. Locking him up?"

Lew looked a little confused. She glanced at Ray. "Didn't you tell him?"

It was Ray's turn to look chagrined if not a little sheepish. "My fault, Doc. I insisted on being locked up. A couple of my buddies were here. We had a nice . . . I mean, I had to wait somewhere, may as well be with friends."

"Jeez," said Osborne, shaking his head. "Honest to God, Ray. Some days I just don't know about you."

As he and Ray walked down the drive to Ray's truck, Ray studied the printout. "Doc, has it struck you that our little friend, the Z-man, seems remarkably unconcerned about helping out with the ATF data? I mean, he seems pretty cool about working with exactly the information that will expose him if he is doing something out of line."

"You betcha that crossed my mind," said Osborne. "The kid is either ignorant or innocent."

"Or so evil, he's fooled all of us, including his old man."

Osborne looked at Ray. "Little late for that thought. What time is it?"

"Twenty after nine."

thirty-one

"Fishing is a perfectable art, in which nevertheless no man is ever perfect."

Gifford Pinchot

Two miles before the turnoff for the Wildwood Game Preserve, Ray signaled right and pulled into a parking lot. The lot served as the entrance to the Bearskin Trail, an old logging road used by mountain bikers, snowmobiles, and cross-country skiers. The trail ran along the back boundary of the game preserve, where it snaked along the Bearskin River.

In spite of the warm, clear morning, the lot was nearly empty, which did not surprise Osborne. Cool nights through the end of June tended to keep tourists to a minimum until after the Fourth of July.

"What are we doing *here?*" Osborne looked over at Ray, puzzled.

But Ray didn't answer. Instead, he relaxed back into his seat, letting his legs sprawl open as he gazed out the window. He didn't seem to be looking at anything in particular. After a minute or so, as if it made a difference, he removed his fish hat and, reaching behind his head, set it down gently on the lure boxes and worm canisters piled in the space behind his seat. Then he crossed his arms and stared out the window again.

"Ray," said Osborne, anxious to get where they were going and knowing it was his duty to ask, "you look like a man with something on his mind."

"That I am, Doc. . . . That I am. Got some curious thoughts to share. V-e-e-r-r-y, v-e-e-r-r-y curious." Osborne knew from experience that when Ray turned his words into a taffy pull, there was no rushing him. And so he waited while Ray continued to stare out the window of the truck, the thumb and index finger of his right hand knitting a curl in his beard.

Finally, Ray inhaled sharply and turned to Osborne. "When I was guiding Hank that day with his blond friend, he had a lot to say about the stock market. Not to *me*, of course. I'm below a tree stump in his food chain. But he did speak freely, assuming, I'm sure, I would have no inkling what he was talking about. As you well know, I have no quarrel with that."

Osborne knew very well. They had both made a few bucks in the stock market, thanks to information Ray gleaned while guiding. More than once, they had sat on Osborne's screened-in porch, sipping fruit juice cocktails and chuckling over Ray's access to stock tips.

They found it amusing that the city boys with their over-accessorized tackle boxes would assume growing up in the Northwoods was tantamount to being raised in a wolf pack. Seldom was it ever in Ray's best interests to correct that impression. Particularly when it involved someone like pushy, arrogant "Answer Man" Hank Kendrickson. "Just feed out that line and watch 'em go," Ray would chuckle.

"At first, I thought he was just bragging, but pre-t-ty soon I could see that jabone was working overtime. He wanted control of her divorce portfolio. Now that I think about it, Doc, he was a lot less interested in her ass than her assets, which explains why he was so pissed when she paid too much attention to yours truly. But it wasn't until that Daniels woman described spoofing this morning that I made the connection.

"Market timing, instant trades: *That's* what he was trying so hard to sell to the blond. He kept it simple so she could understand and, thank you, I have to admit I benefited, too. He went on and on how he had perfected this unique system, using the Internet, that made it possible for him to time the market so closely that he could be in and out in seconds."

"If that's the case, why does he tell everyone he runs a game preserve?"

"That's what I'm wondering, Doc. I am not averse to the concept that this game preserve is a front." Ray's vocabulary always improved when he thought he was on the mark. "Then . . ." he paused for effect, "I happened to have a most interesting conversation as I sat in the slammer last night."

Osborne, forcing himself to be patient, watched a van with four bikes lashed to the roof pull up next to them.

"Y'know Greg Kanuski got six months for four DWIs?"

"That's too bad," said Osborne absently, wondering what on earth Greg Kanuski had to do with the price of pigs.

Ray sat silent.

Finally, Osborne offered up, "I knew Greg's folks. They'd be pretty upset if they were still around. You know the old man didn't drink at all. Did you invite him to our AA group?"

"Nope, I did not. We were discussing women. Greg's real afraid that gal he's been living with is gonna kick him out. You know Marcy Miller, the hairdresser?"

"I know Marcy. She was a patient. Erin's family gets their hair cut at her place. So what did you say? Based on your experience, he has good cause to worry. But, Ray, why does all this concern us right now?"

"One of Marcy's clients is Hank Kendrickson."

Osborne checked his watch. Gritting his teeth, he said, "Ray, we're already ten minutes late. That Hank gets his hair cut by Marcy Miller is no big deal. So the man likes a good hair cut? I know *many* men who get their haircut at her place, including Judge Bellmore."

"Oh, Hank pops for more than a haircut," said Ray, straightening up in his seat and pulling his knees together. He hunched forward, leaning his elbows over the steering wheel as he stared straight ahead. "He gets it colored every . . . three . . . weeks. Greg said he made Marcy go in nights a couple times, he was so worried about his roots. To the point Greg accused Marcy of having an affair with the commode and wouldn't believe her until she let him hang around one night so he could see for himself."

"What color *is* his hair?"

"Black. He gets it straightened, too. Not as often." Ray looked over at Osborne as he spoke. "But it's the facials that Greg thought were really weird."

"A facial?" That *was* odd. Osborne thought only women had facials.

"Right after he moved here, he had facials twice a week to help reduce the swelling from his surgery."

"His *surgery?*"

"Yeah. Before he moved up here, he had a nose job and an inch removed from his jaw, both sides. Greg said Hank paid for Marcy to go to Minneapolis for training on how to massage his face. But that was well over a year ago. He hasn't had any facials for a while. And, Doc, Greg told me this in strictest confidence. Kendrickson paid Marcy ten thousand bucks not to mention his surgery or his treatments to anyone. Said he was trying to avoid an ex-wife with debts in Las Vegas."

"Ray, you can't take an inch out of your jaw. I don't think that's medically possible."

"A portion of an inch then. But a chunk, Greg said a chunk."

"That's different. . . . So what made Greg decide to tell *you* all this?"

"Eh, we were just talking about goombahs. I think he's worried Marcy's a little too interested in the guy."

"I'll bet she is; he's rich."

"Our conversation didn't seem all that important, Doc, until I heard that woman talk about spoofing. That got me thinking, y'know."

While Ray was talking, Osborne remembered the description of Michael Winston. "That fella Gina's looking for, the one she's convinced murdered the woman from Kansas City? He has black hair," said Osborne. "And I remember she said something about Hank seemed so familiar. But she sure didn't recognize him. . . ."

Even as he spoke, Osborne thought of the rock wall in the background of Hank's trout photo. He had missed identifying a landmark as familiar as his own backyard. Light does funny things; it can flatten curves, shave angles. One of his fishing buddies, Larry Knight, a trial lawyer, had a succinct way of explaining his success in trying personal injury cases: "Worst witness is an eyewitness."

"Ray, just how long do you figure Hank Kendrickson has been around? Two years? Longer, maybe?"

"O-o-h, not quite that, I don't think," said Ray. "Two years at the most, I'd say."

"We were due at his place twenty minutes ago," said Osborne. "I'm getting worried about Nick—"

"I'm worried about both those boys," said Ray, reaching for the keys that hung motionless in front of him. He looked over at Osborne, the expression in his eyes as hard as the twist he gave the ignition.

"And what about Gina?" said Osborne as Ray spun the tires backing up.

"What about her?"

"She's the one looking for this Winston guy. She said something seemed familiar about Hank Kendrickson." Osborne thought back to the conversation the day before. "He knows where she's staying, too. Oh, boy. I don't like this, Ray. Not one bit."

thirty-two

"I fish because I love to; because I love the environs where trout are found, which are invariably beautiful . . . and, finally not because I regard fishing as being so terribly important but because I suspect that so many of the other concerns of men are equally important—and not nearly so much fun."

Robert Traver

They left the main road another half-mile farther down. "I know a back way that'll cut five minutes off the trip," said Ray. He pulled into a rutted lane used by hunters. The road twisted down through a stand of aspen and balsam. A wide meadow rolled out ahead of them, the young grass tall and green and glinting with the yellows, reds, and whites of spring wildflowers. On a distant rise, a buffalo ambled into view. They were within sight of the preserve.

Leaving the rutted lane, Ray's truck bounced across the meadow, dipped down through another stand of balsam, and chugged along a berm piled with boulders. The berm ended in a clearing. Ray slowed the truck. From there they could see the rooftops of the Wildwood Game Preserve office, Hank's home, and the outbuildings.

Less than a minute later, they were headed up a well-worn dirt road that ran behind the barns. "May as well park here as anywhere," said Ray, steering toward a grassy area between two livestock pens. "Last time I drove by, they had half a dozen trailers parked out front."

Suddenly he slammed on the brakes.

"What the—?" Osborne braced his hands against the dash.

"Over there," said Ray. "The boys, I see 'em—they're in the woods."

Turning off the ignition, Ray jumped from the truck just as Osborne spotted Nick and Zenner crouched in a thicket of tag alder. Osborne, forgetting the door on his side was hopelessly locked shut, jimmied the handle in frustration. He finally slid across the seat to get out on Ray's side, banging his kneecap on the shift lever as he went. "Goddamnit!"

"What are you two doing out here?" he heard Ray say. The boys stood up and walked out from behind the thicket.

"We, um, had to leave," said Nick. "Mr. Kendrickson got pretty angry at Zenner."

"Yeah, he kinda lost it," said Zenner, looking up through his dark eyelashes, his face rounder and sadder than ever. "But it'll be okay. He always calms down."

"So why are you hiding?" asked Osborne, rubbing his knee.

"He told us to leave," said Nick. "But we waited here. We still got all our stuff inside, and I knew you guys were coming. We were gonna wait for you out in front, but Zenner thought you might come this way, so we hid back here. We didn't want Mr. Kendrickson to see us."

The expression of relief on Nick's face was so palpable, Osborne sensed he had been worried they weren't coming. In spite of his obvious relief, the boy still looked frightened.

"Where's Kendrickson right now?" asked Ray, walking off. Something had caught his eye, drawing him toward a cluster of white pine whose branches hung protectively over a deer feeder. "Nick, take care of that matter we discussed?" he said nonchalantly, throwing Nick a quick look. The boy gave a barely perceptible shake of his head: apparently not.

"He went somewhere in the Rover after we took off," said Zenner.

"So tell me again what he's so mad about?" asked Ray, kicking at something on the ground.

"I don't think I should talk about it," said Zenner. "It's his problem, not ours." Osborne was watching Zenner as he talked. The froggy lids had closed halfway over the kid's myopic eyes. If ever someone looked like they wanted to drop the subject . . .

"Oh no, bud, it's *your* problem." Ray's tone sharpened even as he knelt to examine something in the sand and needles under the pine trees. "I'll give you a choice. You can talk to us or you can talk to Chief Ferris. But if it's the chief you want, then you'll need to have your old man with you . . . and the family lawyer."

"What do you mean?" The heavy lids fluttered, and the color drained from the boy's face.

Ray stood and walked back to where Osborne and the boys were standing. "Don't even ask. Just talk, and talk now." The steel tone was so unlike Ray, even Osborne was taken aback.

"Better tell him, Zenner," said Nick softly.

"Okay, okay. I screwed up. Not being here yesterday afternoon, he lost six million dollars in the stock market 'cause of me."

"What?!" Osborne and Ray exclaimed simultaneously.

"I didn't do it on purpose; I thought he wasn't coming back," said Zenner. "Nick and me, we waited over half an hour—"

"No, no, back up. How the hell can *you* possibly cause him to lose that kind of money?" asked Ray.

"He's got this investment software that I run for him in the afternoons," said Zenner. "He gives me different letter codes and has me do percentages off the numbers that come up. He always does it at the same time, but he doesn't do it every day. So how was I to know he had to have it done yesterday?"

"What time of day is it that he has you do this?" asked Osborne.

"Oh, around three, three-thirty. . . Sometimes it's a little earlier, but then he gets real nervous."

Osborne looked at Ray. "He's got Zenner doing the trades for him at the market close."

"I found blood on those trees over there," said Ray, raising his eyebrows in a question.

"That's Mr. Kendrickson," said Zenner. "He's got three deer feeders and he likes to practice shooting out his office window. See that one way back? He's really good, too. He can take a deer down at that far one with one bullet. He shot a buck last week. It went twenty feet and dropped. Boom. Nailed him in the heart."

"So he's poaching out of season?" said Osborne.

"I don't think so," said Zenner. "I think because it's a game preserve, he can do that any time. That's what he told me anyway."

"What about your guns? You do a little shooting, too?" Ray stood with his arms crossed, legs apart, and his feet planted.

"My guns?" Zenner looked confused. "I don't have any guns out here."

"Where are they?"

"I've got the twelve-gauge my dad gave me and it's in my dad's gun rack at home. Why?"

"That's all you got?"

"Yeah. Why?" the boy asked again.

Ray looked at him in silence. "Okay, kid, tell us about the teeth marks on Nick's shoulders. What the hell is that all about?"

"Oh . . ." The lids fluttered again. He glanced over at Nick. "You told 'em, huh?" Zenner's face changed; the expression grew sullen. For the first time, Osborne caught a glimpse of a hard anger lurking behind the boy's goofy frogginess, a dark and serious center.

"No, I didn't," said Nick. "Dr. Osborne saw them on me when I was sleeping last night. I tried to tell 'em they're just tattoos—"

"He said it's your way of keeping the jocks out of your face. Is that a good way to put it?" asked Ray.

"I s'pose."

"Do you hate those guys? The jocks?"

"I don't *hate* 'em. I just don't want to have to deal with them."

"So this is how you deal with them? Forgive me, guy, but I don't get it."

"I try to scare 'em, okay? It may sound dumb to you but it works."

Nick nodded. "Yeah, he doesn't hurt anybody. . . ."

Encouraged, Zenner's face brightened. "I do stuff to keep 'em guessing, like . . . well, for one thing, I make sure they know that I know more than they do about computers. Anything to do with computers gets respect. And weird. Weird gets respect. Not pathetic weird, Stephen King weird. You can think it's stupid if you wanna, but this is what I figured out. Vampires were big where we used to live, so I made a thing about it when I moved here. Now I kinda have my own group of friends and we do the vampire-Goth thing—"

"Goth? What's Goth?" asked Ray.

"Gothic stuff, like you wear a lot of black."

"They aren't really vampires," volunteered Nick.

"Right," said Zenner. "It's like a *concept,* y'know? Lotsa kids do it."

"*Did* it," said Nick. "East Coast doesn't do it anymore. Where I go to school, it's like five-years-ago shit."

Ray threw him a cautionary look. This was not the time for Nick to show he was cool.

"And the teeth marks?"

"That's our logo. I got these old casts left over from Dad's office. You know those plaster full-mouth models they use to make dentures? We dip 'em in Chinese red ink and press down—they leave marks like you really bit some-one. But they're just tattoos, you don't feel it really. Not like anyone gets hurt."

"But someone did get hurt, Zenner." Osborne stepped forward. "The two women who've been murdered. They have those bite marks on their bodies, on their shoulders. Just like Nick's. The same casts used on Nick were used on the victims. How do you explain that?"

Zenner just stared at him, his mouth open. "You . . . you think I . . ."

"What would you think?" said Osborne.

"And you've purchased over twenty guns in recent months. What's that all about?" said Ray.

"I have?" The boy was stunned, his eyes wide open and locked on Ray's. Osborne did not doubt him for an instant.

thirty-three

*"Some men fish all their lives without knowing it is
not really the fish they are after."*

Henry David Thoreau

As they walked around the old barn that had been converted
into the Wildwood Game Preserve's main office building,
Ray hung back with Osborne. He spoke in a low tone so the
boys couldn't hear. "I think the chief may want to get
Wausau out here fast. I've gutted plenty of deer in my life,
enough to know that what I saw under those trees should be
analyzed. Could be human—decomposing hair and tissue. I
could be wrong, too. I'll find a shovel and scoop some up
before the eagles finish it off."

"I want these boys out of here," said Osborne. "If
Kendrickson is who we think he is, we can't put these kids
at risk."

"I'm with you, Doc," said Ray. "Once they point us in the
right direction, I'll tell 'em to take my truck—"

"That's the door to Mr. Kendrickson's office," said Zenner, pointing off to the left. "He always locks it when he
leaves. The door on the right is mine. He's real paranoid,
too. He had the windows and that door put in so he can see
everyone coming and going." Osborne noticed that even
though it was a sunny, lovely day and the blinds were open,
the windows were shut tight.

"Is there a connecting door between the two offices?"
asked Osborne.

"No. He doesn't let me in there, either."

Ray walked over to the door. He turned the knob. "Yep,

locked." He looked at Zenner. "So there's no other way in, huh? Do I have to bust the lock or break a window?"

Zenner paused for a split second. "I found a way in. It isn't easy, but I snooped around and he never knew. I'll show you."

They entered the office right next door. "So this is my space," said Zenner. The windows to this room were flung wide open. Along the back wall of the small, squarish room were two worktables, cobbled together from sawhorses and unfinished doors. On each rested a computer surrounded by haphazard piles of papers, handbooks, and other junk. Other gear had been shoved under the tables with tangles of cords running to printers and CD-ROM columns. In the far right corner was a third workstation, a larger monitor resting on a beat-up old oak desk. Empty soda cans, paper cups, and McDonald's lunch bags overflowed from two wastebaskets just inside the entrance. The floor was a mess of muddy footprints, sand, and pine needles.

Zenner walked over to the old desk and pulled open the bottom drawer. Sitting there, beside an inkpad, were half a dozen plaster casts, full sets of human teeth, the edges of the teeth stained blood red.

"I keep 'em here," said Zenner. "I didn't want my mom to find them in my bedroom. . . ."

"So someone—anyone—could find these if you weren't here?" said Osborne.

"I guess so, but Mr. Kendrickson never touches my stuff," said Zenner. "He doesn't come in here very often. We're networked so he can pull up what I'm doing on his own screen."

"Did you ever talk to him about your friends and their habits?" asked Ray.

"Ray," Osborne interrupted, "let's hurry this along. I want these boys out of here."

Zenner thought over Ray's question. "Yes," he said, "when I first started here last fall, Mr. Kendrickson was really, really friendly. He'd come in and we'd talk about stuff.

I had some vampire computer games around for a while. So, yeah, he knew about my friends and that stuff."

"He didn't think you were crazy?" asked Ray.

"I always talked about it like it was fun and funny, not like it was real serious stuff," said Zenner. "It didn't seem to bother him. After a while, though, I thought it was a little weird how much he wanted to know. Got kinda spooky. I didn't tell him too much after that.

"Even so, Mr. Kendrickson has always been pretty good to me. But I'll tell you one thing. He's been awful tense lately. And the way he got so mad today, that is real strange."

"Zenner, do you carry a wallet?" asked Osborne.

"Sure. Why?"

"Did you ever leave it lying around here?"

"All the time. Dad gets pretty mad at me, too. He doesn't want me driving without my license on me." Zenner gave him a questioning look. "But I forget it because I hate to sit with it in my pocket when I'm working. My butt gets sore." Osborne could see why. The chairs in the office were old, with wooden seats.

"So you've left it here a lot?"

"I try not to, but yeah. I leave it by my computer at home, too."

"Ah," said Ray. He seemed to be easing up on the kid. "Okay, okay," he said, seeing the harried look on Osborne's face. "Show us Kendrickson's office. We want you guys out of here before your boss gets back."

Zenner walked over to a door in the wall dividing the two offices. It opened to a closet filled with cleaning supplies. Unlike Zenner's workspace, the closet did not have a finished ceiling. Instead, the interior was exposed to the roof beams. Brooms, a mop, and two stepladders, one stool-size and one standard height, were jammed in beside a wall-hung utility sink and a dirty toilet. A can of cleanser, a full bottle of floor detergent, and a half-used roll of paper towels were in a cardboard box under the sink. A pack of twelve rolls of single-ply toilet tissue leaned against a shower curtain that had been rigged to one side of the closet.

Zenner pulled aside the shower curtain, exposing a small anteroom. "This Sheetrock was installed after I started working here last summer," said Zenner. As he spoke, he set up the taller of the two stepladders. "Then Mr. Kendrickson had ceilings put in. But this was all one big room when I started."

As Zenner talked, he climbed the stepladder, then boosted himself up onto a wide wooden beam to look over the wall between the closet and Hank's office. Leaning forward, he lifted two panels from right in front of him, then pushed back and hurried down off the stepladder.

"Take a look," he said to Ray. Ray went up, looked around, then motioned to Osborne to take a turn. Osborne hurried up the ladder, anxious to see what he could before Hank returned. The panels that Zenner had moved left an opening large enough for Osborne to see Hank's entire office.

He scanned the room. It was expensively furnished in hunting lodge style. Fake logs paneled the walls. A weathered hunk of driftwood covered with glass rested in front of an overstuffed sofa upholstered in a Native American pattern.

Immediately below was a clear view of Hank's desk, a heavy oak trestle table with a black leather chair. The desk held an open laptop computer, next to which was a neat stack of folders. A briefcase stood open on the floor beside the chair, and two suitcases were lined up against the wall behind the chair. To the left, just behind the entrance to the office, were three metal cases, familiar to Osborne as the type of case he used to ship his guns in when hunting out west.

Navaho rugs and a black bearskin pelt were scattered strategically across a floor of pegged oak. At the far end of the room was a conference table with four high-backed black leather chairs identical to the one at the desk. The tabletop was carved from a slab of some exotic wood, the surface heavily grained and the edges bark-covered. The slab rested on a solid oblong of black. Overhead hung a chandelier of elk horns.

Opposite the entry into the office was a wall of sliding doors made from solid planks of a bird's-eye maple like Osborne hadn't seen in years. Track lighting ran across the ceiling, the spotlights set to illuminate impressive mounts studding the timbers all around the room: muskie, salmon, deer, pheasant, walleye, and bass. Holding center stage, its angry tusks guarding the wall of doors, was the massive head of a wild boar.

It was the office of a wealthy man, a powerful man, a man who celebrated his prowess in commerce by hunting and fishing only the most challenging prey. If the trophies were to be trusted, Hank Kendrickson appeared to be the consummate sportsman.

"If you want, you can crawl along that double beam down the center of the room," said Zenner, "then you can swing down onto the big table easy. The ceiling isn't very high."

His kneecap still smarting, Osborne had no intention of doing any such thing. "You give it a try if you want, Ray," he said, backing down the stepladder. "Got your car keys? I want these boys out of here. You two go out to my place and wait for us to call." Ray tossed his keys to Nick.

"I'd sure like to poke around if I could," said Ray. "Doc, watch for Kendrickson; I'm going over to see what he's got behind those sliding doors. Zenner, you know what's on his computer?"

"Only what he has me work on. He can network into my computer and all my files, but he doesn't give me access to his." Zenner paused. "I think I know how to hack into his locked files, if that's what you want."

"How long would it take?"

"A few minutes is all, you can tell right away if you can do it or not."

"What do you say, Doc, just two more seconds with the guys? Zenner, scoot over with me," said Ray. "Let's see what you can find."

"No, Ray, it's too risky," said Osborne.

"Doc, even I know enough about computers to know that jabone can erase everything if he gets a hint that Lew is onto him."

Osborne had to admit he had a point. "Okay, okay, but hurry it up."

"C'mon, Zenner, hustle over here," said Ray.

"I-I better not, Mr. Pradt. I tried it once. I made it over, but I almost fell through the ceiling. I'm just a little too—" The boy didn't want to admit it, but his chunky frame wouldn't be the easiest to maneuver across the rafters.

"I'll do it," said Nick. "I know how to hack, and Zenner can walk me through opening the files. Piece of cake. We'll send it over to Zenner's drive in the other room."

"Yeah! Then I'll E-mail to my computer at home."

"Oh, that's good," said Ray. "Doc, did you hear what Zenner said? If Nick can open the locked files and transfer them to Zenner's computer, we'll have it all set up for Lew."

"Just hurry, will you?" said Osborne, caving in. The stress was getting to him. *I'm too old for this,* he said to himself.

"Dr. Osborne?" Zenner called softly from where he was watching the road from the window in his office.

Osborne looked over quickly. "Someone coming?"

"No, but I was wondering. The work I was doing for Mr. Kendrickson . . . have we . . . did I do something wrong?"

"It's nothing you did, Zenner," said Osborne quietly. "But it's looking like Hank Kendrickson may have to answer a few questions. We'll know more later today."

A sudden crash caused both of them to look toward the closet.

"That's just one of the ladders," said Zenner.

"Ray?" Osborne raised his voice. "Don't push your luck, okay?"

All he got in return was a grunt.

Positioned at the windows in Zenner's office, Osborne and the boy could see up the main drive and past the house where Hank lived, all the way to the highway.

"Any chance Hank could come the back way like we did?" asked Osborne.

"He never has," said Zenner. "Only locals know that road."

"Good. You keep an eye out," said Osborne. "I'll check on how Ray and Nick are doing."

He got to the closet just in time to see Nick's feet vanish from the top rung of the stepladder. He waited to hear Nick moving, then he followed him up the ladder.

Ray was moving quickly and easily along the wide beam to the far end of the room. Since the original structure had been a barn, a good amount of space remained even after adding a dropped ceiling. A person of average height could almost stand up beneath the roof rafters. Nick was inching along behind Ray.

As Osborne watched, Ray lifted and moved aside two ceiling panels over the conference table, then swung his feet down onto the table itself. He jumped to the floor and hurried over to the paneled wall. Pushing back the first sliding door, Ray whistled, then shoved the door back far enough so Osborne could see what the boar was so carefully guarding: Dust-free and neatly racked was an entire wall of firearms.

Ray whistled. "Very nice. Older models, expensive." He reached out to grab one, then walked over to the window behind the conference table. The sunlight flooding into the room gleamed off the barrel of the shotgun. Tucking the stock into his shoulder, Ray pointed the gun out the window.

"Yes-s-s," he said. "Someone has a passion for shooting."

"Or for killing," said Osborne under his breath.

"Hey!" Zenner shouted. "Someone's coming! It's the cops."

thirty-four

"The wildness and adventure that are in fishing still recommend it to me."

Henry David Thoreau

"Did you hear that, Ray? Lew's here," said Osborne. He was surprised at the sense of relief he felt. He knew he did not want the boys around Hank Kendrickson if things were going to get tense. The shotgun still in his hand, Ray started for the door.

"The Range Rover is coming, too," shouted Zenner. "What should we do?"

"Did you hear that, Ray?" said Osborne. "Hank's back."

"I better hide, what do you think, Doc?" Ray shoved the gun onto the rack and slid the door shut quickly.

"Yes, hurry."

"Shit," said Nick. He had reached the far end of the beam and was just about to drop onto the table. He edged back. Finding a rafter running crosswise, he angled himself onto it and backed off to the right, just above the gun closet, so Ray could swing up. "Good." Osborne nodded to Nick. Nick's beam ran perpendicular to the one Ray needed, allowing enough space for Ray to crawl back to the closet.

Ray was already on the conference table, hoisting himself up and into the ceiling when they heard voices out front. Carefully, he set the ceiling panels back in place over the conference table and started to crawl across the center beam toward Osborne and the closet. Stepping up onto the highest rung of the ladder, Osborne leaned, teetering, to slide the ceiling panels in front of him, the ones over Hank's desk, back into place.

"Nick, stay where you are," he whispered. "We don't have time to get both of you back." Then Osborne backed down the ladder to give Ray room. The murmur of voices outside grew nearer. Just as Ray started down the stepladder, they heard the door to Hank's office open.

"S-s-h-h." Ray put a finger to his lips as he looked down. He stayed where he was on the ladder, at shoulder-height to the ceiling. At the foot of the ladder, Zenner crowded in behind Osborne, his eyes wide with questions.

"Sorry to walk in on you like this, Hank," said Lew, her voice so muffled that Osborne knew Kendrickson must have insulated the wall between the offices. "You remember meeting Gina Palmer, don't you?"

"Of course. I had hoped to give you a tour of the game preserve, ladies, but I'm afraid an unexpected business trip has come up. I have a five o'clock flight out of Rhinelander today. We'll have to reschedule—"

"We won't stay long," said Lew. "Just a minor business matter to clear up, Hank. Had a call this morning from an official with the NASD. They have a few questions regarding your setup here. I hope you don't mind."

"Of course not. Shall I put some coffee on?"

"No, thank you," said Lew. "I'm afraid I'm coffeed out."

"Nothing for me either," said Gina, her voice louder than Lew's and quite cheery.

"In that case, won't you have a seat?" said Hank.

He must have gestured toward the conference table, as Osborne could hear the two women walk to the far end of the room. Chairs scraped across the floor as if they were sitting down. Then Hank cleared his throat.

He had to be standing near his desk because Osborne could hear him easily when he spoke. "Take a look at this mount, won't you? I just picked it up. This is that beautiful brown trout I showed you the other day, Lewellyn. What do you think?"

Hank's voice still sounded as unnaturally high and reedy

as it had the day before, as if he was still battling a bad cold. Then he must have walked toward the women, because the volume of his voice dropped. Osborne struggled to hear. He could barely make out what sounded like appreciative murmurs.

Suddenly Lew's voice was a little louder. "Hank, I guess Doc Osborne told you I can't make it tonight, but if you have to leave town anyway, that works out after all."

Osborne couldn't hear his response, but he must have looked surprised because Lew said, "Didn't Doc and Ray Pradt stop by?"

"No-o, but I've been running errands, Lewellyn." Again, that annoyingly familiar use of her name.

"Where are the boys, Zenner and Nick? I thought they were working here today."

"Oh, they finished up early. It's too nice a day. I told 'em to go fishing."

"Oh." It was Lew's turn to sound surprised.

Again the voices grew difficult to hear. Osborne couldn't make out any words. He looked at Ray, who shook his head in frustration as the muffled conversation continued.

"I want to hear this," whispered Ray before hoisting himself back onto the wooden beam. Osborne cringed as he watched his friend crawl toward the far end of the room. He didn't like asking the rafters to bear the weight of both Ray and Nick. This was one time he didn't trust Ray's judgment. He knew Ray was no Mr. Fix-it. He might be a wizard in the woods, but he when it came to plumbing, he was lousy. As for carpentry skills? *Jeez,* thought Osborne, *I hope he knows what he's doing.*

Osborne climbed cautiously up the ladder, the better to watch and listen. He crossed his fingers and hoped the soundproofing built into the ceiling panels worked in both directions, or that the few rustles Ray was making would sound like squirrels on the roof. That must have been the case, because no one sitting around the conference table seemed to notice. Nor did they appear to hear the faint click of the other stepladder as Zenner opened it and set it alongside Osborne's.

Zenner climbed up to see what was going on. He waved at Nick, who was fully extended on the beam to the right, his chin braced on his hands.

It took less than a minute for Ray to reach a position he liked. Letting himself down off his hands and knees, he stretched out his long frame and leaned to his right. Moving very slowly, very carefully, he slipped his fingers under one of the ceiling panels. The minuscule gap worked: Suddenly the voices of Hank, Lew, and Gina were easy to hear.

"It appears to be a misunderstanding with your transfer license, Hank," Lew was saying. "You have some sort of a financial organization set up here?"

"Why . . . yes." Hank cleared his throat. "We have a credit union for the game preserve."

"I see. So you can transfer funds from accounts here to other banks? Is that what Sandy Herre arranged for you?"

"As a matter of fact, yes."

"But she didn't tell you that you need a license to transfer funds?"

"Why, no, she didn't." Hank sounded quite concerned. "If I do, that shouldn't be a problem. I'll have my attorney take care of it immediately. Lewellyn, do you mind if I ask what Miss Palmer's interest is in all this?" His supercilious tone made it obvious he felt he was being put in an embarrassing position in front of a stranger. The hint was clear: time to drop the subject.

"Oh, don't mind me," said Gina, very cheerfully. "I'm just along for the ride. I made an offer on some property this morning, and Chief Ferris thought I might enjoy seeing more of the lake country."

"One last question, Hank, and we'll get out of your hair," said Lew genially. "The NASD did ask me to clarify exactly why you have been making international money transfers, and I will need a record of your accounts. I told them I was sure you wouldn't mind."

"Of course not. I can drop that off on my way to the airport later," said Hank. Again, the clearing of the throat. "I'm opening a hunting lodge in Saskatchewan. The transfers are to my subcontractors on the building we have under way up there. I'll have all their names and account numbers for you but, Lewellyn, I'm quite concerned this go through the way I've arranged. If I don't pay these fellows on schedule, they will hold up construction. We have a bit of a crisis up there right now, which is why I have to make this last-minute trip."

"I can't imagine any problem," said Lew. Osborne heard the sound of chairs scraping again. Lew and Gina must have stood up to leave.

"Oh, golly, I do have one more question, Hank." Lew's voice was so friendly. Osborne had heard her sound that way only once before, when he watched her play poker one night after fishing. They had stopped in at the resort down the road from Osborne's place for a fishing report and been talked into playing a few hands. He had been quite impressed: Lew bluffed as well as she cast.

"Gina is helping me update our gun registrations. We learned that young Zenner has been making quite a few purchases of firearms at estate sales and antique stores. He has been using his own name and driver's license number on all except for his very first one. He bought that gun using his name but *your* driver's license. Just want to alert you."

"That little sneak," said Hank. "That kid's been giving me a lot of trouble lately. I've been looking for a reason to fire him. Kid's trouble, gives me the creeps."

"That's not the only problem," piped up Gina. "When I checked the DOT database for your license number, the photo that came up belongs to a man who's been dead five years. Doesn't resemble you in the least."

"You're not serious," said Hank. "That's quite a screw-up."

"We thought so. Do you have your passport handy?" said Lew. "I can use that to correct the records this afternoon."

Hank cleared his throat again. "Certainly. You know, Lewellyn, I moved up here from another state, so I'm not surprised you might have a Wisconsin resident with the same name. I'll drop off a photocopy this afternoon with everything else you need.

"Now, if you'll excuse me," he checked his watch, "my business partners are due here in less than an hour, or I would get everything you need right this minute. But it's up at the house, and I'll have to do a little digging. Say, before you two leave, what do you think of this spot for hanging my new mount?"

Footsteps indicated Hank had walked over to the wall near the door to the outdoors. Ray looked back at Osborne with a grim smile. If ever someone was trying to change the subject . . .

Lew and Gina could be heard walking toward the door.

"That looks good, Hank," Lew said.

"Nice seeing you again, Hank," said Gina, "but . . . do you know . . . something about you is so familiar. I told the Chief yesterday, I'm just sure we've met before."

"I don't think so," said Hank. "But I certainly hope we do so again."

"Oh gosh, Hank, I almost forgot to mention," said Lew, "on those transfers of yours? You must be doing a heck of a construction project, because NASD put a stop on one for sixteen million dollars. The clearing broker in Kansas City canceled it early this morning, just so you know."

"What . . ." Hank's voice dropped to its natural register. "What are you saying?"

"Don't get excited. I assured them you would be happy to straighten this out."

"Why did they stop my transfer?" asked Hank.

"They're confused by some stock transactions issuing from an electronic address identical to the one you use for your money transfers. I believe it's a tax question. You can take it up with them when you're back in town."

"Lewellyn, investing in the stock market is a very sophisticated enterprise." Hank sounded like he was disciplining a child. Osborne smirked. Good. Now Lew would get a good dose of what it was he and Ray despised about the man. "That group—the NASS-whatevers—they must have some neophyte looking at this, because my company is fully authorized—"

Hank stopped suddenly. A long silence. When he spoke again, his voice was quite different: soft, measured.

"Gina . . . no, don't look away." He cleared his throat. "I saw that look on your face. You know, don't you." He wasn't asking a question.

"Yes, Michael, I know," said Gina, her voice so firm it seemed to boom through the room. "You can spend a fortune on plastic surgery, but you can't change your speech patterns. Clear your throat again, won't you? It is music to my ears, you son of a bitch.

"I've got you cold, Winston. You tried to execute a half-million-dollar stock trade and money transfer out of Ashley Olson's brokerage account three days ago. NASD traced it for me this morning."

Silence.

"Hank," said Lew, her voice brisk, "I'll give you a minute to cancel your flight reservations if you wish. You're coming with us."

Ray raised one hand as if to signal to Osborne. Maybe it was the movement that shifted his weight or maybe it was just destiny, but even as he turned to look at Osborne, Ray began to slide. The beam beneath him sagged, tipping him sideways. Down he went through the ceiling. Down and down.

thirty-five

"The outdoor life pleased these old men because they believed any properly obsessed fly-fisherman carried rivers and trout inside him."

Harry Middleton

Osborne held his breath as he listened. A long, long moment he could never reverse. He heard a thud, followed by the sound of papers skittering off the tabletop, the slam of a door.

Then . . . silence. Dear God. Every nerve ending in Osborne's body hummed with dread. He waited for some sound of life. How badly was Ray hurt? How could life turn so bad so fast?

"Always making an entrance, aren't you, Ray." He heard Lew's voice from a distance. She wasn't being funny. "Ray?" she said. No answer. "Ray. . ." Silence.

Osborne went still, as still as he had one cold dawn in his deer stand when he thought he heard a buck but, looking around, had stared straight into the edgy, challenging eyes of a timber wolf. The stalker suddenly stalked.

He did now as he had done that morning: stayed absolutely still, only his eyes moving. As he watched, a few more tiles loosened and dropped. The hole in the ceiling had widened enough for him to have a clear view of the area below.

A slight movement from Nick caused him to glance over to where the boy was clutching the narrow rafter beneath him, his face tense. The beam on which he was balanced looked steady enough, perhaps because it was perpendicular to the one Ray had been on and had had support from another crossbeam. Osborne motioned for him to stay right where he was. He mustered a look of authority for his own face, hoping it would calm the boy.

Looking down, he saw Lew back up to stand behind the conference table. The room was remarkably quiet. She nodded to someone out of his view, said nothing, then raised her right hand to lay her nine-millimeter SIG Saur down onto the table, several feet from where Ray's head had struck a stack of computer printouts. Osborne did not like the angle between his head and his shoulders. Gina joined Lew, her hands held high.

Osborne realized that the fall must have bought Hank the few precious seconds he needed to slam open one of the sliding doors and grab a gun. No wonder Lew and Gina's gestures were so slow and deliberate. Based on Zenner's report that Hank enjoyed firing at deer from his office window, Osborne figured he had a rifle, not a shotgun. Not that it would make a difference at close range.

Hank walked into view, the rifle in his arms leveled at the two women. Keeping his eyes on Gina and Lew, he leaned cautiously over Ray's still form. He paused to make certain Ray was unconscious, then shoved hard, knocking his prone body onto the floor.

"No! Don't do that!" cried Osborne. "You'll break his neck," he added lamely.

Keeping his gun pointed at Lew and Gina, Hank tipped his head slightly to look up into the hole in the ceiling. "Who the hell?"

He looked back at Lew. "Quite a team effort you got here. I underestimated you. I surely did. Dr. Osborne, get your ass down here. And no funny business or one of the girls gets a bullet in her head."

"Take it easy, Hank," said Osborne, trying as hard as he could to sound as flat and even as Lew. Never look a mad dog in the eye, he reminded himself, never let him know you're scared. "I'm coming," he called as he shuffled down the ladder, making as much noise as possible. "No need to hurt anyone."

Feet on the floor, he shoved at the ladder, scraping it loudly across the floor as he grabbed Zenner. The boy was terrified, his breathing shallow and his whole body trembling.

Osborne gripped one arm hard as he whispered in the boy's ear, "Take it easy, Zenner. This is no time to lose it. Understand? I can stall Hank while you go for help. Stay out of sight of the windows, keep as quiet as you can, but get to the highway, flag someone down, have them call the police. But, Zenner, you have to be very quiet. Don't move until I find some way to make a ruckus to cover you.

"Osborne!" Hank bellowed from the other room. "You touch a phone over there . . ."

"My ankle twisted, Hank. I'm coming, I'm sorry."

Osborne loosened his grip on the boy's arm. "Take a deep breath. You can do it. I know you can."

Osborne hurried out the entrance to the computer room, noticing as he went that the screen door squeaked as it opened. He looked down for a rock, hoping to jam the door open so Zenner could get through in silence. But just then Hank's form loomed in the doorway to his right. Osborne quickly raised his arms high as he stepped through the door to Hank's office. Walking to the back of the room to stand next to Lew, his eyes held hers for a brief moment before her focus shifted back to Hank. She hadn't given up.

Turning, he got a good look at Hank's rifle. The man knew guns all right. He was holding a Remington 270 semi-automatic. Damn. Too much firepower, too fast a trigger. Why the hell couldn't the asshole go for a bolt action? A few seconds were all they needed.

"I'm responsible for this, Hank," Lew was saying. Osborne tried to get a look at Ray's face, but his head was hidden behind the solid base of the table. His body lay exactly as it had fallen. There was no way to tell if any bones were broken.

"Doc and Ray work special projects for me. It's my fault they're here."

"You sent these two out to hide in my attic, for chris-sake?"

"Zenner's trick for getting past the deadbolt on your door," said Osborne, anxious to divert Hank's attention. He made a quick decision to bluff and hoped to hell Lew would catch on.

"We've been on to you for over a month, Kendrickson," he said. "At our request, Zenner has been monitoring your on-line activity and reporting back to us. Those nights you were fishing with Chief Ferris? He crawled in here, logged on to your computer, and recorded every transaction you executed."

Lew nodded in agreement. Let Hank think they knew a hell of a lot more than they did. Lead him to believe they have him surrounded.

"You had me cold on the guns," said Lew. "If it hadn't been for Gina's work on the ATF records, you might have got away with everything. I was convinced Zenner had gone over the edge and was getting ready to take out the compe-tition at Loon Lake High. When I got the report on the bite marks, I was almost positive. Hank, you nearly succeeded at setting up a youngster to take the rap for murder."

"Stupid kid made it easy," said Hank, grinning. "He liked to brag about his vampire clique and how they scare the other kids. Then he showed me those plaster casts. All I had to do was press those teeth marks in there nice and hard. Who wouldn't believe he did it?"

The look of pride on Hank's face was fleeting. "So he got into my computer, huh? That explains why he didn't show up yesterday afternoon. Damn you, Ferris. You cost me sev-eral million bucks." The barrel of the rifle shifted ever so slightly.

Uh-oh, thought Osborne. He searched his mind for some-thing to say, anything, willing to sound totally inane if he could buy time. "Hank, we're less than two hours from the

Canadian border. If Chief Ferris agrees, maybe we can make a deal? Give you enough time to get over the border before we—"

"Shut up," said Hank. "No deal. I got you all lined and ready to die. That's the deal. That way I have all the time I need to pack up and get out of here. Lucy's my pal, y'know. I'll give her a call and let her know I'm taking Miss Lewellyn and Miss Palmer here out for a little fly-fishing and dinner afterward. Think she won't buy that? As far as you and your fish freak friend here, the last place anyone would look for you two is out here. You know that."

A moment's silence from Osborne and Lew gave Hank exactly the answer he needed.

"Lucy can't be conned that easy," said Lew.

"I've done it before, Chief," said Hank softly.

Osborne scanned the room with his peripheral vision, looking for some opening. Lew's pistol had disappeared from the table. Hank must have picked it up. The windows were still shut tight. Osborne hoped that would mask the sound of Zenner's footsteps. He prayed the kid was smart enough to remember the door squeaked and try a window on the opposite side of the building, over a spot where he might be able to let himself down onto grass. The only good news was that the ceiling panels over the conference table had ripped open in such a way that Nick's position was still obscured. Osborne knew his beam was one that intersected the wall by the gun racks and ran through the center of the room, closer to the closet than the conference table. He wondered how much of the activity Nick could see. He hoped like hell the boy could hang on in silence.

"What's the deal with all those guns, Hank?" said Lew. "Why so many? You can't take 'em all with you."

"Cream of the crop I can," he said. "Found some fine collectibles up here, too. You know, you backwoods people, you don't know what you got in your own backyard. I picked up some real classics at the auctions for pennies compared to what I would pay on the open market. And the registration system is ridiculous. If it hadn't been for Gina butting in, you would never have tracked—"

"Any Italian shotguns?" asked Osborne, feeling stupid as he spoke. Nothing like making small talk when you've got a 270 about to take out your skull. But small talk could stretch time.

"Brownings," said Hank. "I collect Brownings. The old ones . . . beautiful guns. The carving on some of those stocks can't be duplicated. I'd show you, but I've got the best ones all packed and ready to roll."

He grinned, raised the rifle, and peered through the scope at Osborne. "This is a piece of shit in comparison, but a nice scope." Lowering the rifle slightly but keeping it aimed at the four of them, he walked over to the far window and pushed it open with one arm.

Osborne prayed he wouldn't look up. If he did, he might see Nick. But he didn't. Instead, he backed his way back into the room. When he felt his desk behind him, he stopped. "It's like this," he said, raising the scope to his eye, "Sitting at my desk and shooting out that window, I've nailed four bucks, six does and—"

"And two women?" asked Lew.

"Yes, Lewellyn, two women. Good for you."

"Hell on screens," said a voice from the floor. Ray shook his head as he raised himself up onto his elbows. He looked around at the four of them. A small wave of relief hit Osborne. If Ray was okay, they still had a chance. It might be a small chance but that's all you need for hope.

"Hey, smartass," said Hank, "get up and join your friends." He kept his eye to the scope as Ray struggled up. "And no heroics, you. As much as I love shotguns, I'm partial to rifles for business."

An arrogance had crept into his voice. Hank was pleased. He had everything under control.

"So you're headed for Canada?" said Lew. "Saskatchewan?"

Hank sneered, "Yes, indeed I am. Canada's Club Med for

guys like me. Easiest place in the world to get yourself a new identity, transfer money. I may have time to run my little stock scam once more. Damn! I still can't believe you got onto that. Hey, Pradt . . . hurry up." He waved the rifle at Ray, who was taking his time finding his feet, holding on to the table for balance.

"So you'll stay in Canada?" asked Osborne.

"That's none of your damn business, Doc."

Hank watched warily as Ray, woozy and weaving, tried to remain upright. Hank shifted the barrel slightly, centering his scope on Gina from across the room.

"*Miss* Gina," he said, relishing the words. "You are conspicuous in your silence, my dear. Why so quiet all of a sudden? Does dying bother you?" He oozed fake concern. Hank leaned back against his desk. One thing Osborne knew for sure; a 270 is not a light gun. If Hank's arms got tired, that might not be to anyone's benefit. "Step up front, woman."

Gina, who had been standing quietly alongside Lew, started forward. As she edged past Ray, he sagged against her, knocking her back against the wall. She must have slipped on her heel because she fell, causing Ray to stagger, nearly landing on top of her. Simultaneously, Osborne and Lew reached out to break Ray's fall. In the sudden confusion, Hank jumped up, gun leveled.

"Sorry, I'm sorry." Ray pushed himself back and up. Bracing himself against the table, he swayed forward. "I think . . . I . . . ah . . . broke a couple of ribs," he said between rapid, shallow breaths as if he was afraid to inhale too deeply.

"Get out here in front of me, Gina," Hank ordered. "Right now."

Gina stood up. Her face was whiter than ever against the black of her hair and the black of her T-shirt. She was wearing a pair of close-fitting black jeans that made her look so tiny and doll-like that Osborne nearly jumped at the strength in her voice when she spoke.

"Screw you, Michael," she said. "The only person in this

room with whom you have a quarrel is me. Chief Ferris, Doc Osborne, Ray here . . . they were just doing their jobs. They wouldn't be here if it weren't for me. You and I can settle our score, but let them go."

As she spoke, she lowered herself into the nearest chair. Resting her elbows on the armrests, sitting up straight, she crossed her right leg over her left. Osborne was amazed that she could seem so calm. Then he understood why. The base of the long table obscured a view of her legs from Hank. What Hank could not see—but Osborne, Lew, and Ray could—was her right ankle. Peeking out from below the cuff of her right pant leg was a black leather strap, the strap to the holster for her Airweight .38.

"Get up, I said." Hank's voice tightened. "Get out of that chair."

"I'm not going anywhere," said Gina. "I like it here. Time you and I had a talk, anyway. That's quite the disguise you got, Michael. I could kick myself for not recognizing you the other day. But that beard, the bleached hair, your colored contact lenses or maybe it's the extra fifty pounds—"

"Extreme, maybe, but effective. Got you in my sights, didn't it."

"It's the face, Michael, the shape is so weird. You got more than a nose job, didn't you. Might be kind of a turnoff for those trophy babes you like."

"Shut up."

"I'm not going to shut up. Why should I? I'm going to die anyway. All I ask before you kill me is this," said Gina, her words coming fast and hard. "Help me understand you, Michael. You are a brilliant man. You are a gifted business-man. So before I die, will you tell me just one thing?" She leaned across the table, "Who . . . or what . . . made you what you are? What twisted you?"

A look of uncertainty crossed Hank's face. Osborne worried he would answer the question with a bullet.

Gina pressed on: "You had a good thing going with Ash-ley. What made you steal from her? But you escape and find your way into a legitimate business here. A new life. This is beautiful country. Why muck this up? Why kill two women? Why kill these decent people? Why, Hank? Why?"

"I stole from Ashley because she was an easy mark. Like candy from a kid. But as for killing her? One simple reason." Hank slipped the safety on his gun. "Same reason you'll die. Same reason that kid sister of hers had to die. No one takes from me, no one tracks me down, no one boxes me in. I still can't believe that idiot woman found me. If it weren't for her, you know you wouldn't be here.

"Gina, you are right about one thing; this is beautiful country. And stocked with suckers. Too damn bad you and Ashley had to get in the way of that. But you, Gina," Hank spat, eyes narrowed, "you're special, aren't you. You play a tough game. Humiliation. Exposure. You enjoyed making a fool of me. I'm sorry, but no one does that to me." His face flushed and his voice deepened. He wasn't sorry, he was excited. He was ready.

Osborne braced himself. He recognized the signs. It was why he was very careful with whom he hunted: What makes some men happy isn't the hunt but the kill.

"Okay, all right. But why kill people who haven't hurt you? Like Ray?"

Hank said nothing. He looked through the scope at Gina.

Osborne knew exactly why his friend would die. Take the blond in the boat the day Hank hired him to guide. She wasn't interested in Hank and his money and his stock market acumen. Guys like that are a dime a dozen in her world. No, she was charmed by the man who had everything money *can't* buy: a tanned and healthy body, a sense of humor, a friendly way of teasing, and a wizardly talent for fishing. That was Ray, goofy hat and all. Yep, thought Osborne, Hank would find Ray real easy to hate.

"And why on earth would you kill Lewellyn Ferris?" Gina motored on.

"Gina, don't . . ." Lew tried to interrupt.

"Why?" she demanded. "For God's sake, Michael, look

at the hours she put in teaching you to fly-fish. Treat her as she treated you—as a friend."

"She knows too much," said Hank. "Hell, she set me up. She made me look good." He glanced at Lew. "I opened six accounts off that crew from Minneapolis that we fished with last month. I'll be stripping those accounts later today. Probably clear a good million or more. You're right, Gina, Lewellyn doesn't deserve it; but, like I said, she knows too much." A sly, cunning grin crossed his face.

And that's when Osborne understood exactly what Lew had meant to this man. She was the bait. Her presence in the trout stream, fishing alongside him, gave Hank the credibility he needed. Her being there was more than an endorsement of his prowess as a fly-fisherman. Fly-fishing is a sport where an excellent cast and a choice of the perfect trout fly to match the hatch implies an expertise in all things sporting, particularly business. And if you fish with the head of local law enforcement, even better. Who would ever suspect the police chief's fishing partner of theft or stock fraud, much less murder?

It struck Osborne then that Hank's eyes no longer avoided theirs. He was focused, watching each dead on.

thirty-six

"The best chum I ever had in fishing was a girl, and she tramped just as hard and fished quite as patiently as any man I ever knew."

Theodore Gordon, 1890

"Michael, Michael, Michael," said Gina, wheedling. "C'mon, let's keep this between you and me. I'll help you tie these folks up, we'll lock them in that other room or in a closet where they can't get out for a day or more. You take care of me and get out of Dodge. You're happy, they're happy. How 'bout it?"

Hank squeezed. Everyone jumped as the window behind Gina's head shattered.

"Shit!" screamed Gina as she ducked, banging her head on the table. Suddenly she looked very small and very frightened.

"You can be sure of one thing," said Hank, strutting into the center of the room, "I'm not going to let you ruin this deal, too. Now get over here. I have plans for you."

The expression on Hank's face told Osborne the man was feeding on their terror. He loved it. He didn't want Gina dead quite yet. Her fear was delicious. His control was ultimate. He wanted to prolong the moment. Chances were good Hank would kill them one by one, saving Gina for last. He would be disappointed when she was dead. He might love the con; he sure savored the kill.

The change in Gina was remarkable. Before the gunshot, she had been tough, confrontational. Now she was pulp. Terrified. She stumbled around the table, her hands high.

"I don't understand. What do you want me to do?" Her voice was so soft, Osborne could barely hear her.

"That barrel in the corner, Gina, get the corn scoop."

Gina lifted the lid from a large barrel and reached in. "Like this?" she asked, bringing up a scoopful of corn. Her arm was shaking so badly, half the corn spilled from the scoop, pouring onto the floor with a clatter. The terror was working; she had Hank's full attention.

"You help her." Hank waved the gun at Ray.

"Sure thing." Ray lurched forward. "C'mon, Gina. We'll feed the deer together. That's what you want, Hank? So you can blast us just like you did those two women. That's what you did, isn't it? Shot 'em as they fed the deer. Unsuspecting. Doing what you asked. Being good girls."

"Right on, Ray," said Hank. "What a bright guy. But you are neglecting to credit my marksmanship. Need I point out I've used only two bullets so far."

"Why did you kill Sandy Herre, Hank?" Lew spoke suddenly from where she stood behind the table, opening her hands in a pleading gesture. "What could that young woman have possibly done to you?"

"Yeah, why Sandy?" urged Ray. "I don't need to know why flowers bloom but I sure would like to know why a good soul like Sandy Herre has to die?"

"It's a long story and I don't have time for it," said Hank.

"She got onto your shenanigans with the stock market," said Ray.

"She certainly did not," said Hank, irritated. "No one knew about that until you people sent that crap-ass kid in here. No, I'm afraid Sandy was too much the busybody for her own good."

"Please, Hank . . ." Lew's voice was soft and clear. "We're in your way, I understand that. But Sandy. Why?"

As she spoke, she looked at Osborne. She was buying time. For a fleeting moment she held his eyes. He hoped that she could see what he was feeling. The fear was gone, like the absence of pain, even though a cut is deep and serious.

Why, he didn't know. What he did know was that if they somehow got through this alive, he would hold her closer than he ever thought he could hold a woman.

"All right, all right," said Hank. "Sandy forced me. I had the perfect setup for Ashley. My plan was to take her up Pickerel Creek in a canoe, get her in the water, and arrange for her to slip away. That's a nice remote spot. No one knew she was here to see me, so who would ever go looking for her? I would have a good twenty-four hours to empty her accounts before any alerts were posted.

"At the last minute, I remembered I needed a pair of waders for her. I was looking for a way to lay hands on some with no one knowing, when the perfect opportunity came up. After our Trout Unlimited meeting last Monday, Ralph had an emergency dental appointment and asked several of us to help out in the store. The minute he left, I boxed up some waders, planning to put the box in my car. The mistake I made was writing Ashley's name and mine on a gift tag that I also taped to the box.

"It so happened that was Sandy's day to work with their bookkeeper. Ralph got back while I was out in the alley helping a woman load a new bike into her car. Sandy thought I'd left. She saw the box with my name on the tag, put it in her car, then she drove out here later that day."

"Up to that point, no one could connect you to the woman staying at the Timber Lodge B & B. Is that it?" asked Lew.

"Right. My only mistake."

"Not exactly," said Lew. "You made a several mistakes. You left the box in Sandy's trunk. If you hadn't done that, I might have tied the two deaths together strictly on the basis of the bite marks. That would have set up young Zenner. Although, Hank, you did put your own driver's license down on one of those first gun purchases."

Hank's face hardened as she spoke. "Yeah, that was a slip. But if Gina hadn't opened the ATF files, you would never have caught that."

"You also mailed a letter to Ashley using the postage meter at Ralph's Sporting Goods. Very few people have access to that, Hank. He told me it was you who used the meter for the invitations to the T.U. banquet. It might have taken a few more days, but I would have found you."

"Not until I was long gone. The minute I knew Ashley was heading this way, I made plans to leave. You're just helping me on my way."

"Bottom line here," said Ray, still standing with his scoop of corn, "is Sandy Herre does someone a favor and gets her brains blown into the pine trees. Jeez."

"Hey, you wanted to know," said Hank. He walked toward the door but stopped at the long front window to look out. "Gina, Ray, out the door with that corn. I want to see you go out the door and walk slowly down the path to the deer feeder. I can see you every step of the way through these windows, so don't think you can run for it."

"Third feeder, right? The one way back," said Ray.

"Funny," said Hank. He cocked his head at Ray. "You don't believe I'm as good as I am, do you? Okay, wise guy, third feeder. Now get going."

Gina held her scoop full of corn in both hands. She was still trembling. Eyes on the floor, she whispered as she started for the door, "I'm sorry, everyone. I am so sorry." Ray reached behind her to push open the door.

Then they were outside, the door slamming shut behind them. Osborne watched them pass by the window toward the feeder. Hank stepped nimbly across the room. He seemed lighter on his feet, as if ready to congratulate himself on a job well done. He paused to watch the two figures move down the path toward the feeders. He tucked the rifle stock into his shoulder. The scope was still below eye level.

He chuckled as he waited. "I have a name for this, you know. . . ."

Osborne and Lew said nothing. Gina's pistol lay on the floor between them, hidden from Hank's eyes by the base of the desk. A quick glance from Lew told Osborne she was going for it. Good, she was better with a pistol. He knew what he had to do.

In the next few seconds, he had to make the move that would divert Hank. He tensed, listening for the right moment. The second deer feeder was about 300 feet from the building, the third feeder another 100 feet. He could hear the footsteps move farther and farther away.

"I call this Northwoods Roulette," Hank was saying. "Who do you think I'll take out first—"

"No question," said Osborne. "Ray."

"You are so right." Hank grinned and raised the scope to his eye.

"No!" Nick screamed, his body flying through the air just as Osborne shoved the conference table into Hank as Hank swung and fired at Nick.

Lew had the .38 up and firing. Hank went down.

Osborne leaped for Nick. So much blood was spurting, at first he couldn't tell where the boy took the bullet. He pressed his fingers against Nick's neck for a pulse. If only Nick had jumped one millisecond sooner or later. Hank had shot high and wide, stunned by Osborne's move.

"Son of a bitch," said Lew. She stood over Hank long enough to be sure he wasn't moving. "He's gone, Doc."

"Good. I need your help here."

Osborne looked up at her from where he knelt over Nick. The blood was gushing from his leg. Lew yanked her belt off and handed it to Osborne.

"Just lie still, Nick," he said as he pulled it tight. "Don't move."

He heard Ray and Gina burst through the door. And in the distance, the sound of sirens.

"Ray!" shouted Osborne. "Get to that ambulance. Tell them to call ahead for an operating room. It's an artery. Tell them we need a vascular surgeon." Ray had stopped short at the sight of Nick, surprise and fear flooding his face. He turned and ran to do exactly as Osborne ordered.

Nick, still conscious but very pale, looked up at Osborne. "Is Ray okay?" he whispered weakly.

"He's fine, son. Not another word." Osborne held the belt tight.

"Nick," said Lew softly, kneeling over him. "You'll be okay but you must stay very still. Don't you worry, kid. You'll be okay."

Though her voice was confident, her eyes searched Osborne's for an answer.

thirty-seven

"A lake is the landscape's most beautiful and expressive feature. It is the earth's eye; looking into which the beholder measures the depth of his own nature."

Henry David Thoreau

Ray rode with Nick in the ambulance. Osborne, Zenner, and Gina piled into Lew's cruiser. No one spoke as Lew took the lead, siren screaming. Cars pulled off on both sides of the road as they flew into town. Osborne and Zenner leaped from the car even before it had come to a complete stop at the emergency room entrance. They watched anxiously as the EMTs pulled Nick from the ambulance. He was still conscious.

As four pairs of hands shifted him gently from the stretcher onto the emergency gurney, Nick looked up at Ray. Osborne could barely make out his whisper: "Are you staying?"

"Better believe it, kid," Osborne heard Ray say. "Don't you worry, you're gonna be fine. Now in you go with the docs here. I'm going to call your mother—"

"Ray." Osborne stepped forward. "You stay with Nick. I'll call Elise."

"Doc," said Lew, running over from where she had parked, "if everything is under control, I'll leave you and Zenner here. I'm heading back to Wildwood. I have my hands full out there."

An hour later, Ray walked slowly into the emergency waiting room. He walked so slowly that Osborne broke off his conversation with Gina and Zenner to watch his friend.

Something was wrong. Ray's shoulders were slumped more than ever. A slackness in his features made him look like he was about to cry.

"Ray? What is it?" asked Osborne. "I heard they stopped the bleeding, that his leg would be okay." Zenner sat up straight in the chair beside him, silent and alarmed.

"Did something go wrong?" asked Zenner in a small voice.

"No. Yes. In a way," said Ray. He sat back in one of the waiting room chairs and dropped his hands in his lap. Looking at the three anxious faces, he waved one hand weakly. "No, don't worry about Nick. The bullet went through the calf muscle and nicked an artery. He lost a lot of blood, but he'll be fine. The leg will be fine." Ray rubbed his forehead. "He'll be out of here in three days."

Osborne leaned forward and extended his hand to pat Ray's knee. "You're not telling us something, Ray. What is it?"

"Nothing. I'm just tired. I'm wiped," said Ray. He stood up. "I better check on the paperwork." He started off toward the admitting desk. Osborne jumped up to follow him.

"Ray, wait." He pulled him aside, dropping his voice so no one could hear. "Something is wrong. What is it?"

Ray paused. He looked at Osborne with a soft smile. "Nick needed a transfusion and you know how they always ask the family to give blood. . . ."

"Right."

"Well, Patricia Flynn was the nurse who hooked me up. Her brother is a buddy, y'know. I told her if they needed more blood right away, they could use mine because. . ."

"Right, because he's your son."

"But when she took the bag back to the lab, they told her that I'm Type O and Nick is . . ."

"No match."

"You got it, Doc. And Nick has no idea. He, um . . ." Ray squeezed his eyes shut before continuing, "Doc, he held my hand and called me 'Dad' as they took him into surgery." A tear drifted down Ray's cheek. "So now what do I do, Doc? What the hell do I do?"

"First, consider the fact you flunk biology, Ray." Osborne spoke gently. "It's a common misconception but blood type is no proof of paternity. That's why DNA testing is used today."

At the look of relief on Ray's face, Osborne knew he had to come clean.

"I have something to add to that," said Osborne. "You may be very angry about this but Lew and I . . . well, we felt Elise was taking advantage of you so we arranged for a DNA testing of you and Nick."

"You did? How?" Ray looked stunned.

Osborne told him.

"And the results?" asked Ray when he had finished.

"Not in yet."

"You'll call me when you hear. . . ."

"Absolutely . . . I'm sorry if this upsets you."

"Eh," Ray waved a hand as he started to walk away, "I don't know what I feel, Doc. I need to think about it."

Saturday morning Osborne woke grateful. He lay still so as not to wake the dog, still snoring on the rug beside the bed. Sunlight and the scents of a young summer poured in through the open windows. A soft breeze was cool on his exposed shoulders, but the rest of his body felt cozy under the light quilt.

Like a delicate dry fly tripping along a riffle, pleasant visions drifted into his consciousness: Mallory smiling again, Erin flying a kite with her children, Ray grinning as he flipped the bird through the window of his beat-up pickup, Lew, her eyes eager and excited as her rod bent under the weight of the twenty-four-inch brown. *Yep,* thought Osborne as he inhaled softly so as not to wake Mike quite yet, *it is so nice to be alive. Thank you, God.*

He lingered with the image of Lew . . . Lew changing into her fishing clothes, her breasts . . .

A sudden shrill from the phone beside his bed brought the reverie to a halt. Mike jumped to his feet, tail wagging and front paws on Osborne's chest. "Down! Bad dog," said Osborne, wishing he could sound more threatening than he did as he reached for the phone. Too nice a morning to get mad at Mike even.

"Hey, Doc," said Ray, "I got . . . an idea."

"That's always dangerous."

Ten minutes later, after Mike had peed and been fed, Osborne sat down at the kitchen table. Still in his boxer shorts and bare-chested, he studied the directions he had taken down while talking to Ray. He picked up the phone. First he called the Frahms, then he called the convent and then he called Lew. She had the results of the STR on the saliva samples. He called Ray.

Hospital visiting hours started at four that afternoon. Nick's room was spacious and bright. Nick himself looked good: rested and with his color back. Sitting up against fluffed pillows, his leg was supported in a sling with a slight upward cant.

"You sure you feel up to this?" said Osborne, pausing as he walked through the door, his arms full.

"I feel great," said Nick, shifting himself gingerly as he spoke. "I slept all morning and took a nap early this afternoon."

Ray, his back to the door, was busy over by the windows on the far side of the double room. He turned to Osborne. "They're sending him home tomorrow, Doc. The surgeon checked him over a couple hours ago and said he's recovered in record time."

"Yeah, I'm just fine," said Nick, anxious to reassure them. "I feel pretty good."

Osborne ruffled the hair on the boy's head and patted his shoulder gently. "Oh, to be sixteen again." Then he paused to give him a severe look. "Don't you ever pull a stunt like that again, young man. When Ray and I tell you to stay put, you stay put. You hear me?"

"Yeah . . . okay," said Nick with a sheepish smile. The boy seemed in good spirits but a little subdued, which didn't surprise Osborne. He was, after all, just twenty-four hours out of anesthesia.

"Whoa!" came a loud voice as the door swung open, nearly hitting Osborne in the backside. Gina entered, pretending to stagger under the weight of a long white sheet cake. "Check it out," she said, waving the cake beneath their noses. Lime-green muskies frolicked among blue-edged white frosting waves.

"Wowee, zowee," said Nick in rave appreciation. "I get a slice with a whole fish on it, don't I, huh?"

"You betcha," said Ray.

"Where do I put this?" Gina bustled over to the windows.

Behind her came Joel and Zenner Frahm, their arms full of paper bags. "Party on," said Zenner, popping open a can of soda before handing it to Nick.

"Okay, folks, everything comes over here," said Ray as he spread a paper tablecloth across the top of the empty bed next to Nick's. Reaching into a cardboard box on the floor, he pulled out a stack of paper plates and napkins. Moving aside a small wicker basket filled with plastic knives and forks, Gina made room for the cake. As she set it down, Ray studied the frosting intently. The muskies had bright-orange dots sprinkled across their bellies.

"Now who the hell did that?" he asked. "Somebody doesn't know the difference between a muskie and a rainbow trout . . . or they're trying to cover their ass."

"Lew ordered it from Bernie's," said Gina. "Don't look a gift horse in the mouth, you." She gave Ray a quick peck on the cheek. "Yummy," she said as she sniffed the air. "Do I smell fried chicken?"

Osborne glanced over at the wide sill under the windows. The nuns from Saint Mary's, long the recipients of fresh bluegills from Ray, had been in the kitchen since his phone call earlier that day. Thrilled to contribute to the celebration, they sent over two heaping platters of crispy fried chicken. Along with the chicken had come a large hamper crowded with bowls of potato salad, coleslaw, and a casserole of baked beans crusted with slabs of bacon.

"Where's Lew?" asked Osborne, twisting a can off a six-pack of ginger ale.

"On her way up," said Gina. "She dropped me at the front door."

Ray turned back to arranging the food and setting out the drinks. Osborne watched him. He looked happy, although, for Ray, a little more solemn than usual. Maybe even sad. The expression was fleeting, however. Osborne could see he was doing his best to hide whatever it was he was feeling.

Just then Lew walked in, still in uniform. "Hey, Zenner, hey, Nick," she said, reaching to shake both boys' hands, "Good show, fellas."

"Is it true you nailed that guy with one shot in the heart?" said Zenner, ignoring the compliment.

"Well . . . yes," said Lew, taken aback at the awe in his voice. "I couldn't think of anything else to do."

"Wow," said Zenner.

Lew looked embarrassed. She blushed lightly. "No big deal. Women are better with pistols."

"Yeah. Wow," said Zenner again.

"Yeah, wow," said Nick, equally impressed.

"Boys." Lew's voice took on a stern tone. "I don't like to shoot people."

"Yeah, but—" Zenner started to say something.

"Enough said. Okay?" Lew cut him off sharply.

From the adoring look on Zenner's face, Osborne knew it would be a long time before the boy would find a girl who could measure up to his fascination with Chief Ferris. He might have to compromise.

Two hours later, the noise level was so high, a laughing nurse came by to shut the door. Zenner and Nick were deep into a computer game on Gina's laptop computer, which rested on the food tray for Nick's bed. All the paper plates and dirty dishes had been packed away, and the adults, relaxing back in their folding chairs, were chatting happily.

Suddenly Gina reached around her chair for the case she used to carry the laptop. Tucked into a side pocket was the Federal Express envelope that had arrived on Lew's desk early the previous morning. She dumped the contents onto the empty bed. "Ray," she said, "tell me what you think about this."

She arranged the three photos in a neat line, then stepped back. "Now tell me, please. Why couldn't I recognize Winston?" she asked.

Osborne looked over her shoulder as she laid a fourth and smaller photo beside the others, saying, "Lew gave me this one, too." It was the photo of Hank Kendrickson holding his brown trout at the entrance to Lost Lake. The other three were of Michael Winston. He was dressed for business or a social event and shot from different angles, but always in black and white.

"I'd suggest," said Ray thoughtfully as he ran his finger along the outlines of the face in the photos, "you think like I do when I'm tracking. I look for the outer curves. See the outline of his temples? That's a line that defines and cannot be altered. Here, Gina . . . the brow over his eye socket, the curve of the cheekbone, the shape of the skull. It's easy to be distracted by hair color and facial expressions, but those can be changed. The contours cannot."

"He tried," said Osborne. "He had four molars removed and his jaw shortened."

"Still . . ." Ray set his hand on Gina's shoulder. "I'll bet anything that if you had looked at this man's head *from the back,* you would have recognized him."

"But I would never think to do that."

"Of course you wouldn't. Who would?" said Ray.

"I know I sure wouldn't," said Lew. "That's an interesting point, Ray. I have to remember that."

"Hell," said Gina, "when are you ever going to see a sick unit like Michael Winston around here again?" She glanced over at Lew. "Don't you wonder what makes a person do the things he did? I looked into his childhood when I did the story on him. He seemed to have a normal, upper-middle-class upbringing. . . ."

Lew shrugged. "Gina, if only we knew the answer to that."

Gina picked up the photo of Hank with his fish. "When was this taken? It had to be after he shot Sandy Herre, don't you think?"

"I don't know that we'll ever be sure," said Lew. "My theory is that Hank knew from Sandy that she liked to fish that general area. After he shot her at his place, he studied the gazetteer maps and decided to dump the body back in there hoping, if it was found, that people would think she had had a fishing accident of some kind. He took his boat up to the entrance early the next morning to make sure nothing had gone wrong. He wanted to be sure the body hadn't drifted downstream."

"And he couldn't resist fishing?" asked Joel Frahm from where he was leaning against the windows. "That's pretty cold-blooded."

"That was his cover if he was seen," said Lew. "When no one saw him, he figured he could really cover his tracks by saying he caught that trout up at the Deerskin."

"Which reminds me, Doc," said Ray from where he stood beside Gina, "is Marlene still in town?"

"I'm not sure. Why?"

"I promised to take that little guy fishing."

"There you go," said Osborne, "a promise is a promise."

"What little guy is that?" asked Nick, a petulant tone in his voice.

Just then a nurse opened the door and stuck her head in. "Visiting hours are over in thirty minutes, folks," she said. "Can you wind this down? We have a young man who needs his meds and a good night's sleep."

"Okay, okay," said Ray, moving around the bed to stand beside Nick. "Before we all go home, I have a toast." He reached for the remaining plastic cups and quickly passed them out. Then he poured everyone an inch of Sprite.

"Wait, wait," said Gina, "I have something to say before that." She stood up as straight as she could, though it didn't help much, as she was still the shortest person in the room. "I just want to say that I'll be back in two weeks to close on my new cabin." She tipped her eyes toward Ray. "I am the proud owner of the old Gilligan place, right next door to Ray on Loon Lake . . . and everyone here is invited to a picnic at my place on the Fourth of July."

"Hear, hear," said Lew, "and with that may I say—"

A sudden sob stopped her short.

"I-I-I won't be here," he said and brushed the sleeve of his hospital gown across his nose. "Sorry."

"What do you mean?" said Ray, reaching for Nick.

"Zenner came by this morning and we were fooling around on line and . . . and we, um, we checked my birth certificate," said Nick. He looked up at the tall figure beside his bed. He put his hand over the one that rested on his shoulder. "I know. You don't have to tell me."

Osborne glanced over at Lew. On the phone earlier that day, she had confirmed their suspicions: The DNA test results proved that Ray was not Nick's father.

"Nick," said Ray softly. "Something you need to remember in life: The facts aren't always what they're cracked up to be."

"What does that mean?" the boy sniffled.

"What you did for me yesterday, Nick . . . I may not have been there when you were born, kid. But I want to be your father. I want you to be my son. We proved that yesterday. You *are* my son. I'll be adding on to the trailer, y'know. So you can have your own room. I've checked it out with your mother; she's okay with it if you are."

"Wait, how—?" Lew started to say something but Osborne made a quick move to get her attention. He knew Lew and her dedication to enforcing shoreline restrictions. That would not be a happy chat. Better later. She saw the look in his eyes and dropped the subject.

Ray raised his plastic cup. "A toast everyone . . . to Nick."

After the Frahms had left and it was obvious that Gina was going to wait for Ray, Osborne picked up the cardboard box with the dirty dishes. "I'll take care of these."

Lew waited for him in the hall. She peered into the box in his arms. "Doc, what are you doing with those?"

"I thought I would take 'em home, wash 'em up and drop 'em off at the convent tomorrow."

"Like some help?" She slipped a hand under his elbow as they walked down the corridor together.

"I certainly would," he said. "Perhaps you'll stay awhile? We can discuss Ray's pending violation of your shoreline restrictions." He grinned down at her.

"Nah, let's discuss Ray and Gina," she said with a wink.

I have a better idea, thought Osborne, *let's discuss you and me.* As if she could read his mind, Lew gave his elbow a gentle squeeze.

To:

From:

Shoot
for the
Moon

Written and compiled by Evelyn Loeb

Illustrated by Steve Haskamp

 Peter Pauper Press, Inc.
WHITE PLAINS, NEW YORK

Designed by Heather Zschock

Illustrations copyright © 2001
Steve Haskamp

Text copyright © 2001
Peter Pauper Press, Inc.
202 Mamaroneck Avenue
White Plains, NY 10601
ISBN 0-88088-536-X
Printed in China
7 6

Visit us at
www.peterpauper.com

Shoot
for the

If you shoot
for the moon,
the stars are
within reach.

**The road to success is
always under construction.**

Happiness is reflective, like the light of heaven.

WASHINGTON IRVING

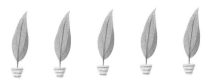

To keep the love
in our lives alive,
we must remain
starry-eyed.

Change your ATTITUDE, and your perception of the problem will change.

He has achieved
success who has lived
well, laughed often,
and loved much.

BESSIE STANLEY

Leave old baggage behind; the less you carry, the farther you go.

Life is what we make it, always has been, always will be.

GRANDMA MOSES

Nine-tenths of life is showing up.

JENNA DAMS

When opportunity knocks, open the door even if you're in your bathrobe.

HEATHER ZSCHOCK

If you **LOVE**
what you do,
consider yourself
a success.

Fear

lessens

as you

gain

greater

understanding.

Freedom is the
ability not to care
what the other
person thinks.

The way I see it,
if you want the
rainbow you gotta
put up with the rain.

DOLLY PARTON

Follow an old path
and you find the
expected. Blaze a
new trail and you
have an adventure.

You can stand tall without standing on someone. You can be a victor without having victims.

HARRIET WOODS

Bring the whole world into your orbit and expand your horizon.

To play great music,
you must keep your
eyes on a distant star.

YEHUDI MENUHIN

Be as fleet as Mercury,
as beautiful
as Venus,
as brave as Mars—
**but always be
down to Earth.**

Love everybody.
It's easier than
having to pick
and choose.

MIKE DOMIS

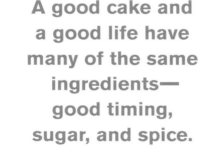

A good cake and
a good life have
many of the same
ingredients—
good timing,
sugar, and spice.

If you never take the
plunge, you'll never
discover the delights
of the water.

You must have long-range goals to keep you from being frustrated by short-range failures.

CHARLES C. NOBLE

If life gives you

lemons,

make lemonade.

Your success
and happiness
lie in you.

HELEN KELLER

Remember the past,
live in the present,
and look forward
to the future.

I never see what
has been done;
I only see what
remains to be done.

MARIE CURIE

Our spirits soar
on the wings
of angels.

SARAH MICHELLE

Success comes in cans, failures in can'ts.

You cannot fly like an eagle with the wings of a wren.

WILLIAM HENRY HUDSON

Try to please
everybody
and you please
nobody.

Success is that old
A B C—*ability,*
breaks, and courage.

CHARLES LUCKMAN

A recipe for success:

follow up and
follow through.

The journey
is often more
satisfying than the
destination.

You are a child of the
universe, no less than the
trees and the stars; you
have a right to be here.

DESIDERATA

We are the
architects of
our dreams.

The only way to discover
the limits of the possible
is to go beyond them
into the impossible.

C. CLARKE

To be happy
with simple
pleasures is no
simple matter.

Dreams are the touchstones of our character.

HENRY DAVID THOREAU

ACTION is often the best remedy for the sick at heart.

To fly, we
have to have

resistance.

MAYA LIN

Never draw the
curtain on the

*window of
opportunity.*

One's destination
is never a place
but rather a
new way of
looking at things.

HENRY MILLER

The world belongs to
those who are loved,
and those who are
loved have the world
at their fingertips.

Tomorrow has an infinite number of possibilities.

I avoid looking forward
or backward, and try to
keep looking upward.

CHARLOTTE BRONTË

Always give
yourself another
chance. You're
the best friend
you have.

Winners never quit, and quitters never win.

TED TURNER

Light one candle and eliminate the darkness; light several and your vision and direction are illuminated.

Only those who dare
to fail greatly can
ever achieve greatly.

ROBERT F. KENNEDY

Remember that it takes many stars to light the night sky.

Climb the stairway to the stars one step at a time.

It is easier to
take your first step
when someone is
holding your hand.

**Keep away
from people
who try to belittle
your ambitions.
Small people always do
that, but the really great
make you feel
that you, too,
can become great.**

MARK TWAIN

Why not go out on a limb? Isn't that where the fruit is?

FRANK SCULLY

To accomplish
GREAT THINGS,
we must dream
as well as act.

ANATOLE FRANCE

Great
expectations
inspire you to
greater heights.

BETH MAYERS

Fall seven times,
stand up eight.

Japanese Proverb

If I have the belief
that I can do it,
I will surely acquire
the capacity to do it,
even if I may not have
it at the beginning.

MAHATMA GANDHI

You can reach
the finish line with
small steps and
determination.

They are able who think they are able.

VIRGIL

Fear stops you in your tracks.
Self-confidence
propels you forward.

Let me tell you the secret that has led me to my goal. My strength lies solely in my tenacity.

LOUIS PASTEUR

We can look at
the world through a
narrow lens and see
the ground or open
the shutter wide and
see the stars.

I'm a slow walker, but I never walk back.

ABRAHAM LINCOLN

Don't be afraid to lean into
the wind, love the earth in
all of its natural glories, and
take care of each other.

TOM BROKAW